Colin Graham is a trained hotelier who became a stockjobber instead. Retired now, he put a history degree at the Open University on hold to write this book. He is married to Jenny, a teacher, and he has two sons—Ross, who is a Ph.D. student in California and Jamie, who is a biodiversity consultant based in Cambridge and London. Of Scottish and Northern English extraction, he is a cyclist and hiker, as well as having a keen interest in the arts and travel. This is his first published novel.

Colin Graham

GLANCE

AUSTIN MACAULEY PUBLISHERS™

LONDON * CAMBRIDGE * NEW YORK * SHARJAH

A CIP catalogue record for this title is available from the British Library.

ISBN 9781035867325 (Paperback)
ISBN 9781035867332 (ePub e-book)

www.austinmacauley.com

First Published 2024
Austin Macauley Publishers Ltd®
1 Canada Square
Canary Wharf
London
E14 5AA

Table of Contents

Homburg

Edward the Seventh had made Homburg hats popular in England when he brought one back from his travels in Europe, late in the nineteenth century, after visiting Bad Homburg, a region of Hesse in Germany. They were fur-felt gentlemen's hats with a single dent in the middle and a ribbon around the outside giving them a semi-formal air. Ernest Bevin wore one every day that he was at work and so that was every day.

"This afternoon please, Mrs Dalton, but not yourself. One of the other ladies or Mr Charlton if he is available. My office, two o'clock and new numbers. Or rather, to be clear, the same numbers on fresh pieces of paper please."

It was June 1944 and this was to be the eleventh ballot. The actual procedure of the ballot was very simple but the ramifications were enormous. It would take no more than a few seconds for a member of Ernest Bevin's staff to fetch his black Homburg hat from the peg where it would normally spend this, and every day, invert it and place ten folded paper slips inside it. Each of these pieces of paper would have a single number on it from zero to nine and on pre-selected days, decided by Mr Bevin, an individual, also selected by him would choose just one of these slips while averting their eyes and then pass it through another pair of hands to the hats owner.

There was no official record of the procedure. Nothing was filmed or photographed or indeed witnessed by a committee and there would be just three people present at the event. Today, it was, as ever, Ernest Bevin and then a senior clerk called Donald Charlton, who had no other official business to attend to that afternoon, and one of the department's secretaries who was a colleague to the not-required Mrs Dalton, a Miss Palmer. Ernest stood by the window, tucked one thumb into his waistcoat pocket, and said, "Ready?"

Jane Palmer cleared her throat as if to speak but merely nodded and Donald Charlton said, "Yes, all ready," and approached the desk where the hat with the numbers in it sat. He too cleared his throat and turning his head away, dipped his right hand into the hat and in his haste, he snared two pieces of paper. He quickly dropped one and only the three people present would ever know the possible outcome if he had dropped the other piece. Only they would know how the now secured slip of paper and the released one could have changed the lives of so many young men. How such an arbitrary action would have agency over so many young lives directly and over so many other lives indirectly?

"Seven," said Donald.

"Seven," agreed Jane.

"Seven it is then," said Ernest Bevin. "The first seven I believe," and he knew these words were made of nothing but were just a distraction from the inevitable consequences to follow.

"Miss Palmer, would you please record the number in the journal and inform Mrs Dalton that I should like her and, in fact, all of the rest of the department at work thirty minutes early tomorrow in order that we may start making the necessary arrangements. Thank you both."

After the two employees left his office, Ernest Bevin lit an untipped cigarette and drew deeply. Nothing on the Somerset farm where he had grown up or in his career to date had prepared him for this. His suit felt tight and his collar and tie constricting. He stared out over the London skyline and a saying came to mind from those Somerset schooldays.

'Homo homini lupus', a proverb meaning 'A man is a wolf to another man'.

He surprised himself that he remembered the Latin version as he had struggled with the language at school but he knew the English translation and its tone and sentiment. It meant that given certain circumstances, skewed permissions or being fearful, trapped or angry then maybe a man, or a woman, could become wolf-like in their actions, especially if they felt there would be no redress or consequences. History tells us that on multiple occasions with excuses, justifications, and rationalisations, human beings have behaved in this manner. Man and the wolf and man as the wolf.

And so that was why, on a wet day in June, in the middle of a war in an office in London Ernest Bevin, the Minister of Labour, randomly selected a number that would start a process and initiate a change that would hopefully help to cage the wolf.

The butterfly effect states that, in theory, the simple action of a tiny creature such as that butterfly flapping its wings could in fact cause a typhoon. It is a form of chaos theory which has its origin in inherent repetition, patterns, self-organisation, interconnectedness, self-similarity, and constant feedback loops.

Ernest Bevin's action, so simple in its execution, can be seen to embrace all of these outcomes despite it being random and literally a game of chance. Let me explain.

Prologue

After the First World War ended in 1918, the coal mining industry in Britain went into a steady decline for the next twenty-one years until the outbreak of the Second World War in 1939. During this period, there was never less than a quarter of miners wholly or partially out of work. Coal was of course still needed for industrial and domestic use but production always matched or exceeded demand. Meanwhile, there was a gradual drop off in the number of men employed by the collieries.

Adding to this decline was the hazardous and physically hard nature of the profession. Many current miners who were themselves sons and grandsons of miners strove to make sure that their own sons did not have to go down the pits or at least had the possibility of not doing so. New industries, education and increased opportunity shone a faint light on the feasibility of young men from working-class areas at least exploring employment that was not hewing coal hundreds of feet below the ground. Then war broke out and for the first few months, there was an urgency to increase production to fuel the burgeoning industries that were essential to the war effort.

As is so often the case in times of national emergency, the country rose to the challenge. Men who were called up to the armed forces were replaced by unemployed but experienced miners. For a few months, the status quo was maintained and then a concertina effect developed, initiated by the fall of France to the enemy and by Italy entering the war on the German side. At a stroke one export market was compromised and another one closed down. Virtually overnight, one hundred mines shut and thirty-four thousand men were made unemployed. The mining industry had slipped back to how it was during the interwar years.

Ernest Bevin came under colossal pressure from mine owners and government colleagues alike. He reacted by doing two things. Firstly, he removed any restrictions on miners seeking work outside of the mines and secondly, he raised the age of reserved professions (those essential to the war effort) from eighteen to thirty. The flood gates opened.

In 1941, approximately two years into the war, it became very apparent that the concertina effect was compressing in the opposite direction. The number of miners had by then dropped by roughly 10% from a high in excess of seven hundred seventy thousand in 1939 to just over seven hundred thousand in the early months of 1941, and coal was in very high demand. Young men, boys really, in their early teens did not want to enter the mines and yet, industry and particular businesses that relied on coal were crying out for more of it. An incredulous government was astonished that a country literally built on coal was facing a national shortage.

Debate followed debate and arguments raged. Solutions were sought and possible ways of increasing production often seemed close but the country and the mining industry were hamstrung with strikes and absenteeism, coupled with inertia and incompetence from ministers and pushback and intransigence from mine owners. Production and miners' numbers continued to drop until a workable solution did present itself, and that was the plan for a second front. Reluctantly, Bevin bowed to the inevitable and compulsory conscription to the pits became a reality.

All that was left to do was initiate the manner of its implementation and this Ernest Bevin explained to the House of Commons on 2 December by telling the full chamber of his new system of random selection based on National Insurance numbers. This was how and why the ballot began. It was a system based upon the 1911 National Insurance Act that had initiated workers' contributions to cover both illness and unemployment. And it was how RP118627A on the wrong day could send a young man down the mines whereas GK4426946A would not, as Bevin's new system was based on the last digit of an individual's unique number. And as Bevin had said earlier, 'Seven it is'.

Exemptions were few and appeals generally pointless, and so Bevin's tombola cranked into life late in 1943 for the first batch of conscripted eighteen-year-olds. Brown envelopes through letterboxes announced the fate of the minority. A new fear was in the air.

Ernest Bevin died in March 1951 as Lord Privy Seal. His reluctance for the position was obvious in his stated, 'I am neither a Lord, nor a Privy nor a Seal', but he was unwell and it was Clement Atlee's respect for the man that he had lowered his work stress by appointing him to this position.

Donald Charlton stayed in post for another twenty years or so until anonymously and with no fanfare, he slid into retirement and obscurity. Unmarried and childless, he did play an occasional game of dice with his nieces and nephews however and the carefully corralled numbers for the game were some dog-eared and tired scraps of paper numbering from zero to nine.

Mrs Dalton retired in the late 1950s to be near her sister in Bournemouth. She always seemed sad and that was because she was.

Jane Palmer married after the war and brought up two children with her husband, Paul, a boy and a girl. Their son, John, enlisted in the navy.

Balloteers

"A pint of mild and a gin and tonic please, George. Ice and a slice."

"You're a funny man, Donald, the last lemon I saw around here was Doreen Cave's rent collector and he hasn't been back in here since all four Cave sisters chased him down the street. One and five pence three farthings if you would be so kind."

Lemons, real lemons, were of course virtually unobtainable during the war.

George chortled. He often amused himself. A former miner himself, he was glad to be pulling pints and not pulling coal trucks.

Donald Charlton poured the tonic water from a small bottle into the gin and the ice cracked and moved. It is generally customary to let the gin drinker dilute the drink to taste but Donald had been in this situation many times and knew it was all in. He also knew that on ballot days, the drink lasted an even shorter time than usual. He picked up the drinks and moved across to where his boss sat at a table near the fire, which was lit and fuelled by coal from somewhere in the British Isles. He placed the drink on the beer mat that coincidentally stated 'Booth's and tonic. Experience it now' and took a sip of his own pint.

"Cheers, Sir," he said.

"Cheers, Donald. Thanks," replied Ernest. "Smoke?"

"Thank you, Sir," and Donald took one, tapped it on his thumb and after having placed it carefully in the corner of his mouth, he rolled his zippo lighter into life to light both the available cigarettes.

They then sat in communal silence inhaling and exhaling until eventually Ernest said, "Dreadful business."

"Yes, Sir," replied Donald, "awful."

Donald knew the workings of the ballot system and he knew the ramifications of the process of which he was so often a part, but his daily life did not touch on the reality of that outcome as it did for so many young men of conscription age. That was until, purely by chance, Susan, a friend of his mother's, who was down in the south visiting her sister, was having tea with his mother one evening when he came in. Susan knew him vaguely but certainly didn't know what his job was or what it involved.

He was in the kitchen dropping off some groceries for his mother and he heard them chatting in the front room and was about to go into the room to say hello when he was stopped by the tone and tempo of the conversation.

"He was due to go into the RAF when the letter came," Susan said.

Susan was talking about a friend of hers and her son who lived in the North-East.

"He had six weeks to come to terms with the situation if you ever can. His mother considered an appeal because he was physically and emotionally a very young eighteen-year-old. But his father would not stand up for him, nor any of his uncles or male friends of the family."

"Surely something could be done?"

"It is a mining community and you just get on with things. He didn't have a boss as he hadn't started full-time employment and the local MP was overrun with approaches from mining conscripts in a similar position. He was caught between a rock and a hard place."

"What if he refused?"

"Absenteeism and desertion were punished with severe fines and possibly prison, and they had little or no money, so they did what so many families did and they got on with it."

"And who was this again?" Donald's mum asked.

"Oh, just a friend," she said. "No. Not just a friend. A friend," Susan changed the emphasis of her statement. "JUST implies an absence of worth and we are all worthy, war or no war."

Both women sipped their tea and exchanged the intimate shared looks of mothers with sons themselves. The known but rarely expressed agony of being a female parent. A mother.

"So on his first day down the mines, she went to awaken him," Susan continued, "and he was curled up in a small gap between his bed and the wall with his jacket over his head, and he was sobbing. She managed to get him up and dressed and in front of some breakfast but he ate nothing at all, which was a new worry to her on top of all the others. How would he do an eight-hour shift with no food inside him? And then they began the walk to the mines because one piece of good fortune was that he could live at home in Gateshead and walk to the Heworth pit where he was conscripted to work."

"She walked him through the kitchen and out through the backyard, past the outside toilet and through the gate onto the back lane, where as yet nobody was moving. He walked with one shoulder rubbing on the wall and his head down. She held his hand. They took a longer route down the back lanes so that she could spend more time with him and so that they might not see any other people at that early hour that might brand him a cissy. Eventually, they reached a corner where there were no more back lanes, no more cover, and here he clung to her and dropping to his knees cried into the buttons of her coat. Eventually, he stood up, up but not erect, and wiping his tears and mumbling a goodbye, he headed for his first day in the pit."

Donald's mum and Susan, her visitor, sat in silence until eventually, the quiet was broken by Donald's entrance.

"Oh hello, Donald, how very good to see you," Susan said.

"Hello, Mrs Court, and how are you?"

"Fair to middling, Donald, fair to middling."

And the silence resumed.

Michael

Michael sat on the steps of the Presbyterian Church in Gateshead with his head in his hands. He was sixty miles away from his home in Jedburgh, which might as well be another continent. He was hungry, cold, and very lonely. He had found a white feather in his overalls at the pit that morning and knew from his schoolboy books that it was the mark of a coward and yet he was not a coward, far from it. He had wanted to sign up, to fight the enemy, to go abroad and fight the enemy, to engage them and to beat them. To help cage the wolf.

And yet, here he was spending eight hours a day, six days a week, a mile underground with other men who on the whole despised him or at best tolerated him, and all because of a number. A number that he could not control, a number that was arbitrary and selected miles away by somebody he didn't know in an office who's location he would never know.

It was dusk and he knew that he had a while yet to wait before he would have the third dip in the, once clean but now dirty, water sitting in the iron tub in the front room of the mining family that he was billeted with. He knew that after eating his dinner, he would still be hungry as he always was, and he knew that his wages only just covered his fares and his board and lodging. He decided to stay on the steps a while longer. He had three shillings left until payday which was barely enough for a couple of pints and he wanted to save that money for Friday just in case anybody would drink with him.

There were two Michaels on the steps. The cheery eighteen-year-old with a family and friends, a school and a bedroom with his posters, his football boots and his things and his dreams, and the lonely, tired, scared, and confused boy-man in his too-big overalls and steel-tipped boots counting the minutes on a cold stone step in the drizzle. He headed back.

Michael, the lad from Jedburgh, finished his time in the mines and left anything connected with his time underground just there, underground. On his last day, he removed and returned the overalls and boots to the storeroom, as it was a government requirement to do so, and then in rarely worn and too tight trousers and jacket, and in unfamiliar shoes, he walked to the Great North Road and hitched his way back to Jedburgh walking the last three miles. His mother on seeing him burst into tears but he did not. He was glad to be above ground and no longer a miner, but he was restless and irritable. Within a month, he had risen early one day and left Jedburgh.

Every morning for that month, Michael stood and, as Mel Gibson had as William Wallace in *Braveheart*, he raised his head and sniffed the air. The wonderful, fresh, cleansing Scottish air. Now tanned and heavier than a few months ago but slightly less fit than he had been when he was doing eight-hour shifts in the pit, he looked and was the picture of health. His hair was longer and no longer matted in coal dust and sweat. His shoulders had a breadth and sturdy set partly from exercise but also from the gene pool to which he belonged. He was now twenty years old and entering his prime.

He looked out across the loch and watched the sun break the clouds and light up the staggering beauty of the highlands of Scotland. He was a borders man born and bred but Scotland was two countries in one, and the less familiar North gave way to majestic mountains, many of which were munros that were in excess of three thousand feet in height as well as glens and lochs and some forest. Michael's ancestors would not have had as far—reaching views as he had now as in previous centuries the country had been covered in trees. Birch, willow and alder were the first trees to arrive, followed by Scots pine and oak.

About six thousand years ago, the warming climate reached an optimum for tree growth, and forest covered most of Scotland to an altitude of about six hundred metres (two thousand feet). Then the decline of the forest began. As the population grew, more wood was harvested and many forests disappeared, making space for agriculture, people's homes and infrastructure. By the early twentieth century, forest cover in Scotland was reduced to around 5%. Michael could see across and up and down and he loved it.

He had never suffered from nightmares about his time underground but he had a tacit understanding of the joy of freedom. His gratitude for being above ground allowed his happiness to stay close at hand like a loved partner or a loyal dog.

So what then of Michael? Of Michael Law to give him his full name.

The month at home had allowed two things for Michael. The first was that despite war time rationing, he had eaten whatever and whenever he could. Griddled pancakes made with powdered milk disappeared as quickly as his mother could make them, along with minimal meat stews and as many eggs as she could negotiate away from the local farmers. The Law family had lived in the borders for many generations and this stood them in good stead when it came to bartering with or, in Michael's mother's case, just smiling sweetly at old farming friends to secure a generous egg supply.

All food, any food, disappeared inside him rapidly and his younger sister and indeed Callum, his father, watched with amazement and a little envy at this daily consumption.

The other thing that Michael did, usually post-eating, was to sleep, sleep, and then sleep some more. At the end of the month, and with no conscious awareness of the change, Michael was sated and a little bored. Dark, dank coal seams were becoming an image from the past and he was getting a trifle restless. His mother acknowledged this change but his father and sister were oblivious. They both had their own lives to lead and though they were happy and relieved to see him home, neither had a maternal instinct for a son.

Michael was neither unkind nor uncaring, but he woke one morning and with the rest of the family out, he packed a small backpack and left a note for each of them. With an air of resignation, his father read and discarded his note. His sister cried a little and read hers twice before putting it in the box where she kept her 'special' things. She would read it one more time many years later when she had children of her own and her son turned eighteen, and therefore, became technically a man himself, like Michael.

His mother, on the other hand, read hers so many times that it needed tape and careful handling to preserve it. Eventually, she made a copy in a neat copperplate hand and kept the original in her scented handkerchief drawer. This was one of three copies that were made before her long into the future death so many times did she feel the need to read it. And this is what it said:

With the clanging of the lift gates, I thought of you. With the screeching of the hammers, I thought of you. When the dust and the noise and the heat threatened to overwhelm me, I thought of you. When I found the white feather and cried at its injustice, I thought of you. When I was alone and scared, I thought of you. When it seemed that the whole world had forgotten me, I knew that you hadn't and never would. I knew that you held my hand even when you were not there, that you loved me close up and from afar, and that you were constant and protecting, and that you were that most precious of people, my mother.

Michael.

He knew that he did not have to say anymore and that if he returned tomorrow, next week, or next year, she would be there for him, but he had no intention of doing so and he didn't. He glanced around his family home, squared those newly broadened shoulders, turned his gaze to the North of the country of his birth, and stepped out.

Richard

Do not mistake the absence of cruelty for kindness. Richard knew this, at least on some subliminal level he did, but outside of his home and his family and the few friends that had not been called up, deciphering the difference had become difficult. He was not alone in this regard but he was a sensitive young man and the daily assault of bad language, impatience, and verbal cruelty tore at him. He was pushed and scolded, then pulled and berated, and it never seemed to ease up.

A different type of youth might have embraced the overt masculinity of the colliery but he wasn't a different type of youth, and so when the explosions came David's emotional explosion along with his loss of temper and physical assault on another miner, was almost as terrifying as the combustion of gas that brought down a section of the roof close to where he was working. Shortly before the roof collapsed, Richard had punched a twenty-year veteran of the pit on his chest and shoulder and it was this action that sent his adversary reeling backwards with Richard in pursuit.

Movies always show heroes and villains punching each other multiple times in the face periodically spitting out globules of blood and rubbing their jaws. Reality, unless you are a boxer in a ring, is far from this. Punches more often than not are wild and do not connect; if they do, it is usually with a turned shoulder, the top of the head or similar. Richard's punches were not accurate but they propelled both men away from the rending roof that had been split open when a miners pick ignited a pocket of methane in the seam close by. Richard's head rang and he could not see anything nor hear much above a constant piercing single note and much more harrowingly, the eldritch cry of a trapped man.

"Fuck, Jesus, fuck," swore Richard.

The trapped man screamed back, "Help me, oh God, please help me!"

Richard fumbled in the dark and touched the man's face which was soaked in sweat partly from the heat but mainly from his fear.

"Don't move," he heard his former opponent shout and he marvelled at the madness of what he said as he could now see that the man was pinned from his hips down.

"I'll go for help," he continued and his charcoal shadow disappeared down the tunnel which was clearing of smoke as the pumps kicked in.

Richard moved closer to the trapped man and sought out his hand which he took and gripped hard.

"What's your name?"

"Peter."

"Peter what?" Richard asked.

"Peter Jennings."

"And who do you support, Peter?"

"What?" He sobbed.

"Footy. What's your team?"

"Who else is there?" Peter tried to laugh. "Always the magpies." Newcastle United to the uninitiated.

"And do you have a girlfriend, Peter?"

"Aye. Karen, a bonny lass who works in the tax office. We are hoping to get marr…" And Peter slipped into unconsciousness.

"What the fuck is happening?" Richard shouted unaware of the frantic activity above and starting to feel fearful himself as the adrenalin in his veins ebbed away. He carried on holding, talking, and being with Peter Jennings.

Richard had six pints of bitter that evening and bought none of them. His opponent bought the first and five other non-conscripted miners bought the rest.

Peter Jennings lived but spent the rest of his life in a wheelchair, pensioned, physically challenged every day but grateful to be alive. Richard visited him once and surprised himself that he could not be more intimate with a man that he had soothed and supported in adversity, and after a difficult twenty minutes, he shook Peter's hand and left him to his thoughts. Both men were secretly relieved at the unsaid but understood end to their relationship.

Richard was only three weeks from the end of his conscription and he had been asked if he wanted to carry on, but his mind had been made up that day in the back alley with his mum and his tears. His mining career was going to be national service only.

On his last day, with a handful of coins and contrary to his nature, he finished his shift and having returned his gear to the pithead office, said some cursory goodbyes and he then stepped into the pub where he had been championed a few months before. He ordered a pint of mild and took a seat away from the bar by the window. Unsure of a second pint, he caught the eye of another young miner at the next table.

"Last day?" The figure said.

"Yes. You?"

"The same."

"Michael."

"Richard."

"Pleased to meet you."

"Are you staying?"

"I have six shillings and one last night of lodging to pay for, which just about clears me out."

"Well, I have six bob too but I live at home so the drinks are on me…if you would like."

"Great," said Michael.

"Champion," said Richard.

The conversation was easy. Mining, football, girls, or rather the lack of them, family, the future, and then it was over.

"Best get back," said Michael. "They lock the door."

"Well, good luck," said Richard. "Perhaps we'll meet again." Though, they never did.

As Michael went to open the door of the pub, he hesitated and then went back to Richard and he held out a book. It was John Steinbeck's *Of Mice and Men*, dog-eared and stained as the result of multiple readings as it had sustained Michael through his time in the North-East.

"Please, take this. For the beers. And for the companionship."

"I couldn't."

"You will."

Michael pulled from his pocket a stub of pencil and inside the front cover, he wrote:

From one ex-minor miner to another.

Good luck on your last old day and your first new day as you close the door and open the curtains.

Michael. Gateshead 16 June 1946.

The lad whom Donald had heard about through his mother's friend, Susan, was the lad who finished his national service and was sitting with his uncle, Walter, in the kitchen of the next-door house. This was Richard whom Donald had helped to create through chance. Four sisters, similar to the rent-man-chasing Cave sisters but not as fierce, lived within a stones-throw of each other in Gateshead. Nan, the eldest, would in due course move to Stockton-on-Tees and live in a tiny cottage with a companion of the same sex free from the taint of post-war moral intrusion. The other three lived cheek by jowl in two-up-two-down maisonettes.

Until the day he retired from the mines, Walter's wife, Dora, would wash his white work shirts by hand, cut all the pearl buttons off them so they wouldn't crack before putting the shirts through the mangle, and then sew all the buttons back on. Every white shirt, every working day. Josie was a spinster. She had come to stay with her elder sister, Ruth, for three weeks while recovering from an illness and had stayed for twenty-seven years. Amazingly in her sixties, she met and fell in love with a local gentleman and after they married, she moved out from her sister's house but only into the next street.

Ruth was Richard's mother. David was his brother. The last digit of David's National Insurance number had not triggered a brown envelope and a demand to be conscripted as a miner. He joined the RAF and flew both figuratively and literally. Richard was demobbed in 1946 and David in 1948, though he would stay in the Far East for another three years in the RAF before he came home. Richard worked for the civil service and stayed in the North-East close to his family.

Their father, Harry, was an impressive man in the area. He was both a magistrate and chairman of the Watch Committee that oversaw policing. He was also deputy lord mayor of Newcastle-upon-Tyne and was generally slated to rise high in the Labour party, perhaps to party leader and maybe, maybe Prime Minister. He had a massive coronary in 1947 and died immediately at the same age as the century. Ruth, his wife, never spoke to anybody outside of her immediate family for the next forty years until her death.

Richard did nothing of any real note during the next fifty years of his life. He had a reasonable marriage, a reasonable job, and a satisfactory income, then later a comfortable pension and two kind but unremarkable children.

However, when his brother came back from the Far East in 1951 with a Vietnamese bride called Anh, and at her bidding when his brother was elsewhere, he did sleep with her, just once, but that sexual encounter brought about a longed-for pregnancy for her and years of uncertainty and suspicion from those close to the previously childless and possibly barren couple. The child was a girl and they called her Sally. She looked like her mother who knew her heritage as did Richard, her biological father and her legal father's brother. David was unsure of something concerning his wife and his brother but not what it was.

David

If men can be called beautiful, then David was beautiful. Richard, his brother, was a good-looking man but David had ethereal beauty. And he smiled most of the time and laughed when he was not smiling. Mothers loved him, particularly his own mother, Ruth, and women loved him or wanted to love him, or at least be physically loved by him. On the basis of his good looks, it would be easy for men to dislike him but on the whole, they liked him too. A glance from David, or a glance at David, were both fulfilling experiences. No brown envelope dropped through the letterbox for David's attention, so eighteen months to the day after his brother's envelope had arrived, and seventeen months after his brother started his first shift at Heworth Colliery, David enlisted in the RAF.

Somewhere there is a black-and-white photograph of a grimy young man in overalls and miners' helmet and a clean-cut young man in blue serge with flying wings and a cap looking confidently into the middle distance. Brothers but not in arms. Close but separated by a single number, maybe a seven. Both were part of the movement to cage the wolf. Both serving their country and both in dangerous occupations but geographically and emotionally hundreds of miles apart.

The fight between Richard and David came from nothing but was years in the making. It was 1962 and Sally had just turned six. David was working for an international bank in Newcastle and was shortly to be offered a promotion and a move to London. He lived in the tranquil and very middle-class suburb of Jesmond with Anh and Sally. Anh did not work but kept a clean and organised home and was a good cook, which were important assets in post-war England. They were content but not happy, loving but not necessarily in love. There was a wrinkle in their relationship, a hairline crack that David could not quite fathom where it lay.

As a bank manager in the making, he was developing a sense of who was and wasn't a reliable customer. The vast majority of his customers were solid but occasionally, there was one that triggered a sixth sense and set David's antennae on alert. Anh did that too. Not often but enough to make him concerned. And then he saw it. A touch, a laying on of fingers and a whispered word between Anh and Richard at their mother's house with the tea in the pot and the scones on a plate. Richard smiled at Anh and Anh then glanced to her left and saw David looking at her. The triangle formed and David, Richard, and Anh, all stared at each other.

In that unbidden moment, unsaid but understood, they all knew. David took one step forward.

"You bastard, you fucking bastard."

"David, please," said Anh.

"And you can fuck off too. All these years, all these bloody years," said David.

Richard offered the classic offender's lament. "Dave, I can explain." David rushed at him and hit him like they do in the movies, full in the face. Richard's face split and blood ran free. He reeled back and sat down like a baby learning to walk and he held his head in his hands partially to staunch the blood but mainly to cover his shame.

"Aaaagggghhhh!" David screamed and raised a fist that both he and Anh knew he would not use on her.

"Aaaggghh!"

Their mother, Ruth, appeared. The mother who had no interest in anybody other than her own family. Richard's wife appeared too, the wife who would never leave him, not now or indeed ever. Ruth spoke to both of her sons regularly in the coming years but never together, and Richard and David never spoke to each other again.

David's anguish held for a few more seconds as anger and then it changed into racking sobs. Eventually, despite multiple entreaties from his mother, he meekly turned on his heel and opened the front door, but not before he had taken the black-and-white picture of the coal miner and the airman and smashed it on the floor.

Within a month, David was living and working in London and Anh was on the way back to Saigon with her daughter, Sally. David would only see his daughter once in the ensuing years but he would speak to her often on the telephone and write to her every Sunday at his dining room table when the single plate had been cleared, washed, and put away.

David's pain was so deep and his belief that there was no way out of his purdah so profound that he often contemplated his own exit from the world. When that day actually came, he was drunk earlier than usual but in a perverse way clear headed. He knew the location and he knew the plan. He took a train and left his car in the drive. He alighted from the train and walked the last mile to the cliff edge and looked down at the crashing waves. With his back to the sea, he walked back ten paces and put on a blind fold. He spun himself round several times and as his brother's friend, Michael, had done by the loch side, he smelt the air and felt the wind on his face to gauge the general direction of the cliff edge.

He took a deep breath and he just ran. It was not a direct run because the spin had angled him away from the cliff but that had been part of the plan. Fear of fear and fear on fear. His sixteenth pace landed on solid ground but his seventeenth did not and, the once beautiful but now careworn and manifestly sad David, dropped over the edge. He touched the cliff only once on the descent before he landed on the rocks below and died instantly. The sea water did not wash clean his face nor did it reset his beauty. Instead, he lay on the rocks broken in body and spirit until hours later, the police and affiliated services processed the scene and the zip of the body bag took him from view forever.

Mike

In a few months, Michael would mostly be known as Mike. His family's formality in the use of his name dropped away and he liked the change. Mike had a carefree sound to it; well, that's what he thought anyway. After leaving the notes in his Jedburgh home, he had walked the short distance to the railway station and it was here that he had his only small but noticeable doubt. It was a feeling of kindness and affection for his mother and the hurt that he was causing her again that made him check.

However, he consoled himself with the fact that this was his decision and not the action of the government, and so he squared his shoulders and approached the ticket office with the confidence of liberty. He had a vague plan that he would head to Edinburgh and look for work. He wasn't quite ready to leave the country of his birth yet but he saw this move as a stepping stone to something new, something bigger and exciting. As he stood in the line, he glanced at the posters on the station wall and one caught his eye.

It was a magnificent print of Gleneagles, known as the 'Riviera of the Highlands', and its bold type and glorious colouring had a dual purpose. Firstly, to announce the impending re-opening of the hotel after its wartime use as a military hospital and then subsequently, with exquisite irony, as a miner's rehabilitation centre. Secondly, it was a recruiting poster for multiple trades to initially help in its refurbishment and then, in due course, for catering and other ancillary staff.

Mike was now at the head of the station queue and instead of asking for a ticket to Edinburgh, he heard himself say:

"A third-class single to Gleneagles please."

"Second class is the cheapest, son," said the man behind the glass, "and if you want that it will be two shillings and threepence."

Mike dug out a florin and a threepenny bit and exchanged it for a small piece of cardboard with blue ink stamped on it, dominated by the words 'Gleneagles. Single'.

Liberty. Freedom. Choice. The joy of it. Mike almost skipped to the platform and twenty minutes later, he was on a train North, with a change at Berwick-upon-Tweed and another in Edinburgh which had of course been his original destination. Twenty years later, Richard Beeching and his infamous Beeching cuts would close hundreds of miles of track in Great Britain along with their associated stations, of which Jedburgh was one. The resultant unemployment would eclipse the numbers that led to Mike's conscription to the mines and the effects would be felt for many years after that.

But this was all many years in the future and on this day, Mike put his backpack on the opposite seat, settled his feet on top of it, and lit a carefree cigarette. He heard somebody whistling and realised that it was him.

"Yes, son?" A big man with a moustache and a clipboard said. Neither of those features were linked but Mike recognised the attitude and the stance. Barrel-chested with legs spread slightly, a compromise between at attention and at ease. Ex-military without a doubt and the second use of 'son' that day which was a mixture of welcome and age definition. John Carnegie was indeed a former soldier, a regimental sergeant-major to be accurate, and he brought all that training and experience to his new role in 'civvy street' as a general manager in the lately assembled hotel hierarchy.

What he lacked in catering knowledge, he more than made up for in discipline and organisation, and in his short tenure, he had become invaluable to the Gleneagles' owners. In the years to come, the moustache would disappear to be replaced by luxuriant sideburns and he would wear his hair longer and slightly relax his dress code but the level of command and efficiency would never waiver and he would cement his position in the hotel. But that was in the future and on this day, he repeated his enquiry:

"Yes, son?"

The reason John Carnegie had to repeat the question was that Mike did not know what to say. His excitement of being on the move and heading for Gleneagles had not included even the most rudimentary plan.

"Err, well, do you have any jobs?" He blurted.

"Yes, we do, son. Did you write to us?"

"No."

"Did you speak to anybody on the telephone?"

"No."

"Did you come in for an interview?"

"No."

"May I ask why are you here then?" John was about to call him son once again when he stopped. "What's your name?"

"Michael Law. Mike."

"Well, what can you do, Mike Law?"

And here Mike paused and taking a huge leap of faith, he said:

"I can hew coal and make a flask of tea and I am quite a good footballer and…"

"Enough," said John. "Conscript miner?"

"Yes," said Mike.

"Good for you. Hard graft and little glory. Bevin Boy then I guess which must have been tough but it's been hard for a lot of people, although as an army man myself, I am glad that I served above ground. Very nice to meet you, Mike. Wait there."

John headed into the hotel and Mike took the opportunity to look at the enormous and beautiful building that was the Gleneagles Hotel with its glorious grounds and golf course.

"Pot man, six pounds a month and live-in with all meals, split shifts with one day a week off, usually not on the weekends. You wear your own clothes but the hotel will provide aprons. How does that sound?"

"Great," said Mike and meant it.

"It's hot and noisy and people get angry but you will be used to all that from the mines, but there are windows and fresh air, and a chance to be part of a team and indeed learn some new skills."

"Finally, and I shouldn't really say this, but if you don't smoke, then I would start as it gives you a few five-minute extra breaks a day."

"Well, I do smoke but thanks, Sir," said Mike.

"John out here and Mr Carnegie in there, but no more sir. Ok, Mike? Oh, and be careful with the lassies, they can be a distraction."

Mike blushed and John pointed him in the direction of the offices where he would sort out his paperwork and his accommodation. Four hours later, he would be up to his elbows in suds and loving it.

Hotels, big hotels are akin to small cities. They have a fixed and a transient population which sways and bustles with ever-changing demands and desires. At their lowest level, they deliver Maslow's basic needs of shelter, food, water, and the capacity to sleep as well as freely available air. Clothing and reproduction are the customer's choice of course, the first encouraged and the second a possible by-product of being in luxurious and relaxing surroundings. Self-actualisation is unlikely but there are nods from both staff and customers to safety, belonging and esteem all tenets of his hierarchy of needs.

Mike was firmly and happily in the food and water department of the hotel, using water to remove the food residue from multiple pots and pans employed in the cooking process and then cleaning the glasses, plates, and cutlery used in its consumption. He was good at his job, diligent, thorough and likeable too, and so it was a shock when he encountered the intransigence, and frankly the obstinance, of one of the sous chefs one evening.

As a live-in employee, Mike was entitled to staff meals which were cooked and plated by the junior chefs and sometimes a sous chef if the restaurant was busy. Mike intuitively knew that the customer was of absolute priority and that staff meals were subject to delay if the kitchen was busy. However, he had been brought up on good manners and respect, and so when one evening:

"Staff meal please, chef, when you are ready."

And he heard nothing back and, in fact, saw no flicker of acknowledgement from either of the chefs at the pass.

"Sorry to disturb you but could I have a staff meal please when you have time."

Again nothing.

"Did you hear me, chef?"

Nothing.

"Chef?"

Gareth, the sous chef, banged down a pan and turned to face Mike. Red in the face from the heat and the pressure of the evening service, but now also furious that he was being asked a perfectly reasonable question, he shouted:

"Look, you cunt, can't you fucking see that I am busy?"

Silence.

"Well, can't you? Fucking potman! Jesus."

Mike stood and stared and then as he had done multiple times in the mines, he counted to ten before turning and heading out of the kitchen door into the welcoming Scottish night. He lit a cigarette and drew deeply as he thought and inhaled and thought some more. Minutes passed and he stubbed the cigarette out underfoot, before picking up the dogend and pushing it into the soft earth of the hotel gardens. He headed back into the kitchen and there was no Gareth at the pass as he was shouting at a new collection of victims on the newly busy banqueting section, where plate after plate was exiting into the main hotel function suite by a skilled and willing line of experienced waiting staff.

These were plates that Mike and his section would be cleaning later.

"Fish and chips ok, Mike?"

Mike swivelled and saw the young junior chef plating the food and wiping the edge of the plate with the cloth tucked into the cord of his apron. As he went to push it over the pass, Gareth reappeared and helped the plate forward with the heel of his hand so that it rested dangerously on the edge. Mike saved the plate but not all of the chips, which he picked off the floor and tucked back alongside the others.

"Alright, cunt?"

"Thank you," said Mike looking directly at the spotty terrified young lad in white who would likely be on the receiving end of Gareth's vitriol later in the service. The irony of this behaviour was that it was often the recipients of Gareth's bile that would be serving him beer at the end of his shift which he thought should be both promptly delivered and often free of charge. Mike was one of many who had been at the end of Gareth's temper. Many took no action, Mike was the exception.

Gareth did not live in. Mike knew this. He was local and lived with his equally bad-tempered father in Auchterarder, a town a short distance from the hotel. Often over the limit to do this journey, he nevertheless drove home every night and on a slackish weekday night when the kitchen was less busy than usual and Gareth had drunk more than he usually did, a police car was waiting on the road as he weaved his way drunkenly home. With due process, he lost his licence and incurred a fine which resulted in a four-mile walk from the hotel to his house most evenings as his equally drunken father would not, or could not, drive the short distance to pick him up.

Mike was the police tip off but his time underground had taught him the need for approbation in disputes and he knew that he needed a face-to-face conversation with Gareth.

He sat waiting on a wall by the winding entrance road one evening smoking a cigarette. The Scottish summers sometimes extended daylight hours virtually to midnight and tonight, the sun was still up when he saw Gareth approaching. There was a check in Gareth's stride and the last thirty yards were measured and he was on alert.

"Evening, big man," said Mike.

"What do you want?" Gareth replied.

"A truce or an explanation, or both," said Mike. "They do not pay me enough to put up with that shit. Firstly, I am aware that your job is frantic and concentrated at times and that you are under pressure. But this is a team game and I am part of the team. A centre forward can't score a goal without his kit and boots, or without the lines being painted or the nets hung or the grass cut. The crowd doesn't cheer for these things but it is part of the process, just like the pots that I wash for you to cook in."

"Secondly, my dad's brother drank too much and was always angry or remorseful as a result. The solution is actually the problem. He lost his family, his career, and his friends until he realised that stopping drinking was the only way to get his life back on track. It's only been a few months but the signs are positive."

Gareth sat down on the still-warm grass. The fight went out of him. He did not cry now but he would in due course.

"What a mess," he said and told Mike of his life.

The sun had packed its bags for the evening when he stopped.

And finally, Mike said:

"Staff meal please, chef."

And they both laughed. Men connecting and understanding each other. Progress.

"You are part of the problem and the solution, I think," John Carnegie said. "I do not know what went on between you and Gareth but I am not a fool. He has decided to move on to pastures new and so as part of the solution, I am asking you if you would like to train to be a chef, starting at the very bottom of course but you would be cooking with the pans and not washing them!"

Mike shook John's hand and they both started to laugh loud and infectiously until a couple of windows opened and the stern looks from within put an end to it.

"Thanks, Mr Carnegie."

In later years, Mike's bistro in Edinburgh would be called 'Mikeys' and his two-star Michelin restaurant would be called 'Michaels'. Both were perennially busy and both treated all the staff from the potman who washed the dishes as he had once done, to the glorious female French head chef who ran his high-end business, with respect and consideration. Oh, and with a good deal of humour too. Newly sober and grateful for the opportunity, Mike's nemesis, Gareth, was a chef in the bistro. He was part of the management team too but his culinary skills were not good enough for the main restaurant and both he and Mike knew this. Not quite friends they were, however, no longer adversaries.

John Carnegie was correct on another matter too. The lassies loved Mike. Not only was he good-looking, witty and fun, but he had something about him. There were several examples of Colpo di fulmine, love at first sight or literally a lightning strike from young ladies working in the hotel as his unwitting charm and laid-back personality worked their magic. Mike was not interested in any long-term commitments, so even though he tried to be a gentleman and behave in an honourable manner, there was inevitable distress and broken hearts.

Mike only had one relationship outside of the hotel and that was with a young lady he met at a ceilidh in the village and the girl's father put an end to that tryst when he arrived at the hotel on his tractor with his dogs.

He was, however, seduced by a tall, elegant American woman in her thirties who was staying at the hotel and who welcomed him into her hotel suite twice in a week and then ignored him after that for the rest of her stay until she travelled by liner back to New York. Here, she would give birth to the child conceived in that Gleneagles Hotel bedroom. Her name was Ellena Goodperson, the definition of which was up for debate as the conception had been a deliberate act and Mike had no idea that she had intended to be or was pregnant.

Ellena had recently ended a horrific and brutal marriage entered into during the years of the Second World War, and as a result of this union and way in advance of later equality thinking, she had changed her name from the masculine 'Good-man' to the non-gender specific 'Good-person'. The child was born in the Upper East Side of Manhattan and was called Tom after Tom Harmon, an American football player and heroic World War Two pilot. There was no connection with Ellena Goodperson; she just liked what the man stood for and hence took his name for her son.

Anh

Anh went home to Vietnam with her six year old daughter, Sally. She was half-Vietnamese and half-English with a father who was the brother of her mother's husband. Complicated but not unusual and over the coming years, she would have friends who were of mixed parentage, although the majority of these would have American fathers and not an English one. Sally was estranged from her father, or at least she thought that she was; it would be in the years to come that the truth would out, and this gave her a distorted and yet sympathetic affinity with the friends whose American GI fathers were unknown, unconnected, or worse, still dead.

The twenty-year war that would colour and influence Anh and Sally's life had started a year before Sally had been born and seven years before their return to Saigon. Officially, a civil war between the North and the South of Vietnam, its actual reach would be global and involve communist Russia and China as allies of the North and anti-communist America as well as lesser combatants as allies of the South. With colonial France withdrawing after its defeat in the first Indo-China war in 1954, the country split into two military forces.

In the North was the Viet Minh and in the South, the state was supported financially and militarily by the USA while the communist-backed Viet Cong operated as a guerilla unit supplied by the North. Escalation into Laos and Cambodia led to the establishment of the notorious Ho Chi Minh trail and the pushback and escalation of involvement by John F Kennedy prior to his assassination in 1963.

Anh and Sally would return to Saigon in 1962. The city was under the control of President Ngo Dinh Diem who wasted enormous US aid and turned an initially thriving metropolis into a huge slum. This alongside the failed Tet offensive of 1968 by the North Vietnamese, coupled with huge urbanisation and a corrupt administration, led to virtual financial collapse, sky-high inflation, a black market economy, and widespread urban poverty. It would only be as the result of a final offensive by the North Vietnamese in April 1975 that Saigon was taken and the war ended.

The city was renamed Ho Chi Minh City and during the chaotic last few months of the war, an exhausted and afraid Anh closed her eyes on the bed in the one-roomed hovel where they lived and never reopened them. Sixteen-hour days in a munitions factory had broken her body and her will. There was no memento of David or Richard and no money, jewellery, or even food. There was just her tired face and a tiny photo of her daughter.

Sally found her the next day as she returned from her less demanding work. She sat cross-legged on the floor all that evening in silent prayer and then covering her mother's body with a sheet, she went out into the newly arrived dark of the night. She headed straight for a bar where American soldiers drank and standing in the doorway, she surveyed the room. There were groups of uniformed GIs laughing and drinking. She selected a small group and painting on a false smile, she approached them in a faux coquettish manner.

"Hey there, soldier boy," she trilled. "You buy me a drink?"

Two of the men grinned but carried on their conversation.

The third said:

"What are you drinking sweetheart?"

"Ruou nep cam," said Sally.

He turned to the barman and ordered two. Over the next hour, they separated from the other two soldiers and he drank three more and she sipped her first one. Eventually, at her bidding, they left the bar. Linh was her temporary name. He was Brad. Of course, he was. He booked a room in a seedy hotel in a side alley and managed a partial attempt at love making before the evening's alcohol took him to sleep. Sally took his dollars and his clothes. Ten dollars went to a burial for her mother. Three days later, she had the necessary forged documents to travel to Canada.

Tom

Tom, he was a piper's son,
He learnt to play when he was young,
And all the tune that he could play,
Was over the hills and far away.

The sightseeing tours of The Statue of Liberty and Ellis Island leave from Pier 83 multiple times a day and for the more adventurous spirit, there is a full circumnavigation of Manhattan Island. The young Tom Goodperson never took the longer trip and in truth, although he was in awe of the enormous statue gifted to America by France in commemoration of the two countries' alliance during the American war of Independence, it was in fact Ellis Island that he travelled to see. Precociously multiple times in his teens, he would tell excited tourists that the statue was modelled on the face of its artist, Frederick Bartholdi's mother, that it represented a Roman goddess and that its frame was built by Gustave Eiffel.

These knowledgeable asides were just employed to kill time and, in fact, Tom had only once alighted from the boat to view the statue up close. It was Ellis Island that he waited for and the chance to immerse himself in the now-closed immigration processing station.

Ironically, the facility had closed in 1954 which was the year of Tom's birth but unlike the twelve million or so immigrants that had arrived there since its inception in 1892, Tom's arrival had been markedly different. He had arrived in the USA in the safest berth of all which was inside his mother as she crossed the Atlantic in a first-class cabin arriving in late Summer in New York. Ellena's one and only full-term pregnancy would be relatively trouble free and that coupled with her height and physique, meant that it was only one persistent passenger that noticed her condition.

"Are you, err, with child?" The preposterous and socially clumsy Connie Darling enquired.

"Whatever gives you that impression?" Ellena replied.

"Well, a lady just knows you see," retorted Connie.

"Does she? Well, if you see a lady be sure to ask her but in the meantime, if I hear you talking about me again to anybody on board, I will put a mark on that unladylike face of yours. Capiche? Now fuck off."

Ellena strode away and with her single cigarette and martini of the day, she patiently waited in the lounge bar for a table for dinner. Several times she had been invited to dine with other couples and families but on each occasion, she had politely refused. Instead, she ate modestly, drank water, and read *East of Eden*, which was the latest of John Steinbeck's novels. She ignored the lascivious glances of the men and the resultant darting looks from their wives, and with elegant ease and a touch of disdain, she exited the restaurant and retired to bed early.

Tom grew inside her and Ellena nightly surveyed the passing ocean from the porthole of her cabin. Waves of pleasure that would dissipate very quickly post-birth and waves of water washing around her and washing by.

Many visitors to Ellis Island talk of the sense of hope that the building engenders even though it has been long closed. It was only after several visits that Tom acknowledged this feeling and realised that this was the reason that he kept returning to its now empty buildings. Empty that is apart from the now many tourists that crowded its floors. But it would never be as busy or as frantic and chaotic as it was during all of its years as a conduit into America.

"A portal," Tom said to nobody.

"Sorry, kid, what did you say?" A kind looking man said momentarily separated from his wife.

"Optimism, opportunity, hope," said Tom.

"Well, if you say so, kid." The English use of son replaced by kid. The man edged away and sought comfort in a hotdog offered to him by his wife.

Tom had neither acknowledged the man nor indeed meant to connect with him. The words were for himself alone. He knew what this place meant and he sensed the pioneers that had passed through its doors in search of a dream. The American dream. He also came to worship at the altar of opportunity without even recognising that calling. 'Take hold, Tom, you son of Scotland. Stand tall and have a go', the ghosts of the past said to him.

"Five minutes, ladies and gentlemen," said the elderly gentleman in the bright yellow baseball cap.

"And then you shall either be on the boat back to Manhattan or be forced to spend the night here. And trust me, there have been a few stragglers who have endured that fate and I use the word fate advisedly as this building becomes very cold when the sun disappears. So step lively please."

"Tom considered adding his name to the reluctant overnighters but was shepherded along by another docent in a similar yellow cap who upon reading his mind, advised him."

"Don't bother, kid. It's cold and dark and as I have seen you here several times before, I suspect that this is a special place for you and if you get caught, then you will be banned from coming back. Why don't you ring me the next time that you are going to make a visit and I will show you the areas that are out of bounds? My name's Don and I work Wednesday through Saturday."

"I'm Tom," said Tom, "and thanks, I will," and he did.

The benches in the Great Hall consist of two sets of rails. Five for sitting on and five for leaning against. Sitting here you can see the upper gallery that runs around the whole building beneath the arched ceiling. And of course, the stars and stripes of the twin American flags. Tom sat with his knees up.

He hadn't been back in four years but as ever, he had been drawn back and was again experiencing that sense of hope that his multiple trips as a child had engendered in him. His breathing was low and steady and he closed his eyes. When he opened them, he chanced to glance up and emerging from behind the material of the furthest flag was a pretty girl. She had almond-shaped eyes, dark hair pulled back in a ponytail, and a ready smile. For the briefest of moments, her eyes met his and then her friend said, "Coming, Sally?" And she was gone.

Ellena's hair was piled impossibly high and she was, as she often was, eight sheets to the wind. She had an uncanny knack for being able to look elegant and poised in public (and she spent a lot of time with her public, her so-called friends and peers) but often when the curtain came down on her soirees and society get-togethers, the mask would not just slip but it would end up on the floor as she staggered about and hurled abuse and vitriol at her housekeeper, or her latest beau, or her son.

"You fucking useless Scottish parasite. All you fucking do is take, take, take."

Tom was in his teenage years, so the opportunity to be anything other than a 'taker' was not available to him. His brain noted the oft-used Scottish attachment to the various insults that he was subjected to but his consciousness dismissed it. In later years, it would make sense but not now.

He lived with his increasingly erratic mother in a glorious apartment in the Upper East Side and was subjected often and randomly to his mother's anger and unhappiness. Occasionally, though rarely, she would make remorseful overtures to Tom but they were insincere and short, and more often than not, followed by a fresh outburst of expletives.

Tom attended Hunter College High School, a fee-paying private school which accepted a fraction of the potential students who took the entrance exam. Even Ellena's wealth would not have moved the dial on acceptance. Hunter College was an academic magnet secondary school where results mattered. Fortunately, Tom was bright. He was popular and diligent as well as a good sportsman.

He kept his head down unlike his mother, who only twice attended functions at the school, once straying onto the football pitch to berate the match officials before being gently escorted away and secondly swaying drunkenly into a valuable sculpture which teetered briefly and then smashed on the floor at a school prize-giving.

"Send me the fucking bill," she shouted before again being steered away.

"Queers and mummy's boys all of you," was her parting line.

Fortunately, she had no real desire to visit the school and so Tom saw out his school days in relative peace. He avoided his mother at home too and as there was always a housekeeper (though rarely the same one as the turnover of employees was staggering) to attend to clean clothes and occasionally meals as he came and went in feral style. There were dollar bills of all values plus nickels and dimes strewn all over the apartment so money was never a problem either. He assuaged his conscience by weighing fiscal probity against parental input.

"I don't want a party, thanks, Mother."

"You ungrateful little shit."

"I am neither ungrateful nor a shit."

"You will be there and you will smile and be gracious. Do you hear me? Do you?"

Tom sighed and calculated. The party was for his eighteenth birthday in three weeks. None of his friends were invited and it was to be held at a suffocating club in the Hamptons. It would be full of his mother's dreadful acquaintances and so-called friends but he thought to himself 'just once more', and so he said:

"Lovely. Thanks, Mother."

Whatever Ellena Goodperson had in mind for him, Tom had his own plans and so he decided to suck it all up and make the party a line in the sand. The event was even more awful than he had imagined particularly as he was the youngest by at least thirty years. He was patronised and condescended to all evening by mostly heroically drunken society people. It was not just the ridiculous evening attire that constricted him but also the atmosphere and attitude. Finally, his mother took him on to the balcony and with the lights of the town glittering in the distance and the surf pounding the beach, she opened her clutch bag and gave him an envelope.

Tom opened it and inside was a roll of hundred-dollar bills and a note which read:

That's your lot. FUCK OFF.

And so Tom did. More of that later.

Over the years at the Hamptons, Ellena, in her self-perceived grandeur, had a habit of having 'just one more drink, a night cap really' on the jetty near her summer retreat. This she did sometimes in company but usually alone wearing an evening gown and stiletto heels. She smoked a cigarette in a tortoise shell holder and drank a glass of Pol Roger from a saucer-style glass, not a flute. Depending on the weather and the resultant swell of the seawater, the planks of the jetty were often wet, and therefore slippery, which was not ideal for a drunken woman in high-heeled shoes. Multiple times she had negotiated the slimy boards, tottering inelegantly.

Often a handrail broke her fall, and several times she ended up on her backside either dirtying or tearing her beautiful dress. Tom would be many years and miles from his mother's side when her luck finally ran out and the sea took the cigarette in its holder, the glass and her body to its depths after a drunken fall. It was a night when she was alone, so nobody saw or heard her demise. Tom would only find out about his mother's death after her funeral, which had settled the decision he would have had to make on whether to attend or not.

Sally

Sally sniffed yesterday's knickers. Women often do.

"Just about," she said to herself.

She then smoothed the near white item (or is it items as knickers is or are plural), laid it over her face and lay back on the bed thinking. There was a bizarrely comforting feeling as a result of being beneath the just about clean cotton and she rode that emotion for a few seconds before twisting to the edge of the bed and slipping them on. She had been in Toronto for just three days, staying in a cheap hotel in the poorest area of the city. She had had no plan except to leave Saigon and now that she had done so, she felt a curious mixture of elation and trepidation.

The circumstances of her mother's death and the hard years of toil in Vietnam sat in juxtaposition to her newfound excitement and she oscillated between these two emotions more savagely when she was inactive, and so she took the cure and became active.

She made a list:

1.   *Work*
2.   *Accommodation*

And then she paused, or rather that was all that she could think of that was relevant to her present position. Sally approached the first item on her list with a good feeling. Even though she only had a visitor's visa, her swift and limited research prior to leaving Saigon had assured her of a solid support network for Asian workers in Canada operating in the black market. And so she set out to an area of Toronto where there were several streets of Vietnamese restaurants.

'Banh Banh' had no work nor did 'The Green Papaya' but at 'Bep Viet' she struck it lucky:

"Xin Chao," said Sally.

The middle-aged man stared dully back at her.

"Cong Viec?"

"Duc?"

The man blew out a smoke ring and broke into a smile.

"Newly arrived honey?" He said.

Sally took a chance.

"Yes. From Saigon three days ago."

"And how is it there?"

"Awful," said Sally.

The man sat down and lit another cigarette. His name was Ngo Quang. He had been born in Saigon but had lived in Canada for thirty years.

"Do you have somewhere to stay?" He asked.

"I am in a hotel in Moss Park," said Sally.

"Not good," said Ngo. "Go and get your things. In fact, wait there and I will get my son to go with you, and when you come back, I will introduce you to my niece who has a spare bed in her flat. You can start work in the morning and we will sort out your duties and your wages then. Ok?"

Sally was amazed.

"Cam on. Thank you. But why?"

Ngo smiled. "Because you are Vietnamese," and then he looked closer at her. "Although not entirely I think, but enough!" Then he laughed. "See you later, lady with no name."

"Sally," she said.

"Sally," he repeated. "Nice to meet you, Sally."

So the first item on her list begat the second item and made the list redundant and, after picking up her few personal items, Sally moved in with Linh and laughed at the irony of the girl's name. The next day, she started to work as a waitress in the family restaurant and she was both busy and to her amazement, happy. Saigon was at hand but also a long way away. The days flew by.

When Sally had been Linh for the night and took the soldiers' dollars, she had also noted down his name and other details from his identity papers when he had passed out. Sergeant First Class Bradley Davis (no E) from Nashville Tennessee. Thirty-two years old. Single. Career soldier. And so an idea came into Sally's mind. Just an idea but within a few days, it had grown wings and now it was building towards being an obsession. Sally was not unhappy but she knew full well that she could not stay as an illegal waitress forever and that was why Bradley Davis Sergeant First Class was rarely out of her mind.

Bradley Davis's mum, Jane, made pies. Lots of them. She loved to make pies, cakes, flans, little angel cakes with wings, and jam and cream but her first love was pies. Her pastry was so short and the fillings so delicious that her husband, Bob, often said:

"Honey, you should do this for a living!"

"Then the pleasure would all be gone," she would reply but she was flattered and, in the midnight hours when her thoughts ran away to Saigon and her only beloved son, she toyed with the idea of starting a small business, partly as a distraction but also to help with the family bills. Bob worked hard as a salesman but the truth was, he was incredibly amiable but really not very good. Steady, as his boss said. At bonus time, the rhetoric was always the same:

"Not bad, Bob, but maybe if you could up your game a bit, chase some new leads, bring a bit of razzle dazzle to the job."

"Sure, Ted," Bob would reply and take the meagre cheque home to Jane.

"Oh, well done, dear," she would say and kiss his cheek.

Bob and Jane. Good-hearted, salt-of-the-earth, blue-collar Americans with a son fighting god knows where, a large mortgage at a horrendous rate of interest, and a handful of dollars in the bank. So back to the pies.

Her best and favourite was the classic American apple pie, like mama used to make. She used honey crisp and King David apples from the North of the state but her favourites were Macintosh. They cut easily, didn't turn to pulp in the bake and only browned a little. Jane used lemon juice to stop the colour change and fanned them out in slivers for the open pie and cut generous chunks for the pastry topping variety. Plenty of brown sugar and a touch of cinnamon. Post-bake, she sat them on the wide kitchen windowsill to cool.

No cartoon-style urchins or cheeky small animals or birds to steal her work as Bob had built a wooden frame that covered up to three pies, allowed no access to beak, paw or fingers, and was so robust that in later years, it would be a two-person job to lift it over the fragrant food. Oh, the pies. The pies.

Letters

Sally sat on her haunches and composed the first of her two letters. Sitting in such a manner was a habit from her upbringing. She would sometimes laugh to herself when a particularly fat customer came into the restaurant as to whether they would be able to emulate this most natural of Asian positions even for a second. Unlikely if she felt kind. Impossible if she was being honest. The letter would be constructed like this in pencil and then she intended to borrow a fountain pen from either Ngo or his wife and sit at one of the restaurant tables between services to write it properly.

This, Sally would have to do three times, as the first effort was riddled with mistakes, the second ended up with a small food stain on the paper as she had not wiped the surface down carefully enough, but the third effort in royal blue ink was a thing of cunning and precision, short and to the point. Later with exquisite irony, she would be given a beautiful tortoiseshell fountain pen with her name inscribed on it when she left the restaurant and in the years to come, it would provide a happy memory of her time in Toronto. She used it often and was always careful to keep it safe.

She wrote:

Dear Brad,

Xin Loi. Sorry. Xin Loi. Sorry.

I can only apologise for what happened a few months ago when we met in the bar in Saigon. I think about you often and wonder if circumstances had been different, whether we would maybe have been able to be more than friends. It is no excuse but my mother had died recently and I wasn't thinking straight and that was why I took your money because I was scared. Please don't hate me but if you can find it in your heart to reply to this letter, it would make me very happy.

Lots of love,
Linh X

Sally sent the sealed letter from Toronto to her friend, Hoa, in Saigon with a cover note asking her to forward it for her so that it would have a local post mark. Sally had done reciprocal, though not identical, favours for her friend and so she was glad to help; in fact, she enjoyed the covert nature of the letters that came to her for posting. And there would be several more in the coming days.

Sally received no reply, which to her mind meant one of two things. Either she had the wrong army address or he did not want to get in touch with her. Sally worked on the basis that the finest army in the world would be able to get a letter to one of their soldiers, so her head told her that it was reluctance and not transit that was her problem, and so she wrote again:

Brad baby,

I wonder if you got the letter that I sent to you. I do hope so. I would really like to see you again and make up for my foolish behaviour. I realise that you are probably quite hurt by what happened but I can assure you that you did not see the real me and I would love the chance to make amends.

Lots of love.
Linh X

Nothing.

Hi, Brad honey,

How are you doing? Please don't hate me as it was such a silly thing and I can now pay you back some of the dollars that I stole from you and maybe we could find another way to write off the rest of the debt? Please, please, please get in touch.

Linh X (actually my name is Sally but I promise that is the last piece of deceit)

No reply.

Oh, Brad baby, don't be mad. Please, please, please write back or my heart will break. I miss you so so much.

Sally X

Sally was in the restaurant when the letter arrived. Sent by Hoa from Saigon and in a US army envelope. The short note was heavily redacted but it said:

Sally, eh? Not Linh.

I don't need the dollars but I would like to know why you did what you did. It can't have just been because I was drunk. Perhaps a coffee and then we can go from there.

Brad.

The meeting was set for a Wednesday afternoon in a cafe that Brad knew and when he arrived, he scanned the tables for Sally and was relieved, and frankly excited, when she waved back. His memory of her was blurred by time and his condition on that evening but she certainly looked different.

"Sally?" He said.

"Well, no," said Hoa, "but please, Brad, sit down and let me explain."

All men, well nearly all men, when presented with a pretty smiling girl sitting at a table in a cafe with the sun on her face and a smile in her eyes would scowl but capitulate, and Brad was one of that majority.

"And you are?" He asked.

"Hoa," she said. "Coffee?"

"Beer," said Brad, and sitting down, lit a Lucky Strike cigarette from a soft pack tucked in his uniform pocket.

"Do you smoke?"

Hoa took one and he rolled his zippo on his thigh and lit hers and his.

"Hit me," he said, "and this better be good."

Most of the conscripted soldiers called up to the Vietnam War served a year. Brad would serve just over two years as a result of excellence and choice. Five months prior to him returning home permanently when the war ended, he would have a compassionate leave of absence of five days for family reasons. On arrival at the Davis home at Five Points in Nashville, his mother offered up all that she had to him which was her love and her baking skills. His father was proud and awkward as many men are but managed to hug his son without crying. Privately, both Brad and Jane would have welcomed a tear but Bob was Bob and a hug was the best of him.

Sally arrived unannounced on the second day and the Davis parents were both shocked and confused. They were less surprised and, in fact, delighted seven months later when Brad and Sally were married. Sally had used the last five months of Brad's tour of duty to woo him by letter and telephone and to win over his parents in a similar way punctuated by two trips over the border from Canada when she cemented her place as their son's fiancée. At the wedding, there was the inevitable suspicion and bitchiness from family friends but less so from Brad's army buddies who had seen first-hand the making of Asian/ American relationships in the chaos of war.

Sally was beautiful and Brad was handsome in a full dress uniform, and they finally consummated their relationship in an enormous bed in an equally enormous bedroom in Hawaii.

Ngo and the family sent money, flowers, and cards to the couple but dared not cross the border én masse with only a handful of legal documents between them.

Three years into the future with no children and a job in finance that bored him, Brad would be a victim of recurring nightmares that triggered an attack on his mother whom he mistook for a Viet Cong soldier as she peaked round the door of the bedroom he was sleeping in while visiting them one weekend. He howled after her as she ran into the kitchen of their bungalow and leapt at her with a cheap Pottery Barn statuette as she pulled the heavy wooden pie frame from the window ledge over her face.

The first blow hit wood and the second never landed as Brad's father launched a heavy pan from the cooker at his son's head. The strawberry preserve in it had long cooled but the metal split Brad's troubled face open. Bob and Jane and their lovely son, pie makers and pie eaters, pillars of the community and kind beyond measure, sat in their own blood and tears on the kitchen floor with jam literally on their faces and their world collapsed.

Sally left in the morning. She was twenty-three years old and a US citizen through marriage, though she would never see her husband again. Hoa suspected that had been her intention all along, to get US citizenship, but sensibly she kept that thought to herself.

Demolition

Big Jim was an enormous man and the owner of the eponymously named 'Big Jim's wrecking crew'. He was well into his forties now but still as strong as an ox and could bench press three hundred and fifty pounds they said, but the 'they' had never seen this feat and, in fact, it did not matter. Big Jim was big in character and heart. His proud boast that he had never had to lay off a man except if he deserved it and he was fiercely loyal and supportive. He had started off in general construction as a hired hand and had commenced his own demolition business over ten years ago.

His mother was a lecturer in period architecture and this had spawned an interest in him, so much so that although he rarely turned down any job, he promoted and sought out demolition jobs that were for period properties. His secret desire on pricing such work would be that the demolition would be aborted and the building preserved, even though this would be financially detrimental.

Big Jim had started off in Los Angeles but had gravitated south to San Diego where the Californian affluence had hit a peak in the 1980s and was doing a good job of maintaining that now. Sunshine and good money. What was not to like? Tom too had headed down the California coast over the past couple of years doing odd jobs and surfing while looking for that elusive direction in life. He was content and untroubled while eating a taco at what he, and many others, considered the finest Mexican restaurant in California, 'The Taco Stand in Encinitas'.

He had one foot on the wall and the last mouthful of a cold beer left in the bottle. He rocked back and accidentally knocked the plastic basket with tortillas sitting on the table behind him to the floor. The guacamole was intact but the chips were everywhere.

"Shit, sorry," said Tom.

"Nobody died," said the large man.

"I'll get you some more," offered Tom.

"Three-second rule," said the giant and swept one huge hand over the tiled floor and returned the full basket to the table.

"Jim."

"Tom."

"Well, our parents didn't agonise over those names," said Jim and they both chuckled and shook hands. Another beer and a bit more time established both their credentials and Tom took a chance.

"Are you hiring?" Tom asked.

"Could be," said Jim. "Hard work but good pay, however, I do need a trial first. Give me a free week and if it works out, I will take you on and pay you for the trial week but if not, we shake hands and say goodbye. Fair?"

"Very," said Tom.

"It's Thursday today, so let's say Monday 7.00am by the lights down there. A red Chevrolet will pick you up, driven by a guy called Rick. If you don't have hard-wearing boots, then buy some, otherwise, it's shorts and a t-shirt. Oh, and bring lunch as we work hard but are done by 4.30pm, so plenty of surf time. Okay."

"Thanks," said Tom and headed for his motel with the intention of finding digs and buying boots the next day.

Fancy Bricks

The work was hard and Tom worried that after his probationary week, Big Jim would call it quits and let him go, but on the contrary, Jim was delighted and paid him for that week and promptly every Friday evening for the next few weeks. The work oscillated between regular demolition work with heavy machinery and several large trucks, to projects that required more care. Tom liked both aspects of the work and pitched in with a will. His colleagues were decent men and all Tom's preconceived ideas of tough-guy construction workers went out of the window.

Several were family men and stayed on after work for only the occasional beer, a couple were single guys like himself happy to be working mainly outdoors with regular paychecks, and a couple were part-timers working to put themselves through college. Friday at 4.00pm, Jim insisted on two things. Firstly, an early finish ahead of the weekend and secondly, a minimum of one pitcher of beer each bought by him and consumed in his presence. You could leave at 4.05pm but you would have your pitcher of beer washing around inside you.

Most of the guys stayed for an hour or so and a couple used it as a springboard into Friday night proper. All of the guys were affable and Tom was often amazed at the range of the conversation. From nuclear disarmament to Shakespeare and onto particle physics with a touch of baseball and football thrown in. The regulation hour flew by and Tom enjoyed feeling part of a unit. New York seemed a long way away.

The next week, Jim called his men together.

"Right," he said. "We have a special project here, so gather around please."

The men sat or leant on their boss's truck and a couple lit cigarettes.

"I recently pitched for the highly specialised demolition of several early nineteenth-century properties in Perry County, Indiana, and this morning, I found out that my tender was accepted. Frankly, I am surprised that as a Californian business, we have been awarded the work but apparently, we have a very high reputation nationwide which is rather flattering."

Jim looked around, took off his baseball cap, and scratched his head. He then continued.

"Clearly, this presents some logistical problems which broadly are machinery and personnel. The quote includes the hire of the necessary plant in Indiana plus the board and lodging for up to six men. I can and may have to hire some local men but I would rather not do so and therefore, the question is really who would be interested?"

Rick posed the obvious first question:

"How long do you think the job will take, boss?"

"Ball park, Rick. Two months. If I was a betting man, I would have a couple of bucks on slightly shorter rather than longer."

"Single rooms or bunking together?" Another man asked.

"Bunkhouse style unless you get lucky, Don, and then you can make your own arrangements," and they all laughed.

"For you married guys and you college guys, it's a chance to salt away some money. For the rest of you, it's a change. As I said, I need six of you so the fairest way is anything over six men, then we draw lots. Under six, then I will need to have a rethink."

Six hands went up including Tom's.

"Well, that was easy," said Jim. "And for the rest of you, there is plenty of work until we get back, and as Todd has not put his hand up, I am going to appoint him to be in charge until we return. Ok?"

They all nodded and as Jim jumped down off the back of his truck, they squared their collective shoulders and set off back to work.

Nor Nor East

The following month saw the six volunteers heading North-East to Indiana. Four of them were on a four and a half hour flight to Louisville just inside the Kentucky border, from which it was a fifty-odd mile drive west to Perry County which sat in Indiana's South-Western corner. Jim drove his pickup along with Tom and he drove it hard. They covered the distance in three days and stopped twice in truckers' motels overnight, where they ate enormously and drank modestly. The many hours on the road gave both of them the opportunity to ask the other one about their lives. Jim was open and candid about his upbringing in Los Angeles and about his parents and siblings.

His father had worked in finance and his mother was a retired lecturer in period architecture. He had two sisters, both of whom had married and both of whom had two children, one girl and one boy. Very average and very normal. His elder sister lived close to his parents in Orange County and his younger sister further North in Portland Oregon. Tom unconsciously probed for a weakness or fault line but there was none. Middle-class white-collar American family. Jim had been an average student academically but a sportsman of outstanding promise until as a seventeen year old, he had stepped in a gopher hole while running full tilt for a disappearing football in a field near his home and tore all the ligaments in his left knee.

The possible pro football career disappeared into the gopher hole too and he embarked on a destructive two years of drinking and recreational drugs until the father of one of his friends from school who was an orthopaedic surgeon repaired his knee over several operations, taking no payment, sufficiently that Jim could play most sports (with the exception of football) to a higher degree than all of his friends from high school. Golf balls and baseballs disappeared from view when hit by him. He became content, married his long-term girlfriend and, although childless, they enjoyed a happy and fulfilled life. Over the next few years, he repaid the surgeon with his own pro bono carpentry skills.

Jim probed Tom:

"And what about you, Tom?"

"Deranged mother. Unknown father. Not sure what my mother is up to and I don't know anything about my father."

"Wow," said Jim. "No ideas…if you don't mind my asking?"

"Well, I know when I last saw my mother and she told me to fuck off on the evening of my eighteenth birthday, I am pretty sure that she meant what she said. There were years of verbal, although to be fair not physical, abuse and I was glad to leave. Fortunately, there was a sum of money involved, not enormous but enough, and I have been happily travelling and working ever since. I have to stress that I went to a very good, if that's the word, school in New York and we lived on the Upper East Side. Now I say it to you, it seems strange, almost as if I am talking about somebody else."

"And your dad?" Jim asked. "If I am not prying?"

"I don't know. I have pieced a couple of things together. My surname is really Goodman but my mum changed it to Goodperson at some point. I believe that she had an abusive marriage and didn't want any connotation of 'man' in her life or her name. There is also a connection to a Jock but I don't know if that's a sportsman or Scottish, or possibly both. I do know that she loved to harangue me about my Scottishness when she was drunk but I have never been there or indeed know anything about the country. One day, I may find out but the truth is, Jim, as of today, I don't really care."

"Sorry to ask."

"Don't be," replied Tom. "But you have got me thinking. Anyway, which shithole are we going to lay our heads in tonight?"

Indiana

"Bloody hell," said Rick.

"Bloody hell indeed," said Jim.

"Carefully?"

"Very carefully."

"All of them?"

"All of them."

The team surveyed the mixed collection of properties that sat in a grove of trees next to a busy highway on the one side and a fast-flowing river on the other side.

"Built when?" Rick asked.

"From 1802 to 1871 according to the documents and plans that I have copies of."

"And the brief?" Rick enquired.

"Core materials to be recycled. Anything wooden that has not got dry or wet rot should be put on pallets. Anything with rot to be burnt. Glass, brick, tiles, etc. to be put in separate skips which will be arriving tomorrow. Clearly, the buildings are too young to have asbestos in them but beware of poisonous materials and other items such as wallpaper which could contain arsenic. Masks, gloves, and hard hats at all times. Oh, and watch out for snakes and spiders."

At this point, Don trailed his fingers on Tom's neck, who jumped a foot into the air.

"You bastard, Don," yelped Tom.

Over the next few days, they laboured and sweated even though the weather was cold. The first two properties came down quickly. A smallish cabin and barn of sorts. Tom was working in the third building which was a slightly larger cabin, more of a family house with a veranda at the front, and was using a crowbar to lever wooden planks from the rear wall in the parlour when he saw something. It was a roll of papers in a sort of parchment sleeve that was yellow with age. It was crisp to the touch but the papers inside looked intact. Tom removed his gloves and gently teased out the papers. There were three pieces of paper and all had writing on them. The first page had what looked like a poem and it read:

Colour departs an Indiana sky
Drowsy birds take wing and fly
Cart wheels turn in softened clay
Toil becomes rest at end of day
As shadows cast their warning light
We hasten home to beat the night
Families united by bonds of love
Offering prayers to god above

The second page had two quotes from a bible and a list of what seemed to be instructions.

Galatians 5:1—Stand fast therefore in the liberty wherewith Christ hath made us free, and be not entangled again with the yoke of bondage.

Exodus 21:16—And he that stealeth a man, and selleth him, or if he be found in his hand, he shall surely be put to death.

1. *Love your parents and siblings whatever their shortcomings.*
2. *Love your country.*
3. *Work hard and keep strong in mind and limb.*
4. *Be honest in all your endeavours.*
5. *Support your kin and neighbours.*
6. *Be happy and enjoy the beauty that surrounds you.*
7. *Keep God in your life at all times.*
8. *Reach out to those in need.*
9. *Respect the law.*
10. *Glory in your liberty.*

And the third page had a short story with a tiny drawing at the bottom of two stick men. The image was of one man chasing the other and made sense after Tom read the story. It said:

The Bully

If he hadn't turned himself, then I would have turned him around myself. By the creek in the gathering gloom, I saw the man/child harming the child/child and the blood ran fast in my veins. I knew the bully from school and was aware of his reputation but this was the first time that I had seen his actions. We were of a matched size but I had the advantage of 'Dieu et mon droit' on my side, and as the younger boy scampered away, we were left alone, matched in size but different in morals. He spat and then swung his fist at me, which I avoided, and then I drove at his midriff and took him down. I have undertaken catch-as-catch-can wrestling for several years now and held him down easily, although he writhed and shouted obscenities at me.

I am ashamed to say that I was so angry that I hit him once in the face but on reflection that might have been the right thing to do. There was a trickle of blood followed by a catch in his throat and then the tears. He was a bully and a coward, and I felt at that moment that he knew it. He came once more to school in the coming days and when he saw me, he looked away. His little victim gave me some meatloaf the day following the event which his mother had prepared and I can tell you that it was delicious.

As Tom sat and read the papers, he acknowledged to himself that the most amazing thing about the three pages were that they all bore a signature on them that read:

Abraham Lincoln 1924

1978

Sally was twenty-three years old and newly separated from her husband, Brad. In the future, she would hear from him once and of him once. The first occasion was to amicably arrange a divorce which was initiated and concluded within a year. There were few assets to be divided and, in fact, Sally wanted nothing from Brad apart from the uncoupling and she satisfied the occasional wash of guilt that came over her by this decision. The decree nisi arrived within a year of her leaving and that meant she was an independent woman with US citizenship and a rather bruised past.

The second occasion when Sally heard of him was when she was idly reading the *New York Times* on the subway one day and came upon an article about the newly recognised condition of Post-Traumatic Stress Disorder formerly grouped under the general heading of shock. Cited and revered was a former army officer now a psychiatrist called Bradley Davis. Sally sighed, reread the article, tore it from the paper, and after carefully placing it in her pocket, she felt a cocktail of emotions. Sadness at what had transpired between her and Brad, guilt at her calculated use of him as a method of securing a right to live in the United States, but mainly a strange pride in what he had overcome and become.

She tucked the article into a copy of the *Of Mice and Men* that her uncle, Richard, had given her mother as a child. The book had sentimental value and also contained a picture of her mother, Anh, plus an emergency ten-dollar note. On a couple of occasions when the nighttime played tricks on her, she contemplated getting in touch with her former husband but each time, the morning would bring reality and the thought would be quietly dismissed.

The Brad that she never saw again remained with his parents in Five Points until they died within eight months of each other in the late 1990s. During that time, he undertook extensive personal therapy sponsored by the army and also trained in psychiatry himself, specialising in trauma work. He never remarried or moved from his parents' home but he saved the sanity of many men and women both in the forces and civilian life through his professional skills. They knew him informally as Brad and clients rarely, if ever, turned down a slice of pie made by him from one of his mother's recipes.

He used the food as a comfort and a salve in particular for the soldiers who identified with the homely gesture as they struggled with their memories. Brad too had conflicting emotions about his marriage, choosing mainly to focus on the kindness that his former wife had shown him in the short time prior to his breakdown. The only photo he kept of Sally was from their honeymoon in Hawaii and it was turned to the wall during therapy sessions.

Sally had several hundred dollars saved and decided to head to New York with only the vaguest of plans. On the debit side of her ledger, she had a father dead from suicide and a mother dead from worry and hard work. She also had a failed marriage. But on the credit side, she was a citizen of the most powerful country in the world, was in good health with a small amount of money put by, and experienced way beyond her years. She had also stayed in touch by letter with the Quang family in Toronto and was certain that if all went wrong, Ngo and Linh would welcome her back with open arms.

And so she mentally flipped the short list that she had made after her arrival in Toronto from Saigon and put accommodation ahead of work for when she arrived in New York.

Four long days of viewing depressing bedsits and shared cramped apartments, eventually led her to a bright two-bedroom unit in Brooklyn where the female tenant was looking for a new flatmate quickly as her previous one had upped sticks and left recently almost without the courtesy of a goodbye. Sally liked her new landlady, Helen, immediately and was confident that she could cover the eighty dollars a month rent when she found a job. Unlike her arrival in Canada, Sally was now able to work legally, so she gave herself the luxury of looking for work that would not only pay her adequately but also interest her.

Helen was unlikely to be a help on this matter as she was an actress struggling to find roles that subsidised her income by waiting tables. However, she was not only friendly but also an incredible social butterfly and very generous, not only with her time but also with her enthusiasm. When Sally started job hunting seriously, Helen pitched in with a vengeance.

"And hot beverages are complimentary but of course, they are to be enjoyed in moderation," said a junior manager who was showing Sally around the tired, and frankly depressing, office of a small insurance company. She was offered the job on the spot but asked for time to think about the role and used it only as the most extreme of backstops.

"No," said Helen.

"Most of the younger staff play chess at the outsize board in Central Park on Thursday evenings and sometimes go for coffee afterwards," offered another potential employer.

"No," said Helen.

"Hair up and demure lipstick only," volunteered another.

"No, no, no," again from Helen.

"We have a strict policy on interoffice intimacy," said another and Sally wanted to scream until:

"It's a serious research position but not a serious crew here. I think we saw the old fogeys off years ago and most of the team are young and fun. Genuinely fun. Drinks and clubbing are encouraged as is laughter. It's a cliche but it is a culture of working hard and playing hard. Thoughts?"

"Oh, yes," Helen enthused, "right up my alley."

Sally stared hard at the good-looking man asking her about her thoughts which were not entirely focused on the job (literally the job) at hand. He had a twinkle in his eye and a way of making political research sound interesting. Perhaps it was? And there was only one way to find out so Sally said that yes she was interested, very interested, and after waiting only three days, a letter arrived offering her the position as a junior researcher on what she considered a fair salary.

Helen was thrilled for her and that night, they celebrated at a very cosmopolitan bar in Greenwich Village, arriving back at the flat with more friends than they had started out with. In the morning, Helen left for yet another audition and Sally gradually removed the various bodies that were sleeping randomly on the floor and the sofa, and set the flat straight again. She headed out into Brooklyn to restock the fridge and food cupboards, returning with an enormous bunch of flowers which she arranged in their only vase on the dining table. The champagne that she had bought took pride of place in the fridge and she planned a meal for the two of them from her purchases.

"Well?" She said, "How did it go?"

"Not sure," said Helen, but she had a quiet confidence about how the audition had gone. Later when the champagne was gone and the alcohol was working its magic, she told Sally:

"I think I nailed it," and they hugged each other. Indeed, Helen had nailed it and within two weeks, she was rehearsing for an off-Broadway production of *The Grapes of Wrath* playing the Joad's eldest daughter, Rose of Sharon. Sally attended the opening night and was amazed and tearful in equal measure at the depth of her friend's acting skill. When Helen came in later from the post-production drinks party, Sally was curled in a chair reading her dog-eared copy of another of Steinbeck's novels *Of Mice and Men*. Helen smiled and made coffee, passing Sally a cup.

"May I?" She said, putting her hand out to receive the book.

"This has been around the block a few times," she said and opened the fly page where the following was written:

From one ex-minor miner to another.

Good luck on your last old day and your first new day as you close the door and open the curtains.

Michael. Gateshead 16 June 1946.

"Who is Michael?" She said. "And where the fuck is Gateshead?"

"I don't know who Michael is but Gateshead is a mining community in the North of England and this book was very important to my mother." Sally understood as she told Helen about the vague origin of the book that she had a need to reveal herself and tell somebody whom she trusted, loved even, about her life, so she put down her coffee cup, ran her hand through her hair, and did so.

"My dad committed suicide when I was young but when he did so, my mother, who was called Anh, and I were living in Saigon. David was my dad's name and he met my mum when he was doing national service and his posting was in the Far East. We lived in a place called Jesmond which is also in the North-East of England after they got married and I think my mum was happy there but something happened when I was five or six years old."

"But you have no idea what happened, Sally?" Helen asked.

"All I know is that my dad's brother, Richard, and my dad had a fall out for some reason and they never spoke again."

Helen looked amazed and said:

"Do you mind if I say something that may not be correct but either way could be painful?"

"Fire away," replied Sally.

"Well, here goes and please, please, please understand that I am looking in as a bystander but there are usually only two things that cause major bust-ups between people, whether they are related or not, and that is money and sex. Does that make sense?"

"It does but there was little or no money, which sort of rules that out, but I do know that through some weird government system, Richard had to go down the mines for his national service and David joined the RAF. I was too young to understand the hows and whys but I got a sense that David was not only the airman but was also the blue-eyed boy and I suppose as the younger brother, this could have grated with Richard."

"Grated!" Helen exclaimed. "I think that would have been enough to drive anybody mad. Sent underground while your brother flies off on an adventure to the Far East, whether it turns out to be an adventure or not. Bloody hell, it would be enough to make a saint commit hara-kiri. And after all that, he brings back a beautiful bride from Vietnam! I take it that your mother was beautiful?"

"Oh, yes," said Sally.

"Which is where you must get it from," replied Helen and Sally blushed.

"Maybe."

"Anything else?" Helen asked and Sally thought before saying:

"Well, I know that my mum and dad were back in the North-East for a few years before I was conceived and this was at a time when there was a post-war baby boom. Of course, I wasn't there to witness this for obvious reasons but before we left the country because of whatever happened in 1962, my mum didn't have another child. So I was an only child born right in the middle of a twelve-year marriage."

Helen stood, went to the window, and looked into the night.

"Do you think that Richard was your dad and not David and hence the enormous fallout if David had found out? Was there ever any suspicion? What did your English grandma say or do?"

"Ruth, my grandma, was a widow and rarely said anything about anything to anybody. She lost her husband in 1947 when he was only forty-seven years old and it broke her. She only had contact with her sisters, one of whom lived next door, and rarely went out, so any family secrets would have been just that, secrets kept in the family."

Sally paused and then continued:

"Do you really think that is possible? Richard always seemed so ordinary, so steady, so boring even, and definitely not a lothario. Normal wife, normal kids, normal job."

Sally lay on the floor with her legs over the side of the sofa.

Helen draped an arm over one leg as a gesture of comfort.

Sally continued:

"I do remember my aunt who lived next door talking to my grandma about how strange it was that a beautiful woman could produce just one child. 'None or many' she said 'but not one, it's not right, it's not god's way'. I was on the stairs and they thought that they were alone. Fuck, do you really think that my uncle is my dad?"

"Possibly," said Helen.

"Do we have any whisky?"

"Bourbon," said Helen and fetched a nearly empty bottle and two glasses.

Sally sat up and leant on her friend's legs. She took a large slug of the fiery liquid and ploughed on.

"Wow. So if we assume that this is true, then it is possible that the Steinbeck book that meant so much to her was because it was Richard's and has nothing to do with the Michael who wrote in it. The novel is a keepsake, her equivalent of dried flowers or a lover's poem."

Helen hugged her friend and they both sat in silence until a New York morning woke them both in the positions where they had finished their conversation, and a stretching Helen said:

"To be continued, babe…but only if you want to."

Finders Keepers?

Jim, Tom, and the crew looked at the pieces of paper with children's eyes. Here were three written items attributed to one of the most famous men that had ever lived. Eight in ten Americans (80%) have a favourable view of the president who freed the slaves and won the civil war, including 56% who have a 'very favourable' view of him. He competed with George Washington as the most important president in America's history and stares down from Mount Rushmore as the preserver of the American way of life alongside Thomas Jefferson, Theodore Roosevelt, and Washington who have growth, development, and birth attributed to them respectively.

Jim emptied a cardboard box that sat on the seat of his truck and Tom carefully and reverentially placed the writings in it, taking care not to have them overlapping. He added the parchment sleeve too and then placed the box back on the seat of Jim's vehicle.

Tom blew out his cheeks.

"So many questions," he said. "Are they real? Do they matter? Did Lincoln live here? And most importantly, what do we do now?"

"Jiggered if I know," said Jim. "But I think we need to get hold of somebody that might know what we have here. What I think is imperative is that we don't touch anything else until we know more and so let's call it a day and perhaps, Tom, you and I can head into town and see what we do next."

"Sure thing, Jim," agreed Tom.

"Guys, can we reconvene tomorrow and hopefully, we will have an idea of how to proceed."

The four other men nodded and after securing the remaining buildings and paying particular attention to the one where the papers were found, they headed back into town to shower and then eat. It was a certainty that today's discovery would be the main topic of conversation over the food.

Jim and Tom decided that the first port of call was to be the sheriff's office in Tell City which was the Perry County administrative centre and so they headed there.

"Can I help you, boys?" A voice said from beneath a Stetson hat.

"We are looking for the sheriff," said Jim.

"Then look no further, gentlemen," said the Stetson wearer and he swung his feet off the edge of the desk that he was sitting behind. "Connor Healey, pleased to meet you."

Jim and Tom introduced themselves and Connor continued:

"Coffee?"

They both nodded and the sheriff poured three mugs of strong black coffee, pulled back two chairs from a nearby circular table, swept the paperwork to one side, and after seating himself on the spare chair, he said:

"Now what can I help you with?"

Tom placed the box on the table in front of himself, lifted the first piece of paper out, and set it carefully in front of Sheriff Healey, who removed his Stetson and pulled a pair of glasses from his waistcoat pocket. He peered at the paper and read slowly from *Colour departs* to *god above* and then blew out a long whistle saying:

"Well, blow me! Where in God's name did you get this?"

After he had read the other two pieces of paper, he rocked back and Jim and Tom told him where they had come from.

After that, dominoes fell quickly and a posse of serious-looking people with serious titles and a significant amount of letters following those titles arrived in Tell City and set up camp, or as they called it 'the operations cohesive' in one of the function rooms of the Holiday Inn Express Hotel and reserved several bedrooms as well. The hotel was glad of the business and arranged for a fax and several phone lines to be hooked up in the bustling function room. The first imperative was to isolate the site and stop any further demolition work being undertaken.

This was done by a county dictate and ensured that Jim was paid in full for the work that had been done and the work that was not to be done. Jim was delighted not only with the early payment of the contract and the resultant free time that he and the crew would have but also with his decision not to ignore the trove and just carry on with the demolition work. He knew that he could not take all the credit and acknowledged the part that his mother's career had played in the subconscious part of his decision and also the gentle urging of Tom as to the possible irreplaceable value of the find. And there could be more, so much more, because as most Americans had learnt at school, Abraham Lincoln was a Hoosier boy from the great state of Indiana.

Jim gave the crew the option of two weeks extra leave on full pay or the chance to head straight back to California and start working on the many jobs that he had in the pipeline. The split was fifty/fifty and the two men with family headed back to the west coast glad of the opportunity to salt away some extra funds while the two single guys hired a car and pointed it North to see what was out there and kick back. Correctly handling the publicity from this discovery could expand his already successful business even further. Doing the right thing was a win/win situation and Jim felt good, he even hoped to include his mother's professional expertise at some point.

A few days after the site had been sealed off and was being carefully examined by experts, Tom came to see Jim.

"Jim, can I have a word please?"

"Of course, you can, what's itching you, Tom?"

"This discovery might be just what I am looking for. I cannot tell you how excited I was when I saw the author's name, the presumed author I mean. How would you feel if I tried to get involved in whatever the clever people are doing here? That might not be possible but being the man who discovered them, there might be an angle for me. What do you think?"

"This is what I think," replied Jim. "You should go for it, and this is what I propose. You found the writings and I think that might give you some rights in law, so how about you take two months leave of which half will be paid and at the end, you can come back to the company or carry on with what you are doing. There is just one condition and that is you spend a week with my ma, Joan, either here or at her home in Los Angeles, and learn from her, but also try and get her involved. She would absolutely love that. Deal?"

"Deal," said Tom, "and thanks."

Bones

"It's the bones you are after, Tom. Not necessarily real bones, which are fascinating too, but the core of the building, what it is built around and what keeps it together, the inner structure. You would never say to a pretty girl I like the way that your spine allows your head to sit at the correct angle so that your features are accentuated by this posture, of course, you wouldn't but that is what it is. Beauty overlays a complex frame. And the same goes for buildings, we see the exterior and the outer layers but it is the engineering beneath that allows the outer edifice to exist."

"I hear you, Joan, and I promise that the next time that I meet a girl and tell her that she is pretty, I won't mention the basis of that beauty is her skeleton."

They both laughed and then Joan said, "And now, down to some serious stuff."

Tom was staying with Jim's mother, Joan, in Orange County while Jim's father, her husband, was away on some golfing jig, close to but not on the beach at Santa Monica. Joan was an energetic force of nature in her late sixties with a zest for life and an encyclopaedic knowledge of her chosen subject. Tom was keeping his promise to Jim as he had managed to get involved in the investigation going on back in Perry County.

After their approach to Sheriff Healey and the first wave of experts had arrived and cordoned off the remaining buildings while making rudimentary examinations of those structures, the whole project was moved up to a state and then a federal level. Although this action disappointed the personnel on the lower rungs of the investigation, the federal intervention allowed for both unity and, most importantly, financial and legal muscle. The excitement generated by the find was national and the cordon had to be widened as sightseers flocked to the area. Lincoln's legacy and mystique with the country had never really dimmed and interest and expectation ran high.

A day was spent assembling a team of experts and a cohort of volunteers to do the manual work. Five experts headed by Professor Simon Cross from

Harvard University and twenty of the volunteers to do the grunt work were retained. Joan and Tom were also included in the team; Joan because of her expertise and the fact that Simon Cross knew her from his student days and Tom because he had made the discovery. The team continued to be based in the hotel in Tell City and both Tom and Joan arrived the Sunday night prior to the work beginning on the Monday morning.

The excitement level was high mainly because a separate panel of experts had examined not only the calligraphy of the papers but also the signature. Both of these had been found to be 99.7% accurate and when the paper and ink test results came back positive for the relevant date, the scientific evidence was overwhelming that all three artefacts had been written by the 16th President of the United States.

"And now to get to the bones," said Joan, "and thank you, Tom, for helping me to get involved."

"No thanks needed," said Tom. "Without your son, I would not be here, so what goes around comes around."

Leverage

"Sally, have you read about this Lincoln thing?" Kyle asked.

Kyle was Sally's nominal boss, nominal because there was a very loose structure at the political research firm where she worked, but he was the boss nonetheless. Kyle had interviewed her for the job and sold it to her and she was glad that he had. She enjoyed the work and the people and was enjoying her life in Brooklyn with Helen. Both were stimulating and fun and there was just one wrinkle and that was that Kyle was gay, a fact that Sally had found out one flirtatious evening at a post-work night out. Kyle had smiled when she leant into kiss him and pulling away, said:

"Sorry, Sally, it's not my trip. You are a lovely girl and it's nothing to do with workplace relationships. I thought you knew that I was gay."

Sally felt foolish and a touch naive, the thought never having occurred to her, and when she told Helen that evening, her flatmate looked at her as if she had arrived from Mars.

"You are extraordinary, Sally. I didn't ever mention it because I thought it was so obvious," and she laughed until Sally begged her to stop.

"Wow," concluded Helen. "You may have been married once but I think I need to educate you some more. We are going out, girl, so get your glad rags on."

"What Lincoln thing?" Sally said.

"The discovery that has been made in Indiana of some things that were written by Lincoln as a young man."

"No. What sort of things?"

"Well, I believe that there is a story and a poem, but much more interestingly, a sort of political checklist and a couple of bible quotes that challenge slavery. Interesting stuff on its own but there might be a bit of agency in it for us if we handled it correctly. Fancy a trip to Indiana?"

Simon, Joan, and the team concluded that on the basis of the first discovery, it was likely that any other items that might be found would be behind the boards that covered the walls of this and two other properties. Of the five buildings still standing, two had been used purely for agricultural purposes. Both of them had stone walls and roofs made of wooden shingles. There was evidence of the loft area being used for the storage of hay and the main part of the small barn being for animals, most likely cattle. The floor was cobbled and the decision was made to preserve them as they were and to undertake a thorough but non-invasive investigation of the insides.

The nature of the discovery in the house meant that it was highly unlikely that anything would have been secreted beneath the floor or in the walls. Both were solid, thick and mortared when they were built. The roofs and lofts, however, were examined thoroughly but only one discovery was made, although it caused enormous excitement amongst the team. On a beam in the barn nearest to the dwelling where the papers were found was a carving that looked like ES9L. Simon Cross was very excited.

Was the 9 actually an 'A' badly cut into the wood or was it a code, or even the result of partial illiteracy? Could it, therefore, be ES and AL? Somebody whose initials were ES and Abraham Lincoln. Were they friends or was this a girl?

Professor Cross's team had already asked for census records going back to 1800 for the properties and that evening, they arrived. The initial disappointment was that Abraham Lincoln had never lived in any of the houses, according to county records, however, he had lived in the area which was common knowledge. And then, there was a reverential hush as the name Eleanor Smith jumped off the page. Aged fourteen in 1824, she had lived here with her parents, Jebediah and Carmel, and her two younger brothers, Thomas and Benjamin. There were three more families that lived in three of the other dwellings and the agricultural buildings were shared between all the families.

None of the families seemed to be related, so it looked like this was an early nineteenth-century commune. There were two Wilson families, which may have been a coincidence as it was a popular name at the time but it was more likely that they were related, and a family called Thomas. In 1824, between these three families, there were ten children; the oldest of which was nine and so it seemed that Eleanor was the oldest child in the community. When old enough, they had all attended school in Spencer County although intermittently.

Lincoln had grown up on a farm in Little Pigeon Creek and although he was only occasionally at school during his teens, he would have likely overlapped with all these families during his time growing up in the area. He would have been fifteen when the papers were written and Eleanor Smith would have been fourteen. Could they have been strictly behaved god-fearing sweethearts? Was ES9L code for Eleanor Smith loves Abraham Lincoln? Or Eleanor Smith's nine lives? Or Eleanor Smith has kissed Lincoln nine times.

The permutations were endless but it was highly likely that she had been the person who had carved into the rafter of the barn and it was certain that Abraham Lincoln had composed the writings and likely that he had an accomplice, probably Eleanor, to secrete them, as she had lived in the house where they had been found.

Professor Cross and his team were very excited and work now started on the three remaining buildings with particular emphasis on the house where the parchment roll and its contents had been found.

Tom was included as was Joan and they both watched as the crow bars gently levered away the boards from the point where the discovery had been made. Four planks down and about a foot above the floor was wedged a straw doll partially eaten away by rats or mice but recognisable, and at this point, Simon Cross called a halt and asked the assembled personnel to step back to where he was in the middle of the room. Everybody was surprised until he started talking.

"I get it. I get it." He said. "I have been puzzled, along with the rest of you I am sure, before we actually started removing the planks about the whys and the hows of what we were undertaking and now it makes sense. Whoever placed the items here, and I think we will find more things, wanted access to them easily and often, but in secret. If you were to sit on a chair right by the wall where Tom made his find, as I have, you would realise that you have all bases covered to hide your treasure. When sitting, the top board is at shoulder height and the next one above it has a trim or sort of cornice covering it."

"You can, therefore, slide the board in quickly and nobody can see it is movable. Also, the papers and doll are all tucked down no further than a hand can easily reach. Finally, from this spot, all the windows are visible, as are the doors, which gives plenty of time to replace any items, slot back the board, and sit innocently when anybody enters the room. This may sound very dramatic but I think that the person hiding these items was scared of losing them or being ridiculed, or possibly even being punished for having them. We must remember that this was many years ago when society operated in a very different way."

"Two further things that I think. Firstly, there may be another hiding place, maybe two, and secondly, I think that the writings aside, we may find a few more items in this cache. So let's carry on looking, shall we?"

Over the next few days, the main house was systematically and carefully examined, mapped, and any items catalogued. Simon Cross was right and wrong in his predictions. They did find what appeared to be another hiding place but this one was more of a secret cupboard and contained a single bottle. Amazingly, there was a drop of clear liquid in it which was likely to be moonshine. Nobody was brave enough to taste it and there was no smell, so it was decided that the contents would be emptied and the bottle labelled as a random discovery. What they did find, which excited the team enormously, was three further items in the original location where the papers and doll had been discovered.

There was an 1801 silver dollar, a flintlock musket, and, most intriguing, a diary with 'Privit Eleanor Smith' on the front. It was concluded that 'Privit' meant 'Private' and that this obviously belonged to, and presumably had been written by, Eleanor Smith. Further examination over the coming weeks in offices far to the East of Perry County would disappointingly reveal a young girl's thoughts from over one hundred and fifty years ago but there was no further reference to Abraham Lincoln and no more intriguing ES9L inscriptions. Eventually, the trail would grow cold and Professor Cross's team would be disbanded.

There would be a small amount of federal money and this coupled with some state financing and money raised by local charities would be enough to buy the main building and turn it into a local museum, which after two years of further donations added a tea room with the obligatory rest rooms. The government took the paper with the bible quotes and the political points and displayed it in the Oval Office but only after boffins in the CIA had finished interpreting what it said. Their conclusions were safe and completely in line with Lincoln's thoughts and actions in later life both as a lawyer and as the president. The other items were framed and put in pride of place in the museum, with the diary open on the only reasonably interesting page which had information on crop and stock prices.

Another booklet that contained a further scribbled ES9L as well as observations and thoughts both of Eleanor Smith's and of Abraham Lincoln's Tom had slipped into his pocket while nobody was looking. The potential ramifications and the excitement would keep him awake at night until the investigation was concluded.

Tom glanced out of the window as Joan's car swung into the compound. It was her last day on the project and she was glad to be heading home. Her husband was flying out to Louisville and they were going to take a lazy drive back across the States to Los Angeles and tick a few places off their bucket list.

A flick of a woman's ponytail and her dark eyes made the connection. It wasn't immediate and it wasn't until Tom was back in the hotel that it resonated with him. Ellis Island, back when he was a teenager, it was under the flag, and just for a second or two, but he remembered how pretty she was and how she had smiled. It couldn't be, could it?

Tom and Joan walked up to the house and saw several large packing cases of equipment and there was a strange empty feeling in the main house, much more so than when Jim's crew had arrived several weeks ago. Tom thought it was because the property that had been abandoned for so long had come back to life, only to be abandoned again, even though it was not in the way that a normal home would have been left, and he confided this thought to Joan.

"Buildings are like people, Tom, they not only have skeletons and organs and an outer skin but they also have feelings and emotions. Well, I like to think so anyway. We have brought this house back to life even if it's for a short while and now we are walking away again. I do hope that Simon's plan to create a museum of some sort comes to fruition and trust me, if it does, this empty space will sing again."

"I hear you," said Tom.

"On another matter, have you decided what you are going to do now? My son thinks very highly of you but I also understand that knocking down buildings, no matter how sensitively it is done, may not be what you want to devote your life to. Whatever you decide, I do hope that we stay in touch and you know that there is a hot meal and a bed for you whenever you are in Orange County." She kissed him, got into her car, and drove away. Tom absentmindedly strolled towards his hired car while scribbling notes on a scrap of paper. He opened the door of his car and swung a leg to sit down in the driving seat and his head collided with the head of the driver already sitting there.

"Jesus," said Tom, rubbing his temple.

"Owww," said the driver, touching a small cut that had appeared on the line of her eyebrow.

Clarity then arrived quickly and Tom realised that in his haste, he had tried to get into what he thought was his car but was, in fact, a similar one. He lowered his head to apologise and looked into almond eyes filling up with tears. They were set in the face that he had glanced at earlier but they were not the ones from his trips to Ellis Island. Those eyes were a young man's folly, an ideal, a dream from his young lonely days as a teenager; these belonged in the pretty face of a girl named Sally. Sally from the North-East of England via Saigon, Toronto and New York.

"I am so sorry," said Tom. "Let me help you."

Sally noticed her anger draining away quickly and wiping the tears and the blood from her face, she smiled and said:

"Thank you. How silly of us."

Tom and Sally. Sally and Tom.

Boys

In the pre-dawn light, Eleanor picked her way through the farmyard to the barn where the cows were lowing and twitching while adjusting their positions in anticipation of their regular morning milking. The faint light shed by the oil lamp told her that her father was already there as usual. As she went to open the barn door, she was gripped by an explosive pain in her midriff which caused her to double over and she grabbed the barn wall to steady herself and then felt a rush of liquid spill down her thighs.

There was just enough light to see a small shape no bigger than a shrew lying unmoving in a pool of blood and other bodily fluids. Eleanor had miscarried and she hadn't even known that she was pregnant. She called out to her father.

"Pa, I need to visit the outhouse."

"Well, don't be long," he replied. "There's work to be done."

Eleanor scooped up the inert form in her hands and scuffed the earth with her bare feet to obscure the bodily fluids standing stark against the dusty ground. She went round behind the barn and down to the river, grabbing an old sack as she went. At the river, she hitched up her skirt, dipped her naked lower body into the ice-cold water and washed herself clean. She then towelled herself with the sack and moving back up the bank, she searched with her hands in vain for the tiny foetus.

"Where are you at, girl?" A shout from the barn came.

Scrambling up the bank, Eleanor shouted, "Coming, Pa!"

After the milking was done and as her father sat on a barrel and lit his pipe, Eleanor said:

"Coffee, Pa? I could sure use some."

"Right you are, girl, and see if your ma has any of those barncakes left."

Eleanor hurried off by way of the river and a short search of its bank in the full light of morning showed the now dry sack but no foetus. It was likely a fox or racoon had come by and taken it.

Eleanor hurried on into the kitchen and brewed the coffee before returning to her father with the pot, two tin mugs and two barncakes. They drank the coffee together and she ignored the pain in her body but later that day, she succumbed to its hold on her and took to her bed early. Her mother looking in on her later had missed her tears and saw only the inert form of her eldest child sleeping off a bug or bout of flu.

Over the next few weeks, Eleanor got her physical strength back but her anger would not cool. She had wanted to kiss the boy, she had wanted to kiss him very much, but she wanted that to be all that happened but he would not stop and he was bigger than she was and stronger too. He had forced her to the ground and pushed up her dress. He had painfully penetrated her so that when she cried out, he had covered her mouth with his hand.

"Shut up," he mouthed but only once as his excitement was over very quickly, and he rolled away saying, "There we are, ok?" Eleanor flew at him with a flurry of blows.

"Hang on, hang on," he cried.

But she was wild with anger and confusion.

"You bastard," she cried, not really knowing what the word meant but she had heard her father use it and then how her mother had upbraided him.

She spat at him and went to hit him again but he held her wrists and the fight went out of her, and she started to sob.

"Sorry," she heard him say but she was running now, scared and ashamed in equal measure. This was not the bully that Abraham had dealt with in his story. This was another boy from a local farm with hormones raging and friends egging him on when they drank alcohol and smoked after church down by the river. He was ashamed too and tried several times to see Eleanor and appease her but she was having none of it. She was sore down below and angry up above.

One evening over at her aunt and uncle's farm, with her brothers and parents mixing in a raucous disorganised happy group playing games and eating too much, she used a visit to the outhouse as an excuse to go into their bootroom. Eleanor knew what she was looking for and took one of the three flintlock muskets that lay amongst the rifles and shotguns that were haphazardly stored amongst the boots and outdoor wear. It would be several days before its absence was discovered and after a thorough search of the property and outbuildings, its loss was forgotten.

"Probably one of the farmhands tilting at crows," said her uncle to his brother. "Idiots and nerdowells, the lot of them. I have a good mind to take it out of all their wages but that would only make them lazier than they are now. It will probably turn up."

Eleanor hid it away with the dolls, the silver dollar, and her diary. It was only in the middle of the night that she thought of using it upon her assailant and so it lay there gathering dust and was soon relegated to an object of curiosity after a tall gangly boy with a serious face and purpose in his manner renewed her trust in the opposite sex. His name was Abraham Lincoln and he was a year or so older than her. He looked like he had been assembled by old men from memory and then stretched on a rack. His coffin face rarely smiled and his limbs articulated like those of a newly born colt but he was kind, intelligent and, most importantly, trustworthy.

Eleanor liked him and then loved him, or thought that she loved him. He was attentive and loyal and had a depth that other boys didn't have. He made her feel safe, so much so that she thought of telling him of her shame with the other boy but changed her mind when she read his story of the bully. She could imagine what he might do to him not only from the story but also because she had seen him wrestle and so far never lose. So her mouth stayed closed and the gun remained where it was, and they spent time together before and after school and chores.

At no time did she feel vulnerable or unsafe, even though her sexuality and growing confidence meant that on occasion, she now wanted to feel unsafe, to be desired, to be a woman.

1982

In 1982, America was emerging from the worst recession since The Great Depression. Unemployment at 11% was a post-World War Two record and the country was creaking. Little did the population know that this was the nadir and the trajectory was now upwards. Tom and Sally were an item. Their unusual meeting in Perry County led to a long-distance romance that was resolved when Tom parted company with Jim and his demolition business and left California for New York to be with Sally. It was not the best time to be looking for work and Tom was now twenty-eight with a potted CV.

However, he had several thousand dollars to his name principally thanks to his work with Jim and his frugal living. Surfing cost nothing and he surfed a lot. Tom knew that he would miss the California lifestyle and the nearness of the sea but he loved Sally more and that made him very happy. He had tired quickly of the Indiana investigation once the excitement of the finds had started to fade and had backed out of any connection with the project after meeting Sally and had returned to San Diego. He had, however, kept the notebook which he had found and not declared that Eleanor Smith had written and hidden, and as the months went by, his anxiety about the theft, if that indeed was what it was, diminished.

From time to time, Tom would wonder about the ES9L on the front of the book and in the barn and he, in fact, spent a wasted morning trying to interpret it with the only result being New York State route 9L, which although constructed along the path of an old military road originally built during the American Revolution had been numbered in 1930 long after Eleanor Smith had died. Tom's conclusion was that Eleanor's education or intellect was poor, that the 9 was supposed to be an 'A' and that it was a child's infatuation for a boy whose initials were AL.

The scribblings in the book bore out Eleanor's limited writing ability and were of minimal interest until at a later date, Sally and Tom decided to investigate Eleanor's life further and then the notebook became pivotal to an extraordinary life.

In the meantime, Sally and Tom did what any young couple that had fallen in love would do and that was to immerse themselves in each other both physically and mentally. Helen had welcomed Tom into the flat in Brooklyn wholeheartedly with her accustomed warmth and kindness. It was a little cramped but all three of them were working and Helen kept unusual hours particularly when she was acting on stage, which was more and more often. She also was starting to pick up film and television work and would regularly spend several weeks away on location.

Her exotic love life also meant regular absences punctuated by intense trysts with both male and female partners as they became 'the one', only to disappear in short order and be replaced by a new lover. In truth, her flamboyance and energy had become wearing but Sally was acutely aware that even though they lived in a rented flat, Helen had been the original tenant and, therefore, had rights of possession. It was, therefore, with relief tinged with sadness, Sally was told by Helen that:

"Time to go, darling. Hollywood beckons."

And it was beckoning her but only with a single crooked finger and not a hearty embrace. The Helen that appeared on the television and graced chat shows in the 1990s had sold her soul to be that person and to those who knew her, it showed when she was off camera. Sally would sometimes see her in the flesh again and it always brought back happy memories of their Brooklyn days.

When she had gone and the last traces of her presence had been removed, Sally and Tom moved every portable item that wasn't fixed or nailed down into the centre of the living room. They then systematically created three piles, 'keep', 'consider' and 'discard'.

The 'discard' was easy and the pile soon contained worn, tired, and ugly items which ended up in a rummage sale locally. The 'keep' was easy too. They needed beds and furniture and practical items such as pots and pans, cutlery, plates, etc. These could be replaced over time and when finances allow. The 'consider' pile took the whole of a Saturday morning but finally, there were three rogue items. Sally yawned and went to make coffee with one of the essential items that had been kept: the coffee percolator. As the liquid gurgled through, she leant on the jamb of the door and watched Tom pick up *Of Mice and Men.*

"Yours?" He asked.

"Yes," replied Sally.

"Do you mind?" Tom enquired.

"Be my guest," said Sally and went to attend the hissing coffee.

Tom opened the fly of the book and read the inscription.

From one ex-minor miner to another.

Good luck on your last old day and your first new day as you close the door and open the curtains.

Michael. Gateshead 16 June 1946.

Like Helen before him had said in this very room:

"Who is Michael?"

"I don't know who Michael is, Tom. But I know who the inscription was written for."

Sally sat down and passed Tom a coffee. She then told him what she knew about Richard, the recipient of the book, highlighting the sentimental value the book had for her mother but omitting the possibility that Richard was her father.

New York

There had been two positives that had come out of Sally's trip to Indiana. The most obvious positive and the one that made her so happy that Kyle had asked her to travel there was meeting Tom. Sally often thought that it was ironic that she had met her partner in such a rural outback, but why not? Now that they were living together, Sally felt loved and supported as did Tom. The second lesser positive had been the amount of traction that her report from Indiana had brought, both to herself and to her firm. Kyle was delighted with what she had written but in truth, she was not sure what political advantage could be gleaned from the writings of a very young but long-dead president.

Kyle kept her in the loop as he charmed and manipulated Simon Cross into aligning a tiny amount of the discovery into the current president, Ronald Reagan's, ideology. Sally was impressed at how Kyle brought the teenage Abraham Lincoln into the modern-day timbre of the GOP so that it seemed that Reagan was father to Lincoln. His skill was rewarded with a personal visit to the White House for Kyle and two of his senior colleagues, although sadly not Sally, and with their presentation to the president of the artfully framed political writings which still sit prominently in the Oval Office.

Kyle's reputation and that of the agency meant a significant increase in business, much of it as retained mandates, which allowed for wider-ranging and more interesting work. Sally was going to be busy and she was content with both her work and her home life.

Tom had taken his time to find what he wanted to do, or rather what he thought he wanted to do. He started work as a cub reporter on the relatively new *Brooklyn Paper* which was a weekly publication that covered mostly issues and events in its eponymously named borough. As it was only published weekly and dealt with local, mainly cultural items, Tom was able to learn the profession in a sedately paced manner. This suited him initially but after a few months working on stories such as the local scout troops annual jamboree or The Brooklyn

Mothers Against Nuclear Arms (TBMANA) annual march and barbecue, he craved a higher level of excitement.

The agency that Sally worked for had been re-appointed late in 1983 to guide the Republican campaign for Ronald Reagan's re-election and as a direct result of this, the firm expanded again and in that expansion, Sally was pushed up a grade both in title and remuneration. She was now a junior consultant with an 18% uplift in salary. Tom was both pleased and jealous in equal measure. As they sat in a restaurant near their home on the night of her news, Tom lifted a glass of champagne and clinked it against Sally's glass.

"Congratulations, babe. Good on you."

"Thanks, honey," said Sally and a silence took the moment away. "You ok?"

"Sorry. Just being human."

"How so?" Sally asked.

"Well, today, I interviewed a woman about how it felt to have lived for eighty-six years in the same house, on the same street in Brooklyn. She had even actually been born there and she showed me the very spot where her mother had given birth, which was right by the fireplace if you are interested. I wouldn't have been surprised if she had gone and got the afterbirth, which she might have kept in a jar for those eighty-six years."

The champagne shot out of Sally's nose and she mopped her face and laughed uproariously until the breath went out of her, then she composed herself but erupted again.

"Oh, Tom," she said, "you are priceless."

Tom's good nature resurfaced and they both laughed again.

"'Eighty-six years, what a fucking waste!' That is what she said to me," said Tom. "I don't think that we can use that as a headline!"

Sally and Tom were sad and amused in equal measure. Sally poured the last of the champagne into their glasses and holding Tom's face in her hands, she looked at him and said, "Well, that's not going to happen to us, Tom Goodman. Tomorrow, we are going to get you on the move."

Young Eleanor Smith

J9ck was the name of the boy that had got Eleanor pregnant, or more correctly his name was Jack. In the second journal, which was now in Tom's possession, Eleanor had written his name so hard that it felt like the pencil was trying to go through the paper. It had then been crossed out and replaced with the word pig.

In 1826, Eleanor had turned sixteen and although she and Abraham were still close, he was busy with not only farm work but also with his studying and a fledgling interest in politics. They saw each other at the weekends and after church on a Sunday but rarely during the week. Constant in the area was a gang of young men approaching adulthood of which Jack was one. Their attitudes and activities were becoming troublesome to not only their families but also to the local residents.

On several occasions, the sheriff and his deputies had been called out to deal with fights and antisocial behaviour mainly as the result of the consumption of alcohol. Abraham was a teetotaller and when he was around, Eleanor felt and was safe, but he was not always around. The elapse of time since he had raped Eleanor coupled with his drinking meant that Jack had twisted the event in his head.

"She was begging me," he bragged to his friends.

"They all want it," chorused the gang. "Every one of them," and of course, they were all liquor brave when in the gang but timid and scared when alone.

Jack carried on, "I have a good mind to go round there right now." The others egged him on but did not want to go with him or be part of it. Jack took another swig of moonshine. "Who is with me?" But the others mumbled, made excuses, and slipped away.

Jack finished the last of the fiery liquid from the stone bottle and threw it in the hedge, turning as he did and heading for the Smith farm. Eleanor's father was still out in the fields when Jack stumbled onto his property but one of Eleanor's younger brothers saw him coming and had a child's instinct for danger. He ran to his sister and told her what was happening. Eleanor sent him to gather his brother and head to the house but not to breathe a word to their parents. She grabbed a long-handled shovel from inside the barn and waited in the shadows. When she heard his advance, she made a noise in the barn and as Jack put his head in to investigate, she hit him hard full in the face.

Jack dropped to his knees and then flat on his face. Eleanor checked his breathing, which was deep and slow. Putting down the shovel, she untied the old horse from inside the barn and looping a rope around Jack's legs, she lashed it to the halter. She then led the horse and its cargo down through the field to the river where she untied Jack and hobbled the horse. While he was still unconscious, Eleanor undid and removed both his trousers and long johns, exposing the limp penis that had hurt her so much when it had been erect. She used the rope to tie him to a tree looping one arm over a branch so that he did not slide down.

She then went to the horse's saddlebags and removed a jar of honey that she had placed there. Moving over to Jack's body, she smeared the honey all over his genitals, which caused a slight involuntary arousal in his penis but did not awaken him. Eleanor then took the wooden bucket from the pommel of the horse and went down to the river where she filled it with ice-cold water. Climbing back up the bank to the tree where Jack was tethered, she took hold of the handle of the bucket in one hand and the base in another, and dashed the water into his face. This woke him and he snorted and shook his head. He looked vacant until he saw Eleanor and then looked down and saw himself. Then he erupted in fury:

"You fucking witch!" He screamed. "What the fuck do you think you are doing?"

Eleanor smiled. "Getting even."

"Getting even? Getting even for what?" Jack spat. "You loved it!"

"Did I? Did I?" Eleanor said. "You raped me, you cowardly fuck, and then I lost a baby into the dust, and where were you?"

"Baby, what baby?" Jack said as the adrenalin left his body and his head started to throb.

"The baby you put in me, you rapist!"

"But I, but I," replied Jack and then the voice of the guilty and of the scared came out of him. "I didn't know. I am so sorry."

"Well, if you had acted like a gentleman, or even a man, you might have found out. You are a coward and a bully, Jack, and this is what happens to cowards and bullies."

Eleanor left him then as the dusk came down and by the time she was back at the barn with the horse, she could no longer hear his screams. When her father came in, he asked what the shouting was all about but she would not tell him, so he ate his supper and smoked his pipe before heading to bed. It was certain that Jack's drunken father would not help his son as he had, as usual, passed out from excessive drinking.

Waking in the night and taking a lantern down to the river, Eleanor slit the ropes on the gently sobbing Jack. The red harvester ants had consumed the honey and bitten him in the process but the well-fed bears inspected him but moved on, however, the smell of their breath and the touch of their fur would haunt Jack for the rest of his life.

At the age of four or five, Eleanor had been taken with her father, Jeb, to Vincennes, which is a city in the county seat of Knox County located right on the border with Illinois. He occasionally visited a livestock market there and as one of his four working horses was now permanently lame, he was reluctantly looking to replace her. As ever in the early nineteenth century, America farming was a hard and financially precarious business and, although Indiana was but a few years away from banning slavery, Eleanor's father would not use indentured workers of any kind.

His faith forbade the enslaving of any man or woman, although he drew the line at intervening in legislation imposed by the government, he just chose not to use them himself which meant crippling long working hours for both himself, his wife, and the one hand that he could afford to employ. He dared not get ill and was grateful when his children were old enough to help with the chores. A day away from the farm was a necessity and not a luxury, although he did treat both himself and Eleanor to coffee and pie on their visit to Vincennes.

Eleanor was wearing what passed for Sunday best as they ate their pumpkin pie and the waitress, seeing her licking the plate while her father visited the outhouse, gave her another slice and filled up the coffee mugs for no extra charge. Eleanor was so full and so happy, she thought that she would explode on both counts when she heard the plaintive wails and the clinking of the chains as a coffle of slaves were driven by.

"What's happening, Pa?" She asked.

"The abomination of slavery," he replied but he kept his voice low as he surveyed the faces of the locals and the slavers.

"Why are they in chains?" She said,

"Quietly, child, there is not much that we can do here," but he was talking to a chair as Eleanor ran towards the crowd. He left the correct coins and hurried after her, only to hear a beautiful young black girl berating the slavers and soothing the other slaves as best she could. Her owner, Benjamin J. Harrison, for this was the term then used, had cheated the young woman into signing a thirty-year indenture on the basis of fraud because she could not read. Her name was Mary Bateman-Clark and despite her physicality and personality, she became too much of a problem for Harrison.

He sold her to General Washington Johnston who sat on the Indiana General Assembly and she was again indentured this time for twenty years through more fraud and deceit. In 1921 after an appeal, and as a result of the freeing of a slave called Polly Strong in 1920 when her liberty became a test case, Clark was awarded her freedom. 'There shall be neither slavery nor involuntary servitude in this state' had been the oft-tested declaration of the Indiana Assembly, and although both Mary and Polly achieved their freedom, their lawyer, a man called Kinney, eventually had to move to the extremities of Indiana to avoid being lynched.

Eleanor saw bravery and spirit as well as sadness and brutality on that day and it remained with her. And as a consequence of that day, J9ck, the farm boy, was never going to be allowed to get away with his behaviour unpunished nor was Abraham Lincoln ever going to be anything less than a hero to her, but until she met up with Lincoln again many years into the future, she would use Mary Bateman-Clark's example and later friendship to shape her own life.

Change

On two separate occasions, Sally had found herself within touching distance of Ronald Reagan, the 40th President of the United States, but only for the briefest of moments before a security man moved her aside or moved the president onwards. She wasn't sure which action had happened because of the slickness of the adjustment. On the first occasion, it was only the back of his head that she saw but she was absorbed with the blackness and seeming plasticity of his hair, all his own of course.

On the second occasion, she looked directly at his face and in a heartbeat, she took in not only his fading matinee idol good looks but also the kindness in his eyes when for the briefest of moments he looked directly back at her and smiled. Both occasions were in the middle of his presidency, the first time was when the agency that she worked for helped to craft a campaign to get him re-elected and the second time was in 1985 when he was undertaking his second term. On both occasions, Sally was impressed with the man and the message, although as ever in politics, many would disagree with her opinion.

Tom, with Sally's help and support, had left the Brooklyn newspaper and now worked for the prestigious *New York Times*. At first, he had struggled with the intensity of the work, particularly as his new employers put out an edition every day of the week including Sundays but also because of the nature of the product and the personnel that crafted that product. In a similar manner to his unknown father starting out in the kitchens at Gleneagles and peculiar to but not exclusive to men in business, there was a distinct rite of passage to be navigated. Tom had good leads appropriated by more experienced reporters and was also given banal tasks to undertake, partly as a test, but also as a show of seniority.

"More bullshit, Sal," said Tom one evening. "Photocopying, checking sources, going through the archives. I want to punch someone."

"Well, don't do that," said Sally. "Keep going."

"I am thirty next month, Sally, and I am being treated as if only the first number existed," complained Tom.

"I know, I know," replied Sally, kissing Tom's cheek. "You will get a break soon, most likely when you are not expecting it."

"Maybe," said Tom and then laughing, he grabbed and tickled Sally. "And there's you chatting with the president."

"Stop, Tom, please, oh please stop," but Tom did not and the tickling became love making and later, both exhausted, they lay on the sofa and ate Ben and Jerries ice cream from the same bowl until Sally laid her spoon down on the table and said, "Enough, enough."

Helen had come back into their life again and was appearing in another play off-Broadway but closer this time to the main drag. It was Chekov's *Uncle Vanya* and with irony, Helen played her namesake, Helena Andreyevna Serebryakova. Tom and Sally attended an evening performance and just before the curtain rose, there was a buzz around them and a tall man with an unkempt mop of hair slid into the aisle seat next to them. During the interval, there was a general whispering as the man was recognised, although Sally was in the dark about who it was. Tom was amazed.

"Who is that?" Sally whispered.

"That is Bob Geldof."

"Who?" Sally replied.

"Bob Geldof, lead singer of The Boomtown Rats, and the man behind *Band-Aid*."

"Oh," said Sally and in the interval, Tom explained everything when there were no audience members telling them to be quiet. "Well, if he is famous, then why don't you ask him for an interview?" Sally continued.

"I don't know, Sal, seems a bit clumsy to me."

Just before curtain up for the second half, Sally leant over Tom and ignoring the 'shhh' noises from behind her, she said, "Excuse me, Mr Geldon, but my husband here is a journalist and would like to do an interview with you. Would that be possible?"

"It's Geldof, and which paper does he work for?" An Irish brogue came back.

"*The New York Times*."

"Good, and does he have a name and a voice?"

Tom rallied, "I do, Bob, sorry. It's Tom. Tom Goodman."

"Well, how about we meet in O'Donnell's around the corner after the show? It's an Irish bar so I won't stand out but you might. For now, I think we had better shut up or we'll be removed."

Bob shook Tom and then Sally's hands and fifteen minutes after the performance had ended, they were all sitting with Bushmills in hand in a corner of O'Donnell's bar.

"Fire away," said Bob.

Going to Mary

Eleanor's father, Jebediah, Jeb, was old before his time. Eschewing slavery or any form of indentured labour had meant that he had worked himself virtually to a standstill. He gauged his age as roughly fifty years old, which was almost exactly right, but he had no paperwork to prove this fact. Carmel, his wife and Eleanor's mother, was slightly younger and much more spritely. Jeb had insisted that she did not do any of the hard labour but that still meant fourteen-hour days doing cooking, cleaning, milking, and any other lighter work around the farm.

In 1829, Eleanor was in her last year as a teenager and her two brothers were in their mid-teens. Both boys were strong, and god-fearing, but not very bright. Neither bothered to attend school anymore and despite entreaties from all three elder Smiths, they would not go.

"We have the farm," both would say and secretly, it was a general relief. It would mean that their parents could cut back on their work load and that Eleanor could leave the farmstead within the next year, which she fully intended to do.

Eleanor felt that God had intervened in her life, mainly because of the love and support of her family but also because of her friendship with Abraham Lincoln as she had been growing up. The trip that she had made to Vincennes when she was a very young child had stayed with her down the years and she often saw in her dreams the stoical determination of Mary Bateman-Clark. With her parents' blessing and picking her way carefully upstate on one of the family horses, Eleanor made the journey North back to Vincennes. The eighty-mile journey took her three days and two nights, the nights being slept in woodland with the horse hobbled and the flintlock in a sack by her head.

She took enough food for the journey and drank from mountain streams. She was never afraid because God was walking beside her. On arriving in Vincennes, she sought out the sheriff's office and he directed her to the Bethel AME Church of Vincennes where he assured her Mary Bateman-Clark could be found. The whitewashed building shone in the sun and Eleanor tied her horse to the rail before opening the church doors and entering the cool of the church's interior. Arranging flowers was an elegant black woman.

"Mary?" Eleanor enquired.

"Yes, I am and how can I help you?" The reply came and Eleanor saw her all over again and knew her once again.

"Could I talk with you please?" Eleanor asked.

"Of course, child, come and sit here while I fetch some cold lemonade."

Eleanor arranged her skirts and smoothed back her hair, and surveying the simple church, knew that she had come home.

Bob

Bob, unwittingly, became the key that unlocked Tom's career. His forthrightness, candour, and sheer force of personality, coupled with Tom's growing journalistic style and experience, produced an article for the prestigious Saturday edition of *The New York Times* that even his self-interested colleagues grudgingly admired, some of them even said so to his face. Their time in O'Donnell's had laid the groundwork for a more formal meeting and the resulting interview needed only minor editing.

The success of the *Band-Aid* single had led to the idea of a live event, which resulted in the staging of dual concerts in London and Philadelphia featuring many of the biggest artists in the music business. Phil Collins, the drummer from Genesis, played at the London event and then jetted over to America by Concorde to appear in the American event.

When Tom had done the second more formal interview, the live events were only in their infancy but his skilled writing, coupled with Bob Geldof's permission, hinted at a global event of profile and magnitude which would become Live Aid.

Tom awoke on the Sunday morning following the publication of his article with a copy of the *New York Times* open at the featured page draped over the bottom of the bed. Sally was already up and brewing coffee, the smell of which drifted through the apartment.

"The new Walter Kronkite," she said. "Coffee?"

It was a poor comparison but Tom got the point.

"Your servant," he said and made a mock bow. "Wow, I think that second bottle was a step too far."

"Well, it's not every day that the editor of the *New York Times* sings your praises, so I suggest you take your hangover as an endorsement of your journalistic skills."

Sally sat on the edge of the bed and having passed Tom his coffee, she kissed him on the cheek and sipped her own. The sun was streaming into the bedroom and Sally had a far awake look in her eyes.

"What are you thinking, honey?" Tom enquired.

"Oh, nothing," she replied.

"Tell me, Sal," said Tom.

"Well…I was wondering how you get the windows of a fifth-floor apartment cleaned, they are filthy."

Tom laughed. "Clearly that was my fifteen minutes of fame done and dusted with."

He embraced Sally, kissed her, and said, "I love you, Sally. I really love you."

"And I love you too," she replied and they turned the words into action before dropping into a lazy Sunday morning second sleep.

"Fuck," said Sally shaking Tom. "We are going to be late."

"Shit," said Tom. "Where are we meeting them?"

"Some place in Greenwich Village that Helen knows. I have got the address somewhere."

Sally headed off to shower and Tom lay back on the pillows again. Helen was always late. Putting his mug atop the unit on Sally's side of the bed, he spotted her copy of *Of Mice and Men* in the cupboard and pulled it out. He opened the fly page again and reread the inscription. He realised that through drink, error or design when he had first looked at the book on the weekend that he had moved in with her, she had said that she didn't know who Michael was but it dawned on him that this could not be the reason that she had the book.

Michael had given the book to Richard, who had presumably given the book to Anh, Sally's mother. It was the original owner that Sally didn't know and that original owner was Michael. When Sally came out of the shower, he asked her about it.

"Sal, can I ask you something?"

"Of course," she said. "It's not a bad thing, is it?"

"I don't think so," replied Tom. "When we talked about this book before, you said that you didn't know who Mike was but you knew who wrote the inscription. That doesn't make sense."

Sally looked puzzled. "Did I?" She said, "That isn't right. I did tell you about my mum being the owner, yes?"

"You did," said Tom.

"And I told you about my dad and his brother, Richard."

"That too," replied Tom.

"It looks like I got my words mixed up, Tom, and I assure you that it was not deliberate. What I meant was that a man called Michael wrote in this book and gave it to my dad's brother after the war and after they had both been miners in the North-East of England. Why he gave it to him, I don't know and who he was, I don't know but the tone of the message implies a mutual relief, almost like two prisoners being released." Sally paused and sat on the bed again.

"Now here is the tricky bit. Helen, who we should be meeting in about thirty minutes, had a theory that Richard, my dad's brother, is actually my father and that is why my mother and I went to Saigon in 1962 and why my father, David, committed suicide. Heavy stuff, I know, and why this dog-eared book was a prized possession of hers that she bequeathed to me."

"Wow," said Tom. "Some story. So in essence, your mother is dead and my mother is dead to me and neither of us knows who our fathers are for certain. Mine through ignorance and yours because of family secrets, although your father, Sally, is one of two men who happen to be brothers, and of which sadly one is dead."

Sally hung her head.

"When you say it out loud, it seems much more acute and, frankly, surreal."

Tom hugged her and said, "One day, we should make the trip to England and find out the truth, and I suppose we could do the same here in New York with my mother if she would talk to me."

Sally rallied herself and addressed Tom.

"Maybe, in the meantime, I am not going to break a 100% record of always arriving before Helen, so get your arse in gear."

Helen was always late for social arrangements but scrupulously punctual for acting engagements. Sally had asked her on many occasions why the two grades of punctuality didn't marry up but Helen would merely shrug and say:

"Darling, I am what I am."

"Yes, Helen, you sure are," and as Helen's current partner had gone to the restroom, she took the chance to ask, "If this is the one?"

Helen laughed. "You never know," she said. "But the truth is, I feel much more heterosexual these days and this particular young lady is a handful even for me. In fact, it might be worth you and Tom getting your coats as I am ending this relationship when she gets back. Oh, and dinner is on me, so don't worry about that."

Sally was shocked and a little intrigued but Helen was true to her word and as a volley of expletives rang around the restaurant, a tiny woman with a Mohican haircut and multiple piercings pushed past them.

"And you two can fuck off as well," was her parting comment.

"Sorry about that," said Helen, "but it's men only from here on in. Back to ours? Or rather yours," she said. "Sorry, force of habit. Fancy letting me get my hetero groove on with Tom tonight, sweetie?"

Sally frowned.

"Your face says no but it's always worth a try. Drinks only then."

Helen put her index finger and thumb into her mouth and a piercing whistle brought a yellow cab screeching to a halt right by her. She leant in and said, "Brooklyn, my dear man, and don't spare the cattle."

Back at the flat, and with drinks in hand, Sally leant towards Helen and said, "Hels, Tom and I have an issue that we wanted to run past you."

"Shoot," said Helen.

"Tom and I have been talking about the Steinbeck novel and the note inside. Do you still think there is a possibility that the recipient, Richard, David's brother, is my father? It was a long time ago but I remember him as being very ordinary. Boring even. Plus my mum never mentioned him or even let slip anything about him. But then again, why would she keep it? It's just a tatty old paperback novel with an inscription from a stranger."

"Well, yes, I do, darling, and of course, there is only one way to find out and that is to ask him, but as we discussed a while back, the ramifications of that are enormous whether true or false. Have you ever thought of trying to identify Michael?"

"Well, yes, we have but then I do think what's the point? What would it achieve?"

"Peace of mind? Closure...I hate that word. Intrigue? Any or none of those."

"Maybe," said Sally and looked to Tom for support, where there was none to be had because he was sound asleep and snoring gently.

Kimberly Smith

Kimberly Smith stood and addressed the house:

"There are two dollars, ladies and gentlemen. The dollar that you have and the dollar that you don't have. I do not see anybody in this house, and I include myself here, that does not have upon their person a dollar or indeed access to a dollar. However, in this country, there are many people who do not have that luxury and that privilege. And yes, I do agree with my colleague, the senator for New Hampshire, that there are the workshy and the perennially unemployed who are happy with that state but they are the minority."

"The majority of the adult population in this great country want to do an honest day's work for an honest day's pay and that is why we need a substantial programme of public works on a scale not seen since the recession of the 1930s and FDR's 'new deal'. We need to spend and invest and do it now. Thank you."

Kimberly Smith sat down and drank in the applause of her fellow senators and was pleased. She was in her third year as a senator for Indiana and her workload had been doubled recently because of the ill health of her colleague, John Tibbs. Secretly, she was pleased because John was a long-term incumbent of the senate and, frankly, an old woman. American politics and American business in general produced numerous senior personnel who remained in post long past the time when they could and, in fact, should have retired. It caused resentment and a scarcity of new blood.

Kimberly had been lucky and had entered the senate at a relatively young age in her forties. She was a lawyer by profession and a staunch advocate of racial equality and after her short time in the mid-eighties as a senator in a male-dominated senate, she had also become a committed campaigner for women's rights. Nancy Kassebaum had followed her husband into the senate as the representative for Kansas but the first woman to be elected without having any family connections was Paula Hawkins in 1980 as the senator for Florida. Paula was also the only female to be elected to office who was a member of the Church of Jesus Christ of Latter-day Saints.

Nancy's position in the state next door to Indiana gave Kimberly a strange comfort and she often sought her council and friendship. What Kimberly was unaware of until 1989 when a journalist called Tom Goodman contacted her, was that she was related to a fierce and dedicated upholder of the rights of black people called Eleanor Smith. In fact, Eleanor was her great, great, great grandmother and in a further twist, they shared the same surname, even though through marriage, and over several generations, the women had taken their husband's names and Kimberly's maiden name was, in fact, Carter.

It was by sheer chance that she had married a man called Smith. Eleanor did not marry until her early thirties. Eleanor kept her established surname of Smith for her political, social, and spiritual work but her marriage certificate said Eleanor Gold.

Helen, of all people, had brought Kimberly into sharp focus. Helen had been asked to play a successful lawyer in a pilot series being made for television. It wasn't a huge part but as Helen put it:

"A ballsy lady lawyer might just put me in the window of one of the big studios, so I want to get it right." She took a drag of her cigarette and ploughed on. "I was watching that Kimberly Smith woman on CNN the other night."

"What the fuck?" Tom and Sally said and just stared before saying, "Sorry, Helen, can you repeat that."

"Oh, fuck off," said Helen. "Jimmy was watching it and I liked her pantsuit."

"Stop, Helen, please," said Sally. "I don't know what's worse, you watching CNN or you liking a pantsuit."

"Right, you two, I need some help and I need some support. Understand?"

"Sorry," they chorused. "How can we help?"

"Could you possibly get me access to Kimberly Smith? With your newspaper contacts and your political ones, Sal, there must be a good chance."

Sally and Tom looked at each other. Tom spoke first. "Do you know, Sal, all in all, it's not a bad idea. I was looking for a new face to interview and she is the woman of the moment, plus with George H. W. Bush now in office and the GOP set fair for another four years, your firm must be casting around for new projects?"

"Very true, Tom, and please, Helen, take this in the spirit that it is intended, but I didn't think a new lead would come from you."

"Win, win," said Helen. "Over to you guys."

Later that night, when Helen had been sent back to Jimmy, who did genuinely seem to be 'the one' and was clearly making Helen very happy, Tom and Sally ate dinner and then sat down opposite each other.

Tom spoke, "Sal, I have been thinking."

Sal replied, "So have I, Tom."

"Oh, well, ladies first then," he said.

"No Tom, after you," said Sally.

"I have been thinking for a while about going freelance, in fact about both of us going freelance, and as a starting point of going back to the whole Eleanor Smith story. Nobody knows about the notebook apart from us and this is the bit that is rather spooky. I have been doing some rudimentary research about Kimberly Smith for a potential article on her and I am as certain as I can be that she is related to Eleanor. In fact, I think that she is her great times three granddaughter."

"That would give us the story of a five generational family bookended by two extraordinary women. Helen, as she did with Steinbeck and the mystery of your father, has an uncanny knack for bringing things into sharp focus. If this were to work out, then perhaps we could move onto the story behind *Of Mice and Men*. What do you think?"

Sally leaned in and kissed Tom.

"Oh, you wonderful man, I was thinking of something similar, but the other way round. Of the book and my life, well our life but your way makes sense. It's an American story that could be fascinating. We have a few thousand dollars put away and we have no dependents or debt, so I say let's do it."

"Great," said Tom.

"So great," replied Sally.

The Winds of Change

The young black boy was christened Four, well to be truthful he was called Four by his parents and the preacher at Mary Bateman-Clark's church in Vincennes anointed him with holy water but as he had been three years old at the time, and both scared and excited, the actual christening was an interrupted affair. He had been called Four by his parents because he was the fourth child. His sisters were called One, Two, and Three, although in later life, they would all change their names to Ophelia, Tabatha, and Theresa respectively, keeping only the first letter of their slave names.

Their parents, John and Louise, were indentured slaves attached to a not unkind, but not kind either, landowner called Duke. The family lived in a cabin on the land and the kindly side of their existence had been that none of the girls nor their mother had been taken advantage of sexually either by coercion or force. The three girls were seventeen, nineteen, and twenty-one years of age, and all three were attractive as was their mother. It was John's darkest fear that one, or all of them, would be raped by a member of the Duke family or by one of the white overseers who worked for him.

Quadroons and Octoroons were still prized slave credentials, although the practice of forced impregnation of black women by white men was on the wane both in the slave states and particularly in Indiana. The older the girls got, the more John's fear receded but this relief was often offset by whippings and all the family bore the scars of what Duke called his 'corrective techniques'.

"If you did what I asked, then there would be no need for correction," was Duke's oft-repeated lament as the bullwhip exploded in the air across some poor person's back. "It hurts me as much as it does you and I assure you, that it is for your good and with God's blessing."

"Amen," was chorused by the overseers and their families gathered for the disciplining and mumbled by the slave families present too.

Duke reset his conscience after a whipping by allowing the slaves an afternoon free of work. Corrections took place on a Saturday lunchtime so the rest of the day meant a form of liberty for the families ahead of the strictly enforced church attendance on Sunday mornings. Most families ate and slept and gathered in groups to socialise. The younger children played and the older children took the opportunity to visit the river and to enjoy the sunshine free from toil. The adolescents flirted and laughed but always with one eye and one ear alert for danger.

Four, unknown to his sisters and parents, had been mixing with three white boys who were sons of employees on the plantation. Thomas and Wesley were sixteen years old, and William, the ring leader, was seventeen. Four was fourteen. William had transitioned from boy to man in the last year and was tall and strong. Thomas and Wesley were starting to show the first signs of manhood with wispy moustaches and an increase in height. William was six feet tall and had not only broad shoulders but also unusually big hands. He was also a Duke.

"You should be a boxer," said Thomas, "with those hams instead of hands." William would cover Thomas's face with one of those hands and rub hard.

"Owww," moaned Thomas and William switched to holding his friend's head in both hands and squeezing.

"Stop, for fuck's sake, Will. Please. Agghh!"

William stopped but showed his strength again by twisting an apple in half and then offered Thomas one of the pieces. Both of the younger boys had tried the apple trick and could not even split the skin.

"Thanks," said Thomas. William split another apple and gave Wesley half and Four the other half.

Four was not a bright boy and he was naive too. He thought that the three older boys just wanted to be friends. He could have been right, they were always nice to him, except for the one time when they had held his head under the water at the river until he thought that he would drown. On that occasion, they said sorry and gave him some chocolate, which Four thought was the best thing that he had ever tasted, and so he forgot the incident and did not tell his family.

After a whipping in September when the people both black and white were heading away to process the violence but perversely also to enjoy the attached afternoon free of work, Four was beckoned by Thomas and he slid away from his family, who thought that he would be playing with his black friends. Down at the river were William and Wesley and the older boy offered Four some moonshine. Four said:

"What's this?"

"This buddy is the nectar of the gods. Try some."

There was a tiny amount left in the stone bottle and Four raised it to his lips and drank.

"Whoa," he said as he screwed up his face.

"Told you," said William.

"Is there any more?" Four asked but the mood changed.

William, egged on by the others, shouted at him, "More? For you, boy? You think you are like us?" There had only been a tiny drop left as the three other boys, and William in particular, had consumed the rest and they were all fighting angrily. Wesley and Thomas held him down and William straddled Four and pressed his oversized thumbs into the gap behind his collarbone until Four screamed with pain. Wesley covered his mouth and hissed, "Shut up, nigger."

William released his grip and rolled off and as quickly as his anger had arrived, it disappeared. He lifted Four up and said, "You got me fighting mad there, boy, sorry about that," but he wasn't sorry, he had just got his control back.

"Right, I'm off. See you, Four. You boys coming?"

Thomas followed but Wesley was being sick behind a tree, and so they laughed and left him there. Four ran home and again kept his secret from his family.

Mary Bateman-Clark and Eleanor Smith read lessons while the preacher conducted the service and the mainly black congregation hung on his every word. He was charismatic and devout in equal measure and even for the younger attendees, the time passed quickly. John and Louise were in the seventh row on the left which was the pew that they preferred along with the girls. Four was to join them later when he had performed a chore that the Duke family had asked him to do; they had even leant him a horse so that he would be back in time for church.

The main doors to the building had been left open as was the side door so that a breeze could blow through on this hot September day. The rains had held off and the men in their Sunday suits and the women in their elegant dresses and holding parasols against the sun's rays promenaded on the dusty street as well as the boardwalks that kept them free of mud during the wet winter months. Four trotted up on the Duke's horse whose bridle was now being held by Wesley. Thomas and William walked on the other side of him. At the hitching rail outside the church, they stopped and John caught sight of his son outside and breathed a sigh of relief. He didn't see the other three boys because of the sunlight and the congregation behind him blocking his view, so he didn't see them loop a rope under the horse and tie his son's ankles together.

Nor did he see Thomas shake pepper into the horse's eyes nor did he see both Wesley and William thrash the horse's flanks with supple willow branches. John and the whole congregation heard the horse with Four aboard scream and gallop into the church, blinded and terrified, and they heard the sharp crack of its front legs as it hit the dais and smashed to the floor unable to rise. Four was trapped under the thrashing horse with a broken leg and broken ribs as well as extensive damage to his face.

When, eventually, a gun was found and the horse was shot, Four had thankfully blacked out. It took eight men to lift the horse off him and to get him to the doctors to set his leg and bind his ribs before stitching his face. Later on, the doctor would administer laudanum and remove three broken teeth with the blacksmith's pliers.

Even Duke was shocked by what had happened. The two other boys' fathers were sacked and the cost of the medical work and the horse was taken from their wages but in truth, this was nickels on the dollar compared to the actual cost. Thomas and Wesley's fathers beat their sons in the manner that they had thrashed the horse before they left to find work in the slave states to the south, taking their contrite sons with them. William's father was scared of his son and dared not do anything other than shout at him, but Eleanor Smith was not scared of him and so after all three boys were only found guilty of public affray and bound over to keep the peace, she sought him out.

Though he looked down on her physically and laughed in her face, a tiny part of him knew that she would not leave this event unavenged.

The congregation over the next few days cleaned and repaired the church and in due course, Four recovered sufficiently that only a small limp would show when he was tired and a gap would show in his mouth when he smiled, which surprisingly he often did.

Upper East Side

Kimberly Smith assured Tom that it was because of convenience and not avarice that she had requested that they meet for lunch on Madison Avenue on the Upper East Side of Manhattan. She further explained that she spent so much time in Washington that she rarely had time to visit her mother who lived in the area and that she could kill two birds with one stone, and although this was a request by her, Tom knew that it was really a condition. His editor raised his eyebrows but signed off on his expenses in advance for a booking at Paola's Osteria and, as a lover of food himself, was secretly envious of Tom's choice.

"And your mother?" Sally asked on the morning of Tom's lunch with Kimberly Smith.

"What about her?" Tom replied.

"Is it not time to make amends, or at least try to?"

"It's been seventeen years, Sally, I don't even know if she is still living there and to be honest, if your mother tells you to fuck off, then the message is quite clear."

"Just wondering," said Sally and a seed was sown.

Tom had had no contact or information about his mother since his eighteenth birthday party and, although he occasionally wondered about her and indeed whether she was still alive, he had closed the door on her a long time ago. Annoyingly, Sally had opened that door a fraction and he found himself interested enough to peek through the crack.

"I allow myself veal and foie gras once a year and today is that day for the veal," said Kimberly Smith.

"Costata di vitello please."

"And would madame like grilled or Milanese?" The waiter asked.

"Milanese," Kimberly replied. "Oh, and broccoli di rapa too please," she added.

"And for you, Sir?"

"I would like saltimbocca alla romana with some spinach, please. Oh, and a bottle of Barolo too."

"Very good, Sir," and two minutes later, the same waiter was pouring a small portion of the wine into a glass for Tom to taste.

"Delicious," he affirmed and the waiter filled Kimberly's glass a third full before filling the residue in Tom's glass to the same level.

"Cheers," said Tom.

"Salu," Kimberly replied before adding, "Now, I hope that you are going to paint me in a sympathetic light."

"I'll try," said Tom. Getting out a small tape recorder, he said, "Do you mind?"

"Not at all," was the reply.

Tom weaved back and forth with his questioning and Kimberly was compliant and erudite with her replies. She had grown up in Kansas and had studied law at Yale University where she qualified with a first. She had trained in New York City before joining a practice in Indianapolis where she had reached the level of partner after six years. All in all, her life had been one of high achievement with a happy marriage and two children, an advert for the American dream. Tom saved his last two enquiries for the end of the meal while they were drinking coffee.

"This has been great, Kimberly, so thank you so much and obviously, we will give you editing rights prior to publication, which will hopefully be in the next two weeks. Could I ask you one final question and a favour too please, both of which you can say no to?"

Kimberly drained her coffee cup. "Fire away but I reserve the right not to answer and if I do answer, then I really must be on my way in ten minutes."

"Of course," said Tom. "Easy one first…a friend of mine is playing a female senator in a film production and was after some pointers on how to approach the role."

"Glad to," was the reply.

"And secondly, have you ever heard of a woman called Eleanor Smith?"

"Eleanor Smith. No, I don't think so. Why?"

"Well, my wife and I are thinking of writing a book about her life and we think that you are her great, great, great, great, great-granddaughter."

"Interesting, tell me more."

"She was a civil rights advocate, anti-slavery campaigner, and a feminist before the term had been coined. Born around 1810 in Perry County, Indiana, and lived most of her life in Vincennes, also Indiana. But of course, you would know where both those places are, so pardon my clumsiness. It is believed that she knew and indeed was friends with Abraham Lincoln in the 1820s and kept that connection, although intermittently, through to 1865."

Kimberly stared at Tom, then spoke:

"Right, Tom, now it makes sense. I have been puzzled about your familiarity and the penny has just dropped. You were the guy that discovered the Lincoln writings a few years back."

"Guilty," said Tom.

"Wow. Now that is interesting, and presumably quite a story. There is, however, one catch. I am a Smith through my husband and my maiden name is Carter."

"Which is as it should be, the maternal surnames obviously change through the marriages and you being a Smith is a coincidence. Eleanor Smith was, in fact, Eleanor Gold when she married but kept her maiden name for her work. It was my clever girlfriend that worked all that out and is a former flatmate of Helen, the actress who is after your help and a political researcher to boot."

"Shit," said Kimberly. "I must rush, but yes to both questions. Get Helen to ring me and we can take it from there, and as for your project, come and see me in Indianapolis. Here's my card, just ring my secretary and we will sort out a date. Oh, and thanks for lunch."

Kimberly exited the restaurant and Tom blew out his cheeks, poured the last of the wine into his glass, and lit a cigarette. He smiled inwardly and rose to find a payphone to ring Sally and let her know.

"Tom Goodperson?" He heard a voice say as he walked along.

"Tom Goodman actually, but what can I do for you?"

"Do you not remember me?"

Tom had a vague memory of the man's face but not his name or why he knew him.

"Sorry," said Tom.

"Sandy Carmichael, I was your mother's lawyer."

"Well, blow me," said Tom. "And dare I ask how she is?"

Sandy took a breath and then said:

"You mean you don't know?"

"When your mother gives you five thousand dollars and tells you to fuck off, the message is pretty clear wouldn't you say."

Sandy played with his cufflinks and then said:

"I am sorry to say that your mother is dead and has been these past seven years."

It was Tom's turn to be stunned.

"Dead? How?"

"A fall, Tom, drunk I am afraid, and she drowned."

"Shit. Long Island I guess then."

"Yes. Long Island."

"Bloody hell. And the body?"

"Buried in Trinity Church cemetery."

"Wow. All these years." And despite himself, he heard his voice say, "And the estate."

"Gone I believe, apart from a small parcel of securities which I think may be in your name. Do you have five minutes? My office is just around the corner."

"Sure," said Tom and he followed Sandy Carmichael down two blocks and into a glass and chrome building, where they took a lift to the sixth floor and entered the reception of Gooster, Frane, and Carmichael.

"Susan, could you look out the file on Ellena Goodperson please and bring it into the Eagle suite."

"Of course," said Susan and in ten minutes, she had done just that.

Sandy picked up the file and scanned the pages inside.

"Hmm," he said. "Let me ring our firm's broker. Chuck," he said. "How are you? It's Sandy Carmichael here. Could you give me the value of six securities you are holding on our behalf both capital and income please?"

"Sure. I'll call you back." Normally, Chuck would give this to a junior but Gooster, Frane, and Carmichael were valued clients of his and so after checking the figures, he rang Sandy back.

"Initial investment in 1972 of ten thousand dollars per security. All income reinvested. No capitalisation issues or takeovers. Current valuation as of 12 Sept 1989 is $289,442 in the name of Thomas Goodperson."

Sandy told Tom and Tom sat down.

"Wow," he said. "Is that really mine?"

"Only when you sign this document and I draw a cheque for that amount in your name. I am so sorry that I had to be the one to tell you about your mother but I hope the money is some sort of compensation."

Later at home, Sally asked:

"How did your day go?"

"Interesting," said Tom. "Let me get a drink and tell you."

Time to Go

"That prick is driving me mad," said Sally.

"Which prick?" Tom asked.

"The prick with the fancy title and the attitude."

"Whose name is what?" Tom enquired.

"Ron Barnaby the third, or elder or junior, or some similar quasi-familial bullshit that he tacks on to the end of his name," blurted Sally.

"Aaaahh, that prick," said Tom. "And what has he done now?"

"It's not so much what he has done as what he is with his Ivy League glasses and his chinos and his V-necked sweater draped over his shoulders just so."

"You don't like him then?" Tom asked.

"He's a…a…a double prick with a flake and raspberry sauce."

Tom held up his hands in mock shock. "Mercy," he said and grinned.

"Don't you make me laugh, Tom Goodman, don't you dare," said Sally as Tom rubbed pretend tears from his eyes and pulled a childish lip.

"Don't," she said. "Don't," and then she laughed. "Aaaggghhh. That man!"

"Well, dear lady, I have some news which may make your nemesis disappear over the horizon." Tom picked up the bottle of wine that he had just opened and poured some of it into two glasses, one of which he gave to Sally. "Sit yourself down."

Sally did so and while taking the wine, she tucked her legs under her body on the sofa, and said, "Thanks," before taking a large swig.

"Ok, Tom, as you would say, shoot."

Tom took a sip of his wine and then placed it on the table next to an armchair which he lowered himself into.

"Firstly, I had a very profitable and enjoyable time with Kimberly Smith. Not only is she successful but she is also much more than a political animal. She has a breadth of interests and causes which hopefully, I can do justice to in my article about her, but she is also decent and, this may sound a bit wacky, but she seems to have a soul. She was really interested in Helen's role as senator and agreed to help her as much as she could, but she really came alive when I mentioned the possible Eleanor Smith project."

"Great. Now is she pretty?" Sally asked.

"More handsome," said Tom.

"That's ok then," said Sally and chuckled. "But it's good that the Eleanor Smith story got her attention. Was she aware of the name and that she was her descendant?"

"Well, that's where it got interesting. Firstly, it was when I explained that the fact that she and Eleanor had the same surname was just a coincidence and here she just gently slapped her own forehead and said 'of course, it's always the maternal surname that changes', and then when I went on to the outline the reasons for the potential book, a light came on and she said that she recognised me from the Lincoln papers. Rather flattering I thought."

"Well, Tom, you have had a good day, so we'll just have to keep her on the side until we are ready to press the button on Eleanor and to that end make sure that, you write a truthful but sympathetic article on her. Ready to eat?"

Sally made to rise and Tom reached over and touched her arm.

"There is something else," he said. "As I was leaving the restaurant."

"Was it good?" Sally enquired.

"Fabulous, but hear me out, Sal," and Sally pretended to lock her lips together and throw away the key.

"As I was leaving the restaurant, I bumped into a man called Sandy Carmichael who was my mother's lawyer."

"Wow," said Sally, managing to speak without retrieving the imaginary key.

"And he told me," said Tom. "He told me," and there was a catch in his voice. "That my mother is dead and has been for seven years."

"Bloody hell," said Sally. "Oh, Tom, what a shock." She moved over to where Tom sat and put her arms around him. "How do you feel?"

"I am not sure," said Tom. "Shocked, sad, but a lot of relief."

"I'm sure," said Sally. "What happened?"

"She drowned on Long Island. Drunk, as ever, and alone. Nobody saw or heard her. It must have been that nightcap ritual on the jetty that she did when she was there. I never understood it, I just thought it was an excuse for more booze, which it probably was."

Tom paused and looked out of the window and into the night.

"Closure?" Sally enquired, and standing behind him, she put her arms around his waist and her cheek on his back. "At least you know," she breathed. "Now come and eat."

In the morning, Tom awoke and the New York sun streamed in through the drapes which Sally had opened before heading into the kitchen to make coffee. It was a Saturday and the weekend stretched ahead of them with only the vaguest of plans. Sally brought in two mugs and putting Tom's down next to him, she rounded the bed and climbed in next to him.

"Morning, handsome. How are you doing?" She asked.

"Good, thanks. Sal, I need to tell you a couple more things, neither of them bad."

"Shoot then," Sally aped Tom's style.

"When I was in my teens, I often used to go to Ellis Island on the ferry. I loved the history of the place, its formality, and its purpose. I loved the possibilities the building offered up to people coming to a new land. I think part of that was because of my arrival in America, not the poverty as that was never the case, but of being a stranger in a new land. The building to me always had a feeling of hope, even though it had been closed for a few years."

"Oh, Tom," said Sally. "How lovely."

"There was one occasion when I was sitting in the old processing hall, which has an upper balcony running right around the perimeter, and emerging from behind one of the huge flags was a pretty girl and her friend said to her 'Come along, Sally' but she stopped for a few seconds and her eyes met mine. She smiled at me and in that moment, I fell in love with her but then she was gone and even though I went back there several more times, I never saw her again."

"Tom, you will make me cry, but it couldn't have been me because I only arrived in America a few years later."

"I know that now. But when I met you in Indiana. When we literally bumped into each other, I did think you were the same girl for a while at least, even though I never told you so. It was only after we got to know each other and you told me about your life, that I realised that you weren't the same girl and that it was a dream, or a vision, or maybe even a premonition. She has gone now but you haven't and that's ok. It was a lonely young boy's folly and I love you very much, Sally. Very much."

Sally said, "How lovely, Tom, and how lucky am I to have been a dream and a reality with a man I love. I love you, Tom Goodman."

There was a pause as they held each other and enjoyed the moment. Then Sally said:

"And the other thing?"

This galvanised Tom.

"Well, Sally, Sandy Carmichael who told me of my mother's death, also told me of a legacy, that by good fortune, I now have in my possession to the tune of a shade under three hundred thousand dollars. So you can tell Ron Barnaby to go fuck himself and you and I can go on an adventure to find the real Eleanor Smith."

Sally jumped out of bed and opening the window, shouted:

"Fuck you, Ron Barnaby. Fuck you!"

Eleanor

The woman within the girl.

On her second visit to Vincennes and on her second sighting of Mary Bateman-Clark, Eleanor stayed for a whole week, and this time, she not only got to see the lady but she also got to meet her, talk with her, and be with her. It was almost a religious experience for Eleanor and she delighted in her time with Mary and her family. Mary had married Samuel Clark in 1817 and added his name to hers. Samuel was an enslaved person too and also from Kentucky. He would be William Henry Harrison's horse handler at the Battle of Tippecanoe in 1811, when Harrison led government forces against Native Americans and his life and love would be bound up with horses.

The future events with the slave boy Four, the desecration of his wife's church and the cruelty to the horse that had to be put down on that day would be a driving force in his life and the action and the aftermath were never far from his thoughts. Eleanor was eighteen when she made this second visit to Vincennes in 1828. Mary was thirty-three years old and had already given birth to eight of her twelve known children. On her last day before returning to Perry County, Eleanor knew where her future lay and promised Mary that she would return as soon as she could to be a part of what would turn out to be the first mixed-race community in Indiana.

"Godspeed, child," said Mary as she passed her a cloth package containing food for the journey.

"But, Mary," said Eleanor. "I can't take this, you have so many mouths to feed."

"Hush now, girl. Some of the ladies from the congregation did some extra baking and this is the result. It's nothing but a bit of grease and flour and maybe some bacon but it should get you back down south. Now mind you, keep that gun close by at night and hidden by day and stick to the back roads."

"Oh, thank you, Mary, and you Samuel and all you children," she said as seven smiling faces looked up at her and one sleeping bundle gurgled and was oblivious to the event.

"I will return," said Eleanor, "but until then, look after yourselves."

They all waved and Samuel put his arm protectively around his wife and the whole family walked slowly back to the church.

"What do you think then, Mother?" asked Samuel.

"That girl has fire in her belly. She is going to be somebody important one day."

"Do you think that she will come back?" Samuel said.

"I do, Samuel, yes, I do but," and she looked up at her husband. "I don't think that she will stay forever."

In three months, Eleanor did return. This time she travelled by stagecoach and came with a carpet bag full of clothes and a smaller bag with her important items in it. This she had kept below her dress amongst her petticoats and it contained one of the two silver dollars that she had somehow acquired, some paper money that her parents had given to her, a notebook with some writing in it, and in a square of oilskin, a lock of hair and a message from 9braham. The '9' was crossed through and now showed as Abraham as Eleanor had corrected her spelling over time.

She would never know how many intelligent minds had deliberated over the use of '9' instead of 'A' when, in fact, it was literally a spelling mistake. The message had been written by Lincoln a year earlier when he was twenty years old and she was nineteen. He was a year or so away from moving to Illinois with his family but his intelligence and thirst for knowledge kept him busy. He knew from the rare occasions that he and Eleanor met up that her future lay elsewhere, and so he wrote:

Kind Eleanor,

You stand with those that do right, and with me, and bathed in God's light we see what is correct and how it should be employed. Never be afraid because I am only the softest whisper away.

Ever your Abraham.

Eleanor had left the gun, her dolls, a diary, a notebook, a silver dollar, and Abraham's other jottings hidden in her secret place unaware of the '9/A' conundrum that future intellectuals would agonise over their relevance. They were just things that she did not need at this moment. Just things.

Fore

It was a Thursday and shepherd's pie was on the menu in the quaintly named 'nineteenth hole' at The Gosforth Park Golf and Country club, and as a result, the early tee-off times disappeared quickly so that the aged and almost exclusively male golfing community could get back to the clubhouse to secure a portion. There was a strange comfort for English golf-playing males of a certain age in the traditional minced beef and mashed potato dish. Memories of school dinners and national service as well as meals provided by mostly now-dead mothers were triggered just by the mention of its name.

The smell and the taste of the dish temporarily turned old men into little boys and had them waiting patiently in line ever hopeful of an extra spoonful from Betty or Susan who worked in the club's kitchens.

Richard was no exception and as a non-driver, he would get his wife, Joceline, to take him down to the course early on a Monday so that he could book a pre-9.00 slot for his four-ball. His three playing partners were glad of this arrangement and Richard had only failed them once and only by twelve minutes when a diversion near his home had meant a delay in getting to the club and the earliest tee-off time still available was 9.12 am. Fortunately, after they had putted out on the eighteenth green and the obligatory fifty pence wagers had been settled, there was still sufficient pie left for all four of them to have generous portions.

In fact, if they could have stood the tension, there was merit in being slightly later than usual as Betty scraped the dish enthusiastically and all four men got not only an extra spoonful but also the remaining crispy bits from along the edge. Alan wiped his mouth and ventured the idea of a slightly later tee-off time in order to secure larger portions but the four men were in agreement that their collective hearts could not stand the tension. And so normal service was resumed and in return for Richard's diligence in securing the correct Thursday tee-off times, he was dropped back home by one of the other three men in rotation.

Richard could drive but he just chose not to and his wife, and on occasion his two children, were resigned to the situation. He rarely commented on the skill of the allotted driver but experience told them that his hand on the dashboard and a clearing of the throat were a sign to reduce speed.

Richard had retired in 1988 at the age of sixty-two. A civil servant all his life, he had a much desired but limited final salary pension and made no fuss when government changes brought forward the date when he could stop work. Diligent but unremarkable, he was one of an army of unsung bureaucrats who toiled behind the scenes either directly or indirectly for the government. He and Joceline had settled into a pattern of life acceptable to them both of which shepherd's pie Thursday was a feature.

They saw both of their children regularly as they also lived in the North-East and they were secretly hoping for grandchildren. However, although both children were with partners, neither had achieved that situation yet.

"Plenty of time," said Richard.

"Yes, dear," said Joceline.

Forty years away from his national service as a Bevin Boy, Richard still occasionally had nightmares about his time underground but he never talked about it and was not a member of any affiliated organisations. When he did awaken in an anxious state. Joceline would calm him by holding his hand until the moment passed and more often than not after he fell asleep again, she would slip out of the bed and quietly head downstairs. In the kitchen. she would make herself a cup of tea and look out of the window into the dark of their small but neat garden.

Occasionally, there were stars in the sky and she would wonder at the universe. Mainly, she sat with her regret and sadness. Regret at her ordinary life and sadness at the never again mentioned affair that Richard had with his brother's wife. She knew of the short affair and of the child and of her brother-in-law's suicide. She knew of the sadness and of her own cowardice, and she often wondered about Anh and Sally and what had happened to them but it would have been disloyal to try and find out. Her life was one of forgiveness and compromise and, therefore, regret.

Occasionally, on warmer nights when she didn't need a dressing gown and she was standing at the window in just a nightgown, she would touch herself down below but she stopped short of masturbating in case Richard came downstairs, as he had on occasion, or one of the neighbours was about early and might be looking through the window. In her imagination, before probity took over, it would be David, Richard's brother, who loved her and took away her pain.

And so they went on. Trips to the local pub for dinner, always early to get a certain table, golf games, and occasionally dinner at the golf club too where, thankfully, the strict booking system negated any anxiety about table selection. Low-fat spreads replaced real butter, and bacon and eggs were moved out in favour of muesli and fruit. Checkups for newly researched potential late-life ailments became a regular feature and as a consequence, the local GP surgery was visited on a just in case basis and awarded with Christmas gifts for all the staff not just the doctors.

Betty always received an ornamental dish of Brazil nuts as she not only dispensed shepherd's pie at the golf club but also kindness and appointments for the NHS. Golf, health monitoring, television shows as long as they were of merit, but never to be recorded in advance, and gardening filled their days, and many would envy the structure of those days; and then:

"Gleneagles," said Joceline.

"Pardon," said Richard looking up from his newspaper.

"I would like a mini break at Gleneagles."

"Whatever for?" Richard asked.

"Because we have been to Scotland every year of our married life and always self-catering and before it is too late, I would like to have a bit of luxury."

"Oh," replied Richard.

Joceline felt emboldened.

"And before you mention the cost, I know that we have just had a life insurance policy mature and I also know that the hotel has a weekend break deal at the moment." Emboldened, she pressed on, "The upside of having joint policies is the enhanced benefits, the downside is that I am on the document and, therefore, have access. And in addition, you left your paper open with The *Daily Telegraph's* offer."

Richard was boring but not unreasonable and, in fact, not mean, just cautious, so he said:

"Of course, we should go. When were you thinking of as I will have to tell my golf buddies?"

"After Easter," said Joceline, smiling and then closing her eyes to imagine yet another protracted and painful way of terminating his golf partner's lives.

And so they booked a long weekend at 'The Riviera of the Highlands'.

Petticoats

After serving their function on the stage coach to hide her valuables, Eleanor's petticoats were the first thing to be dispensed with. Cumbersome, hot and restricting, Eleanor had always hated wearing them and back in Perry County, it was only on visits to church that she acquiesced to her mother's requirement to 'dress like a lady in the presence of the lord'. Both of her parents were liberal in nearly all of their views apart from this one of her mother's and the slightly stranger, though less physically irritating, habit of her father's to tap all the children's front teeth gently with the handle of his hunting knife to check that they were sound.

This too happened on a Sunday but in the evening just before bedtime, and in later life, although now excused from the ritual, Eleanor would subconsciously use a knife from the table to tap her own front teeth especially when she was deep in thought or bored.

"Good teeth, good health," Jeb would state after all the children had been examined. Free of her father's inspection, Eleanor developed a strange nostalgia for it but not for the petticoats. Not the petticoats.

The women of the town, well to be accurate the white women of the town, frowned upon anything that was considered unladylike and after one of the grander dames noticed her slimmer figure, she made it clear to Eleanor that her attire was 'not that required of a lady'.

Too early to forcefully make her opinion known, she pleaded poverty and when that was overturned by the delivery of several sets of petticoats, she changed her excuse to a skin complaint which she endorsed to two representatives of the town by showing them a rash on her upper thighs. Both women blushed and withdrew and were not aware of the application of the baby's breath plant that Eleanor had administered that morning. It cost her a couple of days of irritation and the application of calamine lotion but she was left alone, petticoat-wise, by the good ladies of Vincennes after that.

The only male that chanced to make a remark was told to:

"Go and eat hog shit," and he too left her alone after that.

Unencumbered by conventional clothing, Eleanor struck a strangely masculine figure in the town and working on the basis that there is no such thing as bad publicity, she chose not to adopt a low profile. Eleanor was here as an agent of change. That had been a pledge to herself and to her parents. Her younger brothers were initially pleased that they no longer had to sleep in bunk beds and even though they still shared a bedroom, they each had a single truckle bed, but over time, they missed their elder sister. They missed her protection and her humour but mostly they missed her kindness. This had been transferred to Vincennes and they were to be the beneficiaries.

On the first night in her new home, Eleanor had slept on one of the pews in the church despite the entreaties of Mary to stay with them.

"There's ten of you already," she said, "and on top of that you had no idea that I was arriving today despite my paying for a telegram to tell you of my arrival, which never arrived." Here, she made a mental note to get the money back from the postal service.

"Come to dinner then, child," said Mary.

"Gladly," replied Eleanor and that evening, after having made the short trip from Clark's cabin earlier in the day with blankets and a pillow, she returned to their home to eat with the family and despite having two younger brothers of her own, she was not prepared for the chaos and the noise of eight children jostling and pushing but mainly laughing as they fought to get their favourite seats at the table. Samuel at last achieved a semblance of order with a pretence at anger which was patently not real, however, hunger now directed the children's behaviour and they quietened down enough for their father to say grace. As they all held hands, Eleanor included, Samuel said:

"Lord, we give thanks for the bounty that you have provided.

For food that stays our hunger,

For rest that brings us ease,

For homes where memories linger,

We give our thanks for these."

Collectively, they all said Amen and then Mary and Samuel between them passed around dishes of collard greens, grits, oatmeal pie, mashed pumpkin, homemade bread, and a stew made with a stringy old hen that Samuel had dispatched that morning. The stew had been hastily made in Eleanor's honour within minutes of her unexpected knock on the door that morning. Meat of any kind was a luxury but milk wasn't and so there was a large milk pudding with biscuits to follow. All eleven people at the table, young or old, eventually rocked back in their chairs or on the benches and with wide smiles, blew out their cheeks. Samuel broke the happy silence with an enormous belch, and Mary said:

"Samuel, manners please, we have a guest."

One of the youngest children started to giggle and within seconds everybody at the table was consumed with gales of laughter. Mary, eventually, dried her eyes and, addressing the table, said:

"Chores. Off you go before it gets dark."

There was a chorus of 'Nooooo, Ma, please'.

"Off you go," repeated Mary. "And if you do your chores in time, and properly mind. I think we can prevail upon our guest to read you a story." She turned to Eleanor and said, "I hope I wasn't being presumptuous."

"Not at all," said Eleanor.

"And in the meantime, coffee I think."

"I'll get the coffee," said Samuel. "You ladies take a seat on the porch."

"Why thank you, kind sir," said Mary, making a mock courtesy and she took Eleanor by the arm, as women will, and within seconds, the two of them were rocking gently back and forth in the swing seat on the stoop engaged in conversation.

Samuel took his time with the coffee and with the back door open, he lit a pipe and stared out into the night sky. The evening was warm and the sky was clear so that the stars stood out sharply. He identified the North star and with the tobacco drawing perfectly, he puffed away contentedly. Eventually, there was a cry from the porch. "Have you gone to Louisiana for that coffee, Samuel Clark?" Mary demanded and smiling, Samuel lifted the pot and three tin mugs from their hooks and made his way outside to join his wife and her new friend.

All three of them knew that whatever their friendship became, it would not be easy but it could be pivotal. Samuel felt the chemistry between the two women, one white and one black, as he poured the coffee and kissed his wife's cheek.

Freelancers

"Hels baby, do you want your fat back? Flat, flat I mean," said Sally who was a little drunk.

"Fat back, Sally, fat back. Are you implying that I was once a bigger girl than I am now?"

"Flat I mean, Hels. Sorry, I think I am a bit tiddly."

Tom and Helen raised their eyes to the ceiling and then laughed. Jonny, Helen's reasonably long-standing partner, just smiled. Three meetings with Helen's best friends were not quite enough to be fully intimate with them and he was very keen not to upset his girlfriend.

"Coffee," said Tom more as a statement than an enquiry, "and then we will give you our news."

He set off for the kitchen and Sally headed for the loo. Ten minutes later, all four were back in their former positions, Sally with her arm linked through Helen's.

"I think you better handle this, Tom," said Sally and this time, all three were in accord and so Tom said:

"Sally and I have decided to give up our jobs and to embark upon a project of which, Helen, you know a bit about, but, Jonny, I don't think you do, so here goes. You, of course, remember the whole Indiana demolition situation from a few years back where I found, by luck I must stress, some papers written by a very young Abraham Lincoln and hidden by a girl he knew when he was growing up in a place called Perry County."

"I do. Jonny, honey, do you?"

"Vaguely," said Jonny. "Can you expand please?"

"Of course," said Tom. "Long story short, I was living in California as a bit of a surfer dude and working for a demolition firm that specialised in character buildings. The owner, partly because of his mum who was a lecturer in architecture, but mainly because of his firm's skill and reputation, got a job in Indiana and one thing led to another and I, just by being in the right place, found some things written by the young Lincoln. There was a big fuss and lots of media attention and one of the papers ended up in the White House. That you may know, Jonny." Tom nodded at Helen's boyfriend and he nodded back.

"And then, it all went quiet again until your girlfriend was auditioning for a part as a no-nonsense female senator." Helen licked a finger and smoothed her eyebrows to indicate gravitas. "At which point, all three of us had a sort of crossover moment and a woman called Kimberly Smith came onto our radar."

Tom paused and asked them all, but really Jonny, if it made sense. All three nodded.

"So," said Tom. "I arranged to interview Kimberly and did some research with the help of my politically involved girlfriend and, fuck me, Kimberly Smith turns out to the several greats granddaughter of a woman called Eleanor Smith."

"And Eleanor Smith is who?" Jonny asked.

"Eleanor Smith is the girl that Abraham Lincoln was writing poems and stories for and she was the person who had hidden these writings in the boards of her home."

"Wow," said Jonny.

"Wow indeed," said Tom. "Anyway, Sally and I had some good fortune with a slice of inheritance, and I won't sadden you with the details of that and have decided to try, and I emphasise try, to write a book about Eleanor Smith who, from our initial findings, had an extraordinary life."

"One thing," said Jonny. "Smith would be a male line name, not a female one."

"Ah, Good spot, Jonny, and it shows that unlike my girlfriend who is nodding off, you have been paying attention."

"I am not," said Sally. "Quite," and she lay her head on Helen's shoulder.

"Smith is pure coincidence. Eleanor married a Gold but kept her maiden name for her work and Kimberly is a Carter who just happened to marry a Smith."

"Gosh," said Jonny. "Cool stuff and fascinating too."

"So finally to my earlier point, Helen, and you too. Jonny, Sally and I are going to buy a Winnebago and live in it while we research the book and so we will be giving up the flat."

Helen piped up, "Well, I think it's the end of an era then, gang, as this lovely man," and she pointed at Jonny, "has asked me to move in with him. And not that I am avaricious or anything but he has a rather lovely three-bedroom apartment overlooking Central Park."

"End of an era then," said Sally.

"Or the beginning of a new one," said Helen. "Oh, and by the way, I have had lunch with Kimberly Smith and I now know how to take on those old fuckers on Capitol Hill, so watch this space!"

Pride and Dignity

'People aren't supposed to own and sell other people like so much cattle and such.'

The term indenture comes from the medieval English 'indenture of retainer'—a legal contract written in duplicate on the same sheet, with the copies separated by cutting along a jagged (toothed, hence the term 'indenture') line so that the teeth of the two parts could later be refitted to confirm authenticity (chirograph).

Mary Bateman had won her freedom on 6 November 1821 at appeal and Samuel Clark at some point afterwards but certainly well before Eleanor's arrival in 1829. Officially, Mary Bateman-Clark's court case had ended indentured servitude but in the same way that wars, religion, and politics are not absolute in their scope and parameters, neither was Indiana's legislative decision. Official documents lay out the terms and conditions of treaties and agreements but they are enforced by people and they are usually the same people who were part of the decision processes prior to significant change.

Mary and Samuel had gone about their married life since their release from indentured servitude with caution as the yoke of slavery still hung over the state along with the added threat of being taken against their will down south where there were no indentured workers, just pure slaves. There was still a minority, but a strong minority, that stood against the Indiana anti-slave legislation and the Clarks were very aware of this section of the white community and the ongoing mantra that the legislation only applied to indentured servitude undertaken after 1816 when the law had been implemented.

Mary knew that changing a person's opinion, to literally get them facing in the opposite direction, was a long and challenging process. Samuel said to her:

"Do you know how old you will be when you have everybody in this town singing from the same song sheet, Mary?"

"The same age as will be if I don't," was her reply and he loved her all the more for saying it.

Her home was her sanctuary but the church was her office, and the morning after Eleanor's arrival, she made her way to that office with a mug of strong coffee, some biscuits, and gravy in a dish under a cloth. Their home was less than a hundred yards from the church, so the coffee stayed hot and the biscuits stayed warm.

"Morning, child," she said.

From beneath the blankets, she heard Eleanor say, "Morning, Mary. Is it light?"

"It's so light that it is thinking of getting dark again," she replied and smiled that Mary Bateman-Clark smile.

"I have brought some coffee and biscuits, honey, but I will give you a minute to, to, well you know."

"I do indeed and where do I go…to you know?"

"There is a bucket out the back and a water pump too. Anything…err more solid than that, you will have to visit our outhouse."

There was a strange awkwardness in Mary's need to discuss bodily functions, a trait not isolated to Indiana, but a country-wide reluctance that continues to this day. Eleanor yawned and shuffled off and Mary took the opportunity to shake out and fold the blankets. She then absentmindedly brushed the pew with the back of her hand before taking the opportunity to kneel at the altar and recite her first prayer of the day. It was always short and to the point.

In love

In family

In God

We go forward

Amen

"Dies primus," said Eleanor on her return. She had twisted her long hair into a ponytail and scrubbed her face with the cold water. She reached into her bag and lifted out a skirt and a blouse which she lay on the pew next to herself. She then lifted her nightdress over her head and Mary, despite having given birth to eight children with all the attendant nakedness of all of them and indeed herself, found herself embarrassed anew.

Eleanor smiled and smoothing her clothes, she asked, "Did you mention coffee and biscuits, Mary?"

"Indeed, I did." Holding Eleanor's hands and looking into her eyes, she said, "Dear girl, you are very welcome here."

"Thank you," breathed Eleanor.

"And when you have finished your breakfast, we shall set about finding you somewhere to stay and some work, if that is satisfactory to you?"

"Thank you again and yes, that would be wonderful."

"Finish your breakfast then and I will come back in a while."

"Oh, and dies primus, what does that mean?" Mary asked.

"It means the first day," replied Eleanor. "A friend of mine, a male friend, taught me a little bit of Latin; he is very clever and he will be a famous man one day." She meant Abraham of course but that would mean nothing to Mary so she kept his name to herself. One day, she would tell the Clarks about him.

Mary headed off back to her home and Eleanor took the coffee and the biscuits on to the church steps. The sun was glancing off the nearby roofs and the day had the promise of warmth and brightness. Eleanor said to herself, "So much to achieve, so much to change, I hope that I have the fortitude," and then she bit into one of the biscuits and her tastebuds took over her brain.

Later that day, Mary was good to her word and arrived at the church with a song on her lips.

"How was your breakfast, child?" She asked.

"Delicious," said Eleanor. "As good as my ma's and she can sure bake."

"Praise indeed," replied Mary. She came up the stairs into the church and closed her eyes reverentially in the cool interior just for a moment, and then said, "Now, come with me, Eleanor. I hope that I have found you somewhere suitable to live and possibly, just possibly, some suitable employment for you."

The two ladies walked down the street away from the church and past the Clark's home. As they approached the end of the street where the dwellings gave way to open countryside, Mary led Eleanor down a track by the side of the last house to a small cottage that could not be seen from the road. Here, she smoothed her dress and knocked on the door. It was opened by a handsome black woman in her later years who took a split second to recognise her caller and when she did, her mouth broke into a wide smile showing even white teeth.

She sang out, "Mary Clark, as I live and breathe, to what do I owe this honour?" Mary was about to reply when she was enfolded in the woman's ample bust while she said, "Now where are my manners? Come in, come in." It was at this point that she saw Eleanor, and took in the fact that she was white, and her smile slipped slightly. Mary introduced Eleanor and assured her friend that she was one of the good ones and made the necessary introductions:

"Eleanor, this is Dolores."

"Pleased to meet you," they both chorused and Mary held the hands of both ladies.

"Iced tea I think on this hot day," said Dolores. "And you are very welcome here, child," she continued.

Dolores led the two ladies into her small but immaculately appointed home. The floors were bare boards but they were polished to a high gloss and there were brightly coloured rugs at the points where feet would come to rest. The walls were whitewashed and there was a small collection of pictures on those walls, a few ornaments adorning the dining table and a chest of drawers against the wall. At the far end of the room was a range with a fire going in it and Dolores said, "I am just doing some baking. That's why it's so warm in here, so perhaps we should take our drinks outside?"

"Lovely," said Mary. "We'll find a spot in the shade."

Dolores opened a small larder door which was located away from the fire, here its thick walls kept all her food and drink items cool even in the fiercest summer heat. She took a jug of iced tea down from a shelf, removed the cloth that covered it, and placed the jug and three glasses on a tray which she brought out into the yard where Mary and Eleanor were swaying gently back and forth on the swing seat. She then filled the three glasses, passed two to the seated ladies, and kept one for herself. Finally, she rolled a small barrel over from behind the barn, blew the dust off it, and perched regally with glass in hand.

"Would you be more comfortable here?" Eleanor asked.

"Probably, honey, but this old arse of mine has seen more than splinters, I'll do."

There was a pause and then gales of laughter. The ice had been firmly broken.

It was decided that Eleanor would pay Dolores two dollars a month for lodging and five cents a meal but only on the days that she ate with her landlady. She would occupy the small back bedroom which had a stand with a jug and a basin for washing and a chamber pot for night time ablutions as Dolores didn't like to be disturbed when the final candles had been blown out. She would attend to her own laundry, be expected to help with any heavy lifting and the chopping of firewood, and most importantly, have her own key. Dolores too had no doubt that there was an abundance of work for a strong girl like her and they would attend to that after they had finished their iced tea.

"One last question," said Eleanor and here she looked at both women in turn. "What about the colour issue?"

"That, my dear girl, is not going to change because of the arrival of one more soul in this town, be they black or white. That is an ongoing situation," said Mary.

Dolores looked at her friend and just made a noise, "Yup."

Winnebago

"Who is that?" Sally asked.

"That, my lovely intrepid adventurer, is our target."

"That's Eleanor?"

"It sure is."

"Where did you get the picture from?" Sally asked.

"Yesterday when you were having your goodbye lunch with Helen, I took myself off to the New York Public Library, and after a good deal of research, I managed to find this picture in an old reference book. Taken in or around 1887/88, this is Eleanor Smith, or Eleanor Gold to give her married name. We hopefully will be able to confirm her birth date when we get to Indiana but based on the year 1810, she would be seventy-seven or seventy-eight years old when this picture was taken. The librarian kindly let me borrow the book to get a photocopy."

Staring back at them, in a classic Victorian pose, was a handsome woman in a long pale dress with her hair up and her hand resting on the back of a chair. The picture was in black and white but the dark drapes meant that her light-coloured attire stood out and it was clear that she wore no petticoats.

"Wow," said Sally. "What a cool woman."

"I thought that we would stick it to the dashboard as a talisman. I have ordered two photographic copies but I am not sure if they will arrive before we leave. Isn't she a babe though?"

"I am not sure that a revolutionary, anti-slavery feminist devotee can be called a babe but hey, yes, she is a babe."

Tom and Sally had both left their respective jobs on good terms. It was now 1990 and both of them had entered their mid-thirties, Sally being slightly younger than Tom. Kyle had said to Sally:

"Anytime that you want to come back, Sal, there will be a job here waiting for you."

It was not a promise that he could, in fact, keep but as it turned out, he would never have to as Sally did not return and in fact within a year, Kyle himself would be gone, taking a job initially for George H. W. Bush's administration and then subsequently, and unusually, transferring to the Democratic Bill Clinton team, where he remained and rose through the ranks during the president's eight-year tenure. The late twentieth century was ushering in tolerance and understanding on multiple issues and Kyle's sexuality was never an issue or an impediment. Sally kept in touch with him and on occasion used her feminine charm and his position and connections to circumvent problems.

Tom was sent off in the usual way that journalists do and that was with an excessive drinking spree in one of the many haunts that the *New York Times* employees used on and around the eighth avenue headquarters. In a similar way to the business that Sally had left, journalism was also changing, although somewhat reluctantly. There were more female journalists and the content and style of the newspaper were softening. There would always be a fraternity culture to the business and drinking and long lunches were still high on the agenda, however, the smarter writers noticed, accepted, and then embraced a more sober and ultimately, a more professional world.

Tom liked a drink but saw it as a reward and not a catalyst. On several occasions during his time at the paper, he had wearied at the tiresome gatherings in dingy bars and so now, like Sally, he was glad to be moving on.

"First thing that I am going to do, Sal, is lose seven pounds," he told Sally in the morning after his leaving drinks. She prodded his belly and replied:

"Ten minimum I would say," and during the resultant giggling and then love making, she teased him further by climbing on top of him. "I don't want some fat old man crushing me." Tom was mostly amused but also somewhat embarrassed, and that evening saw him in a running kit heading towards Central Park.

Within a week, Tom was five and half pounds lighter and hadn't touched a drop of alcohol during that week. They had given notice on the apartment with a touch of regret but mostly with excitement and anticipation. During that week, they visited three RV lots and bought a three year old Winnebago which they had serviced and professionally cleaned by a specialist company. All of the furniture had been sold either on Craig's List or given to friends, including Helen, who nostalgically kept and then installed the big mirror that had hung by the front door and had seen multiple versions of herself and her friends.

Tom and Sally kept a couple of pictures, some kitchen items, and a handful of books, most importantly, *Of Mice and Men* by John Steinbeck with the inscription by the unknown Michael in the flyleaf.

On their final weekend, and as the Winnebago was being valeted, they checked into a hotel and decided to play tourists in their adopted city. After breakfast, Sally waited for Tom in the lobby who arrived with a guide book and a backpack.

"Ready to see the sights, babe?" He said.

"One thing, Tom, and please do not get mad, but do you think it might be worth visiting your mum's grave as a sort of bizarre thank-you but also by way of closure."

Tom looked up to the light filtering through the upper casement windows and at the dust motes swirling there, and what Sally had said felt right.

"Absolutely," he said. "Let's go there first."

Sally smiled, rose, kissed him, and loved him even more.

"It's a lovely day, so shall we walk the twenty blocks?"

"Lead on, Sal," and she did.

The Tartan

One of Ellena's friends shouted:

"What's under your skirt, big boy?" and they all grabbed each other and giggled.

The Scottish marching band had finished its drill and the parade was breaking up. As the girls were turning to walk away, there was a heavily brogued shout of 'this' and as one sixteen young Scotsmen formerly in ranks of eight but now in a line faced the girls and lifted their kilts in unison to show sixteen sets of genitals of varying shape and size. They held the pose for a few seconds and then dropped their kilts and it was now their turn to laugh until a very stern sergeant-major appeared, reprimanded them, and restored order. He then marched straight over to what he correctly assumed were the majority of the girls' parents and in his finest Govan accent, apologised on behalf of the Black Watch and threw them all an impressive salute.

The parents, like their daughters, were somewhat in awe of the soldiers in skirts and chorused that there was not a problem, just high spirits. One of the fathers was an ex-military man and he thought to himself that it must have been an assault on the senses to have been waiting to engage the enemy, to hear the pipes and drums, and then see row after row of highlanders with bayonets fixed emerging out of the mist or over a ridge.

The sergeant-major returned to the offenders and, in a deep authoritative voice, said: "I know, lads, that this is a bit of a jolly, but you are at all times a soldier of the British Army and must behave as such." He then added, "However, it's a good job it was a warm day or otherwise there would have been nothing for those lassies to get excited about." A smile then broke under his impressive moustache and he marched away.

In an unusual but extraordinarily generous invitation, the Black Watch pipe and drum band had been invited to take part in a New York parade and they had gratefully accepted. The threat of war was in the air and similar opportunities were likely to be rare in the near future, so permission had been easy to procure.

It meant a week in a Manhattan hotel for forty soldiers and their officers. The event was to be held half way through the week which allowed for three whole days or R and R. In one room was Private Jack Gow and his friend, Finlay Croan. Both were pipers. Both were twenty-two years old and both had turned their national service into a career.

Jack was from Auchterarder, a town close to the world-famous Gleneagles Hotel, Finlay was from a Glasgow tenement in the depressed Gorbals area of the city.

Ellena Goodperson was eighteen in 1938 when the Black Watch came to town. She was the daughter of a well-to-do family living on the Upper East Side. Virginal, shy, and privately educated, she was somewhat naive. When Jack Gow shone his dark Celtic eyes on her from beneath his impressive busby, as she was giggling with her friends, she blushed and adjusted her hair. When he smiled, she felt her skin grow warm. When he walked over to her and removed his head gear to reveal a shock of dark hair, she did not know where to look but she knew what to say when he asked her name.

"Ellena."

"Ellena what?" Jack enquired.

"Ellena Goodman."

"And are you?" Jack asked. "Good?" And the implication was clear.

Ellena blushed anew. Later that day, she met Jack without her parents' permission to show him some of the sights of New York. And she did so on the second day too, staying on into the evening when they kissed in Central Park. After a dinner for the Black Watch held in the mess of one of America's finest regiments, Ellena snuck out from her home and waited self-consciously in the lobby of Jack's hotel for his return. He bribed his roommate to disappear for a couple of hours and Ellena saw and felt what lay beneath his kilt, but it was not until several weeks later that she became aware of what their coupling had produced. Even though she had kept in touch with Jack by letter, she felt both alone and very scared.

Vincennes Days

Eleanor awoke on her second morning in Vincennes and could feel her landlady in the building. She could also hear her singing as she moved about the cottage.

Lord I turn my face to thee
Guide me so that I may see
All the beauty thou does impart
Which fills my soul and warms my heart

Eleanor had not heard the song before and so did not know the words but after Dolores repeated the verses several times, she got a sense of the rhythm and within a week, knew the words and would sing along too. On this first morning, though, it made her a little homesick and she wondered if she had done the right thing, but as she took in the music and drifted with her thoughts, there was a cursory knock at her door, and a smiling face said:

"Coffee, honey," as a statement, not an inquiry, and at that moment, all her doubts dropped away.

"Thank you, Miss Cain," she said.

"Dolores, always Dolores, Eleanor," she replied.

"Thank you, Dolores," and she took the tin mug with its steaming contents and made to rise.

"First day lie in," said Dolores. "Grits and bacon in fifteen minutes, that alright."

Eleanor sipped her coffee, smiled, and said, "More than alright, a feast." She carefully put her drink on a pretty tile which sat on the table next to her bed so that she did not mark the wood, closed her eyes for five more minutes, and then almost leapt out of bed to greet the day. The bacon and grits were better even than her mother's and after eating, Eleanor poured cold water into her basin and washed her face, neck, and hands. There was a small mirror on the wall and staring back was a pretty young woman with hair tied back, clear skin and clear eyes, and a determined set to her face. "With you, Lord," she said into the air and then went to help Dolores with the dishes.

"First day is chores free too," said her landlady and despite Eleanor's protestations, that was how it was to be. "Now help me with my bonnet and we will go and see Mary, and see about some work for you."

Dolores looked in the mirror too and tucked a stray lock of hair under her hat.

"Hmmm," she said. "The boys used to form a queue to dance with me, but I am not so sure that they would now." She was bigger by quite a few pounds than when she was a young girl but her skin was still smooth and her teeth pearly white, and the years had not diminished the sparkle that she had in her eyes.

"Still beautiful," said her companion.

"To the blind and the daft," she replied and chuckled. "But thank you."

"Were you ever married?" Eleanor asked.

"Was never asked," was the reply. "No, that's not true, I was asked once but the boy was a drinker and I had a father who was a drinker, so I turned him down. I do not regret that decision as the girl he married was often seen in church with a black eye or worse and there was rarely any money, and therefore, rarely any security or love."

"Oh dear," said Eleanor.

"He died of a thing called a portal haemorrhage I believe, which is nasty but the truth is, she and we are the better for his going. Her parents took her back in along with the three children that she had given birth to and she lives quietly with them and spends a good deal of time at the church. You will no doubt meet her. She is a lovely woman but you can see the sadness in her eyes."

Dolores closed and locked the door and then pointed up into a tree on the edge of the yard where a glorious red and orange bird sang its morning song.

"Northern cardinal," she said.

"Cheer-a-dote, cheer-a-dote-dote-dote, purdy, purdy, purdy," she continued. "They are my passion, birds that is, and in this part of Indiana, we are blessed with many and varied species. I will teach you about them if you like, and I am afraid that if you don't like them, you will have to put up with me talking about them. That's just how it is."

"I do like them. Very much," said Eleanor and the two ladies waited until the song finished and the bird flew away.

"Right. No more idling, to Mary and the church," said Dolores linking her arm into Eleanor's, the two ladies, different in age and the colour of their skin but friends already, stepped out into the road.

Road Trip

It is eight hundred and thirty-six miles from New York to Vincennes by road and almost a parallel route East to West through Pennsylvania and Ohio before tailing down through Indianapolis, then heading due south to Vincennes. That would be the route to take if you wanted to get there in the shortest time, but as Sally pointed out:

"Eleanor has been dead for over a hundred years and Abraham Lincoln even longer, so I think that we can indulge ourselves and take a more circuitous route."

"Absolutely," agreed Tom and moving the occasional tables and pot plant to one side in their hotel room, he spread the map out on the floor. The excitement of an unfolded paper map is a special thing and Tom knelt just below the Gulf of Mexico and smoothed the folds as flat as they would go. "This is fine for now but I think that we should get state maps or at worst a map of the Eastern side of America so we can drill down into the details."

Sally agreed and came round to position herself just below Florida. She had lived in the United States for the majority of her adult life and Tom for the entirety of his life, but when they looked at the map, both the enormity of the country and the fascination with its many and multiple geographic locations took them over.

"Do you think that you could name all of the states?" Sally asked.

"Forty, maybe forty-five," replied Tom.

"And their correct location?" Sally further asked.

"Twenty-five, maybe thirty," said Tom.

"I am about the same amount. It's amazing; for instance, did you know that Indiana has a shoreline on Lake Michigan? Or that the Eastern Wisconsin border is in Lake Michigan? Or that Louisville is in Kentucky but it looks like it just sneaks into Indiana? Or that Fort Wayne…"

"I get it," said Tom. "There's a lot to learn and for us a lot to see, so on the basis that our ultimate destination is Vincennes with a hundred-mile trip to Perry County somewhere in the mix, how would you like to proceed?"

"Well, how about this for a rough plan?" Sally said. "New York to Philadelphia, as I have always wanted to see the Liberty Bell and with the presidential connections that we hope to expand on, or at worst just write about, there is a solid tie up there. Then on through West Virginia and even though it won't be the fall, it will still be stunningly beautiful, Knoxville, Nashville for a bit of musical input, Memphis to pay homage to the king, and finally up through Tennessee and into Indiana. We can decide nearer the time if we want to visit Perry County on the way up or to go straight to Vincennes and then head south again later."

"Sounds great," said Tom. "What about Washington DC as we head South-West?"

"Not really sure. I had quite a few trips there in my political days, you did too. Shall we give it a swerve?"

"Absolutely. Liberty Bell and then into the boonies. Drink?"

"Yes, please," said Sally. "Want to talk about your mum's grave?"

"Not really," said Tom, but with a glass of wine in his hand, his brain decided otherwise and Sally just listened.

"She was always, always either depressed or angry and inconsolable, not that I ever really knew what to console her about. Anything would set her off and I think it was really only her money that kept any people in her life. The longest period that any housekeeper stayed was about four months and most of them were much less than that."

"Oh, you poor thing," said Sally. "And her parents, Tom, what of them?"

"Her dad was a successful businessman and I think that her mum had been in the theatre but gave that all up when she got married. She was an only child too and both her parents died before I was born. And of course, she was almost always drunk, which made her argumentative and cruel, plus she surrounded herself with sycophants and bores who encouraged or ignored her behaviour, particularly as she was picking up the bill."

"It sounds awful, Tom. And I know that I have asked you about this before but you really have no idea who your father was?"

"No. There is no name on my birth certificate. The only hint of who he was would be when my mum ranted about a bloody Scots bastard…either Jack or Jock…but no more than that."

"Well, Tom, you could use some of the money to get a private detective to investigate. If you are interested, that is?"

"The truth is, Sal, that I am not sure that I am. But, hey, you never know. Thanks for listening and coming along to the grave. I love you very much."

"And I love you, Tom Goodman."

She kissed him and held his hand.

"And tomorrow we are off on our adventures. Hooray!"

Lovely Eleanor

And she was lovely. Everybody thought so but one of the church choir said, "The nicest person you could ever meet, but she doesn't suffer fools gladly."

Another replied, "And I certainly wouldn't want to cross her." Eleanor had that rarest of gifts that she could switch from stern authoritarian to a little girl in a heartbeat and she often did. Those who came to know her well spotted the signs and adjusted their behaviour accordingly, but those who didn't know her so well could be disarmed in a heartbeat, only to be under her fierce gaze a moment later. It certainly kept the people that she came into contact with on their toes but it also meant that when the town council were looking for teachers to start a mixed-race school, it was Eleanor to whom they turned.

On her second day in Vincennes, Eleanor had left Dolores on the steps of the church, and as would become their custom on meeting and parting going forward, they hugged each other.

"Morning, sleepy girl," said Mary in jest. "Is the bed too comfortable?" To which Eleanor smiled and pretended to yawn.

"Morning, Mary."

"How is that terrible landlady?" Mary asked in a voice loud enough for the departing Dolores to hear, to which she just waved over her shoulder without turning around.

"Just fine, and thank you so much for setting me up in her home, I think that I am going to be very comfortable."

"I am pleased, child, and now to the second pressing concern, some work for you. I visited last night with the Ford family who farm two thousand acres to the west of here. They have five children and a mainly livestock business to run and are in desperate need of some help both on the farm and with the children. The eldest child is eleven and the youngest four, so there are no babies to manage and they employ four hands on the farm, three are black and one is white, and they are all married males and none of the three are slaves or indentured. They are good people and I think that you could be happy there."

"It's about a mile and a half walk from Dolores' cottage but two of the men travel from Vincennes, so there is a very good chance of getting a lift most mornings as they both have their own horses and carts. Early start at 6.00am for milking and all done by 4pm when the eldest children are home from school to help out. They provide a midday meal and the pay is six dollars a month for a five-day week with a goose or similar at Christmas. How does that sound?"

Eleanor took Mary's hand, touched her face, and said:

"Thank you so much for your kindness, Mary. I am blessed. I did the milking on the farm at home as well as other general chores, and as for the children, I have two younger brothers at home for reference."

"Wonderful. Wonderful," said Mary. "I said that you would head up there this morning to meet everyone and perhaps you would like to come to church this evening and then to supper afterwards."

Eleanor smiled and pointing, said:

"This way."

"That way," replied Mary. "And see you at six o'clock tonight and perhaps one final thing, would you read the lesson this evening?"

"Gladly," replied Eleanor and she smoothed her skirts and headed off towards the Ford farm.

The last hundred yards or so was a compacted dirt drive up to the farmhouse which was surrounded by fields. Behind the farmhouse were several barns and outbuildings. It was late morning when Eleanor arrived at the house and she saw long before she arrived at the stoop the shape of a woman rocking and sewing in the warmth of the morning. She looked up and rose when she saw Eleanor and smiling, said:

"You must be Eleanor? You are very welcome here, come up on the veranda and have some lemonade while I fetch my husband."

"Thank you, Ma'am," said Eleanor.

"Sally," said the lady. "And my husband is Tom."

"Thank you, Sally," she replied and Sally turned and headed into the house and came back with a jar of citrus sharp lemonade which she gave to Eleanor. A tall black man passed around the corner of the house carrying a pitchfork and Sally called out to him:

"Joseph, have you seen Tom?" And as he made to reply, Tom emerged from the house and looking at Joseph, he held a finger over his lips to stop his reply and stole up upon his wife whom he grabbed around the waist and swung gently from side to side.

"Here I am, my sweet," he said and Sally turned to pretend to scold him.

"Tom Ford," she admonished him and slapped his chest playfully. "Whatever will people think?"

"They will think that we are a happily married couple and they would be right," and he kissed his wife. "Now how can I be of service?"

"I want you to meet Eleanor Smith," she said, "who is here about the general duties vacancy on the farm."

Tom turned to look at Eleanor and in an instant, and although she did not yet know it, she had been employed. The Fords asked her several questions but not for references as Mary and Dolores had already made positive statements to them and by the time the lemonade had been drunk, Eleanor was the farm's new employee. Tom shook her hand and Sally took the newly released hand and laid it over Eleanor's other one, and clasping them both, said:

"Welcome to Ford farm, Eleanor, we do hope that you will be happy here," and she was.

Michael

Michael was not some bastard Scot, nor was he the son of some bastard Scot but he did have a son who was part Scottish and a bastard by the definition of marriage. Michael did not know of Tom and Tom did not know of Michael, although clearly the son knew that he must have a father, even though the father did not know that he had a son. Clear? Sort of.

In 1990, Michael was sixty-four years old and was defined by two main criteria. Firstly, he was a bachelor and secondly, he was a very successful businessman. His Edinburgh restaurants and in particular the Michelin-starred 'Michael's' had been a success for many years and along with the equally successful 'Mikey's Bistro' had spawned a catering business that included pubs, a food factory, and an events business. 'Michael's' was booked up weeks in advance and 'Mikey's' rarely had an unused table. As for Michael's marital status, tying the knot had just not happened.

Not only was he eligible and wealthy, but he was also attractive, intelligent, and urbane. Over the years, there had been several partners but in essence, he was married to his business and happily so. He lived in a beautifully appointed flat in the new town which was within walking distance of both restaurants and was big enough to contain an office from which he controlled all of his interests. He also had a cottage in the borders which he visited regularly but rarely, and mainly when his sister and her husband urged him to 'take a break'.

His parents had passed on recently and in their honour, but mainly in his mother's honour, he had prevailed upon one of his chefs to create a dessert using powdered egg as a tribute to her efforts when he had returned home after his national service as a Bevin Boy. The truth was, his mother had rarely resorted to the powdered egg because of her contacts with the local farming community but it became a signature dish for 'Michael's' and so its derivation was never questioned.

John Carnegie had only recently retired from his position as general manager at Gleneagles and he regularly took the train from Gleneagles station to

Edinburgh's Waverley station travelling first class. He would emerge in gloriously tailored splendour like some 1930s film star pausing for a couple of seconds on the carriage's footplate before descending to the platform to receive his public. He wore a beautiful tweed three-piece suit, a Homburg hat, and carried a silver-topped cane. His hair was grey and luxuriant and he had grown another moustache to compliment the sideburns he had sported since his army days. He looked just like the retired cavalry officer that he in fact was.

John walked, or rather marched, the five hundred yards along Princes Street and up onto George Street before entering Michael's restaurant. Any new staff were in awe of this glorious customer but it would always be one of the long-term staff that pricked the balloon by throwing a mock salute and crying, "Atten…shun."

There would be a pause and then John would throw his hat and cane at the waiter before himself crying, "I want to see the manager," which would bring his friend and protege running.

"Your usual table, Sir?" The two men looked at each other sternly until they both cracked a smile and hugged.

"Good to see you, laddie."

"And to see you, John, give me five minutes and I will join you."

The two old friends sat down to eat together.

"How are you enjoying your retirement?" Michael asked.

"Busier than ever," replied John. "I think you have to either hide away or else leave the area completely to entirely disassociate yourself from a career as intense as the one that we chose. To be fair, I didn't want to leave the hotel entirely and now I can pick and choose what I do. I am like a retired famous footballer such as Bobby Charlton or Bobby Moore that they bring out on match days to chat to the fans."

"Bobby Charlton, eh?"

"You know what I mean. I am grateful really as it keeps me busy and the truth is, I love the old place and it has been good to me."

"I hear you," said Michael. "I sometimes feel the younger staff members' eyes on me, particularly at board meetings, but I have no plans on retiring yet."

"And how is Mrs Carnegie and all the other Carnegies?"

"They are well, thank you, Mike. Again they keep me busy…and poor. And I suppose that no lady has taken your eye yet? It's never too late, you know."

Michael laughed. "A happy bachelor; thanks, John."

"Well, from memory, you could probably fill this restaurant several times over with disappointed lassies."

"Maybe," said Michael.

"And along that line of thought, a strange thing happened at the hotel last month."

"Really? What was that?" Michael asked.

"There was an American guy staying, an investigator of some sort apparently. He wanted to see registration records from a period in the 1950s to ascertain if a certain lady had stayed at the hotel. I happened to be in the building for a management meeting and one of the under managers asked for my advice. It is, as you know, a legal requirement to not only keep but also to share such information with regulatory authorities. Her name was Ellena Goodperson and she stayed for a week in autumn, or fall as he preferred to call it, of 1953."

"He described her and what with the description, the unusual name and the fact that she was a single American lady, I have a vague recollection of her. Do you remember her?"

"Indeed, I do, John. She invited me to her room on two occasions and we had sex. She was clinical in her demands but wasn't going to take no for an answer, not that I had any inclination to turn her down. There was little or no intimacy or conversation and after the second occasion, I never heard from her again. All I remember was her saying 'done' on that second occasion and I paid it no mind as I was twenty-six years old and, frankly, flattered by the attention. I was going to ask her about the parting comment when I next saw her but of course, I never did."

"I remember making some cursory enquiries after getting her details from the records too but in truth, I just put it down to a single woman and single man in a hotel bedroom of which there must have been thousands, if not millions, of examples over the years. Strange though."

"Strange indeed, laddie, but I have his card at home if you want to follow it up or indeed if I hear anything further, I will let you know. Now what are the specials today?"

Ford Farm

Eleanor was waiting for her good luck to change. It wasn't that she was a pessimist by nature, it was just that she was a farmer's daughter, and that was the life she had been brought up in.

"There's livestock and there's dead stock," was one of her father's favourite sayings and it brought realism to the life of the farmer. She was now working on another farm, so she was acutely aware of the problems of the profession yet again first-hand. But after three weeks, there had been only the most trivial of issues. On one occasion, a young heifer had managed to get out of the tiniest gap in the rail fence that surrounded the farmyard but had been brought back by a neighbour's son. For this, he was rewarded with a large slice of apple pie made by Sally and as he ate it, he could not take his eyes off Eleanor. Tom had joined them for this mid-morning break and noticed the young lad's direction of gaze.

"We are over here," he said to the youngster, which brought a rebuke from Sally as the hectic colour exploded in the boy's face causing him to force down the last of the pie before mumbling his thanks and his need to leave before stumbling off down the track. After a polite silence and once Tom had flagged that the boy was no longer in earshot, all three of them collapsed into good-natured laughter, so much so that the other hands arriving for coffee and pie just looked at them and then each other in mystery.

But the main source of Eleanor's good fortune was her friendship with the three ladies who had helped and supported her during her short time in Vincennes. All three were kind beyond measure but also practical and resourceful. They were also not to be trifled with as Eleanor had seen on several occasions not only on the farm and in the church but also in the community of Vincennes. Sally Ford had intervened on a racial matter with the full support of her husband when it was likely that Mary and Dolores would have had to avoid confrontation because of their colour.

Lying on her bed having blown out the candle one evening, Eleanor saw the possibility of adding her support to her three new friends in the ongoing post-slavery changes that would burden not only Vincennes but also many towns and cities across America in the months and years to come. But for now, she was enjoying her work and her involvement with the church.

It was one evening after a busy day working at the farm that Eleanor came into the cottage to find Dolores sitting at the kitchen table holding what looked like a scrap of cloth. She did not hear Eleanor approach and therefore she did not wipe away the single tear that rolled down her cheek. Eleanor watched her for a few moments and then scuffed her feet on the floor to announce her arrival. Dolores immediately tucked the item into the blouse, wiped her face, and painted on a smile.

"Evening child, how was your day?"

"Fine, just fine," she replied. "And how was yours?"

"Fine too, thanks. Hungry?" She moved to fix some food at the range.

"Dolores, are you alright?"

"Just dandy, honey," she lied and Eleanor knew it was a lie.

"Dolores," she said, drawing out the syllables into a question.

"Oh, Eleanor," she said and sitting down again, the tears started to flow.

So Eleanor came up behind her, laid her head on the older lady's shoulder, and held her and finally said, "Would a sympathetic ear help?"

"I think so. It's been a long time in the dark," she said.

Eleanor moved Dolores to the battered old armchair and stoked up the fire even though the day was still warm. She then made coffee and brought her friend a steaming tin mug of it. Finally, she curled up at the feet of her friend and smoothing her skirts, she said, "What ails you so?"

Dolores touched Eleanor's head and began.

"He was lovely. Handsome, strong, kind and thoughtful but…white. His parents didn't mind the colour difference and nor did mine but everybody else seemed to, and there was name-calling and whispers, but thankfully no violence. The worst of it was when friends avoided us or crossed the road when they saw us coming but we were happy, or at least I thought we were. And then I noticed the change in myself, a physical change, and I knew that I was pregnant."

Eleanor's mind quickly travelled back to her miscarriage in the dark, by the river, on her own, and as only women can, kindred women who have experienced the conception of a child, she immediately sensed an empathy rising in her.

"I was so happy, despite the obvious problems, not only of colour but also that we were not married, but I thought that love would overcome those issues."

Dolores now mentally reprimanded herself and Eleanor sensed the change and so pushed her for details.

"So what happened? If you don't mind telling me."

"Well, it was a lovely summer's day and I was wearing my Sunday dress and I had brought a picnic down to the river. The sun was hot and the river was cool and we were drinking lemonade and lying in the grass when I told him. When I did, there was a pause and his mood changed, but as I said he was not a violent man but within ten minutes, we were walking back to town in silence. I never saw him again, well not as his girlfriend, and his parents sought me out after church and told me that if I kept the baby, then they would deny that it was anything to do with their son."

"'Best get rid of it' was his father's advice. My parents were supportive but realistic and my father took me aside the next day and suggested, well told me really, to terminate it. This was eighteenth century Virginia bear in mind."

"Virginia. Virginia, Dolores. Jesus," blurted Eleanor blaspheming. "Apologies for taking the Lord's name in vain," she followed up.

"I know, child, I know. So as you can probably guess, I had no choice. My father took me to a woman fifty miles away who dealt with these things and gave both her and me some money, and told me not to come back for a month, and so I didn't."

"Then what happened?"

"I never went back, never saw my parents, nor my siblings, nor the terminated child's father again. It took a full month for the effects of the abortion to heal and the woman's clumsiness and lack of skill meant that it would be unlikely that I could ever conceive again but, as I told you a while back, I have never been married and one pregnancy out of wedlock is enough for anybody."

Dolores then pulled a tiny pair of knitted baby boots from her blouse.

"These," she said. "I bought for myself lest I ever forget as if I ever would, but they remind me that I could have been a mother."

"Oh, you poor thing," said Eleanor and touched Dolores's cheek. "What happened after that? If you don't mind me asking," she enquired.

"That, my dear girl, is a story for another day. Now supper I think and a glass of that cider from the jug in the larder to steady our nerves. Thank you, honey, you are an angel."

On the Road

There was drink, and sex, and a little bit of jazz, but strictly no drugs, as Tom and Sally went on the road. The photocopy of the marvellous septuagenarian Eleanor Smith had been replaced by a glossy 8' by 6' photograph of her that had arrived by special delivery at their hotel on the morning of their departure.

"It's a sign," said Tom.

"It's a stroke of good luck, Tom," replied Sally but she too was happy with the outcome of her (secret) chivvying of the photographic archive company.

The image of their quarry stared back at them from the dashboard where it had been carefully Scotch-taped. In the shelf below and to the left of the steering wheel were two other treasures, Sally's copy of *Of Mice and Men* and now another book, this one was Jack Kerouac's seminal tome, *On the Road*. Tom saw himself as a disciple of the authors and had taken to apply brylcreem to his hair and wearing white t-shirts in his honour. Sally saw this as a phase and rather than try and correct Tom's image, she waited for the infatuation to pass, which it did.

With a full tank of gas and the large paper map, Tom took the first turn at the wheel and they headed from Manhattan out onto interstate 95 for the hundred-mile two-hour drive to Philadelphia. Both of them wanted to see the Liberty Bell as a sort of talisman for their trip but neither wanted to stay too long in the city, so they parked as close as they could in an overpriced lot and walked the final blocks to go and see it. Tom was amazed at the security that surrounded it until Sally, backed up by the attendant guard, pointed out that it was not to stop the antiquity being stolen, which would be almost impossible because of its weight, but because of the risk of damage or vandalism.

The inscription on it reads 'Proclaim LIBERTY Throughout all the Land unto all the Inhabitants Thereof', which is a biblical reference from the book of Leviticus (25:10), and the guard further added that even in the land of the free, there are elements that do not want symbols of emancipation to exist. As they left and he saluted them, Sally told Tom that the bell was a rallying point during the Cold War for both pro and anti-communist feelings. She said:

"When you know that, then maybe a glass surround and a guard is not enough."

"Maybe," replied Tom. "But I have a good feeling about our visit and seeing such an iconic symbol of American Independence."

"So do I," replied Sally. "But a couple more things, sweetie. Please, please, please do not use the term iconic and secondly, let's get the fuck out of here. I feel like we are going to get mugged at any moment."

Tom laughed. "No more use of that word and I am with you, let's leg it."

They quickly marched to the RV and this time, Sally took the wheel and they headed out of Philadelphia not really talking until they had left the city behind. The target was to hit West Virginia that evening where they both felt that they would be away from the big cities of the East coast and then to slow the trip right down. This they did with ease as traffic permitting, you can always travel at a good speed on the wonderful interstates and highways of America. It was not even dark when Sally waved an imaginary flag and called a halt for the day.

They didn't bother to find an official RV park but Sally just pulled off the interstate into a rest stop and they decided to take their chances that they wouldn't be moved on by any state troopers. America was a country full of people on the move in pickups, RVs, Harley Davidsons, compacts, saloons, in fact, any vehicle that you can name, and even though the overnight laws are strict, there were many more travellers than police so cautions and fines were rare. Tom cooked and Sally sat with a cold beer while he did so. She had picked up Steinbeck's book for the umpteenth time and reread the fly page.

It was the minor miner that resonated with her and yet again, her mind drifted back to what Helen had said to her in Brooklyn:

"Perhaps your dad's brother is actually your father," and she thought again that nobody keeps old paperbacks unless, of course, they are of sentimental value. She thought about throwing it in the trash and putting the photo of Anh, her mother, in her wallet, the emergency ten-dollar note that used to live there too having long ago been spent. Instead, she decided to use her spare time on this trip to try and find out who this Michael was for curiosity's sake if for nothing else.

"Tom, do we have any half-decent paper that I can write a letter on?"

"What?" was the reply.

"Writing paper, Tom, do we have any?"

"I have a New York Times pad somewhere, you could cut the header off that if you like. In the meantime, come and eat."

Sally finished her beer and came back to the van where Tom had reversed the passenger seat so that there were two places to sit opposite each other across the small table. He had made pasta and a salad.

"Fancy," said Sally and the food tasted delicious, all the more so for being served in the fresh air and woods of West Virginia.

"To our adventure," said Tom, passing a glass of wine to Sally and then clinking his glass against it.

"Cheers," replied Sally and when they had eaten and she had cleared up, she brought Tom a cup of coffee. In the meantime, he had found his journalist pad and Sally set about writing a very vague letter to a made-up address in England. To add to the unlikely outcome, she had given Helen's address in New York and so now had to find a telephone to inform her that if by the remotest chance, there was a reply and a letter arrived at her friend's addressed to her, she was to keep hold of it. She was determined to ring Helen every week to find out if there was a reply and of course to chat to her friend as women are like to do.

She wrote:

Dear Sir,

I am trying to trace a coal miner called Michael who left his employment on 06/16/46 (she changed this to 16/06/46 later remembering that the month and day were detailed in reverse order in England). I know that he left on the same day as a miner called Richard Gordon. I am sorry but I do not have Michael's surname but I believe that they both worked in the same pit in or around Gateshead, and that they were conscripted for national service which would make them twenty years old at their exit. I know that this is somewhat vague but I would be grateful for any information, please.

Yours, Sally Gordon.

P.S. I live in the United States and my address is at the top of this page and I enclose an SAE for your convenience.

She then made up an address in England that might, just might, get to the correct location. She had remembered a colleague of Tom saying that the Royal

Mail in Great Britain tried to deliver every letter even if it was vague as dad, the big house, Wales. Sally's attempt was:

The National Coal Board (Northern Division)
London
England

Amazingly, the letter entered the civil service mail system where it was moved slowly but logically to a department that could at least consider the request.

Yes, Miss

As Eleanor ascended the steps of the church, there was a posse of children attached to her which grew as she entered the body of the church. Fords and Bateman-Clarks jostled for position, grabbing at Eleanor's skirts and trying desperately to get one of the two pole positions where they could hold her hand. Other children from other church-going families joined the throng and it was only the intervention of the parents that restored some sort of order and enabled the service to proceed, although Eleanor had an adoring young audience on either side of her as she sat on the front pew.

"You are either the Pied Piper of Hamelin in disguise or otherwise, you are missing your calling," said one mother and several of the other parents nodded their heads in agreement.

"A trifle unfair to imply that all these children are rats," replied Eleanor but she was secretly flattered.

The next Sunday, she was approached by a group of parents again as she left the church with her usual admirers. The children were shooed away and Eleanor was led into the shade where Mary took the lead.

"Eleanor honey," she said. "Some of us have been talking and we are wondering whether you would consider opening and running a mixed-race school using the church as a school room?"

"Goodness," Eleanor replied. "Where has this come from?"

"Well, sweetheart, the town is expanding rapidly and therefore, proportionately, so are the number of children, and in addition," and here Mary took a deep breath. "We are hopefully moving away, slowly I know, from racial intolerance and prejudice." Mary paused again and listened to the collective amens from the other adults. "And so, with the council's blessing, we would like you to take the lead in setting up this important institution."

Eleanor took a deep breath herself and looking at her employer, said:

"Sally, what about the farm?"

"With the children in your care, we would have more free time to concentrate on farm work and farm hands we can always find, BUT the main point is that we think that you would be a wonderful teacher. So what do you think?"

Eleanor sat on a tree stump and smiled. Mary knew that smile and was expecting the next comment.

"Could I have the afternoon to speak to Dolores please?"

Mary was correct in her assumption and so her supporters agreed to meet at the church after evening prayers and when they did so, they saw their target and her mentor smiling and laughing, and they knew that they had their girl.

The hard work was about to start.

"Which part of the church am I going to be able to use?" Eleanor asked the next morning.

"My thoughts, and I stress that they are my thoughts, are to use the body of the church for lessons but to use the small room in the transept for the chairs and books and anything else that you will need. It will be good discipline for the children to put away their things at the end of school and I am sure that you will have willing hands to help set it up in the morning. We have twenty-two chairs but as yet no desks but two of the fathers are carpenters and have offered to make the desks in their spare time."

"As for books, I have prevailed upon the town council to order what we need from Louisville, Kentucky, and here I will need your help in making the right selection. So Miss Smith, if you are of a mind, I think we should take a leisurely stroll up to the town hall and get the ball rolling."

"A question, Mary," said Eleanor.

"Yes, Eleanor, and what is that?"

"Did you always think that I would take this job?"

"God told me so, child, he knew."

God needs to be careful, thought Eleanor, *or he will be taking orders from you*. But this stayed as a thought and she replied:

"Praise God then."

The two ladies turned right after descending the church steps which was the opposite direction to Dolores' cottage and walked the hundred yards to the town hall. Here, they were ushered into a beautifully appointed room with a central table, carpets on the floor, and impressive pictures on the walls. Both ladies shared the same thought and it was that the large table could seat all the children that had so far enrolled in the school but they kept this to themselves and waited by the window until three men entered the room. Two of the men were white and one was black. The older white man was clearly in charge and the other two men deferred to him.

He graciously asked Eleanor and Mary to sit on one side of the table and when they had done so, the two junior men sat opposite them and he sat at the head of the table. His name was Calvin Dark and he was the town clerk but aspired to be the town mayor, and so there were few meetings that took place without his presence. Calvin Dark was a married man with no children and Mrs Dark was a shrew of a woman, tight, irritable, and unfailingly nosey. Between them, the Darks seemed to have an interest or a view on almost everything that went on in Vincennes. They were to be either courted or avoided.

"The council has approved a budget of sixty-three dollars and fifty cents for books and sundry school supplies. This is a six-monthly allocation that can be reviewed up or down." Calvin put the emphasis on down. "We would like to create a board of governors in due course but are happy for the school to proceed on an ad-hoc basis for the next few weeks. When you have decided what you need to order, one of the two gentlemen opposite you will telegraph that order through to the suppliers in Louisville and they have promised delivery within two weeks. Any questions? No? Good." He concluded before either lady had a chance to speak. He rose which prompted the two other men to do the same.

"Gentlemen, would you be good enough to see Mrs Bateman-Clark out please, and, Miss Smith, might I speak to you in private for a moment?"

Mary shot Eleanor a glance but received the reply:

"I will see you back at the church, Mary, I am sure that Mr Dark won't keep me long, will you, Sir?" And she smiled in his direction.

"But a moment, madam."

Mary followed the two clerks out and the last man closed the door quietly. Eleanor was standing now and saw Mary walking back to the church through a window as she also studied a painting of a grand old man with magnificent grey hair and beard.

"What can I do for you, Mr Da…"

Calvin Dark grabbed Eleanor's hair and twisted it while driving her face against the wall.

"Now you listen to me, missy, if you think that you can just turn up here with your peasant ways and your liberal views and mix all the nigger trash in with decent white children, then you have another thought coming. Sure, we will do this for a bit to appease those who want an end to segregation and suppression but you mark my words, when this experiment is over, we will not be back to square one, we will be back behind square one and you and your kind will beg us to reinstate the status quo. Do I make myself clear? Do I?"

He twisted Eleanor's hair again and pressed her harder against the wall but not in such a way as to mark her face. Eleanor nodded and when he let her go, she was annoyed to feel a tear on her face.

"Now straighten yourself up," said Calvin Dark.

Eleanor did just that and as she did so, she saw his pudgy face transform into that of J9ck, the rapist, and she almost felt sorry for him, a portly, angry racist. He would not be left with honey on his genitals overnight by the side of a river but he would get his comeuppance. But for now, Eleanor just patted her hair and smoothed her skirts again, and did something that made the hairs on Calvin Dark's neck stand on end; she curtsied.

Montani Semper Liberi

The seal bears the legend, State of West Virginia, together with the motto, 'Montani Semper Liberi' (Mountaineers Are Always Free). A farmer stands to the right and a miner to the left of a large rock bearing the date of admission to the Union, 20 June 1863.

"Do you want to hear two things that I know from my research so far, Tom?"

"Indeed, I do," he replied. Tom was at the wheel of the RV and Sally had her feet on the dashboard either side of the black-and-white picture of their heroine.

"Firstly, give or take a few weeks, I think that the state that we are in was admitted to the union at the same time as Eleanor Smith met up with her childhood friend, now president of the United States, prior to his Gettysburg address in Pennsylvania later in the year. That year was 1863."

"Secondly, John Steinbeck based the novella *Of Mice and Men* on his own experiences working alongside migrant farm workers as a teenager in the 1910s, before the arrival of the Okies that he would describe in his novel *The Grapes of Wrath*. The title is taken from Robert Burns's poem *To a Mouse*: 'The best-laid schemes o' mice an' men/Gang aft agley' (The best-laid plans of mice and men/Often go awry)."

"Wow," said Tom. "I knew about the Gettysburg address, November 1863 I believe, but I had no idea that Eleanor met Lincoln only just prior to that date. Impressive, Sally, very impressive. Nor did I know that Steinbeck's novel was taken from a Robbie Burns' poem, however, I can see where your thinking is going on this one."

"You know me too well, Tom," said Sally smiling. "I have a book with a Scottish attachment and you, might, just might, have Scottish blood. I think that we should also look to find out who Michael is and try and trace your father as a sideline to Eleanor. That's why I wrote to The National Coal Board about Michael and that's why I think that you should try and trace your mother's movements around the time that you were conceived. It would be fun. There might be another book in it."

Tom laughed. "We haven't started this one yet; all we have is a picture of Eleanor Smith and some ideas. But I get your point," and he daydreamed a little until the edge of the road brought him back to the moment. Perhaps.

West Virginia is world renowned for being beautiful in the fall but it is equally beautiful for the rest of the year. Tom and Sally took their time travelling across the state through the tree-covered Appalachian mountains, detouring down to the south to visit the town of Harpers Ferry which lies in the Shenandoah Valley where the Shenandoah River meets the Potomac River and is the site of a famous civil war-era raid.

Surrounded by a national historical park, the town looks as it did in the nineteenth century, with many of the buildings open to the public as living-history museums. Tom was particularly interested in visiting these museums as a precursor to seeing the one in Perry County, for which his expectations were not very high, but as Sally said:

"Tom, you could be wrong, you know. The central theme of the Indiana museum is the most celebrated president in American history." But Tom was still not sure.

West Virginia was a joy to them both and they sought out high points amongst the forest to take in the views. On the evening of their last planned day in the state, before they headed west into Kentucky, Tom was reading a traveller's guide to America and called out to Sally who was emerging from the treeline.

"Hey, Sal, it says here that one of West Virginia's most unique tourist stops has been named as one of the forty most beautiful places in the United States. According to *Insider*, Prabhupada's Palace of Gold in Moundsville, West Virginia, is one of the most beautiful places in the United States."

"Best we go and have a look then," said Sally. "And as Eleanor Smith was technically Eleanor Gold, then a palace built by Hare Krishna monks to represent Gold must be another sign."

"Or," said Tom, "it might just be interesting."

"Tom."

"Yes, babes."

"Before we head off, I need to tell you something, something important, something that I haven't known how to tell you."

Confessional

"Do you know why people sit in circles, Tom?" Sally asked.

"Pardon?" He replied.

"Circles, Tom, why do groups sit in circles?"

"Give me a for instance," he said, lifting his head from the book that he was reading and marking the page with a scrap of cardboard. Tom hated turning down the corners of pages in paperback novels, even cheap pulp fiction ones.

"The knights of the round table, AA meetings (not that I have ever been to one) native American pow-wows, that sort of thing."

"No, I don't," said Tom.

"To see and be seen. It means that you are observed and can be check for authenticity and truth while being monitored yourself. Very much like the use of the conch in the Lord of the Flies. It's both a supportive thing and a check on honesty."

"Wow. Interesting," Tom replied. "And your point, Sal, because you always have a point," and he smiled both to himself and to Sally.

"Come here please, Tom," and Tom stood up but with a little less savoir-faire.

"Can we form a very small circle please as I need to tell you something and I want you to look directly at me while I do."

Tom was now concerned and walked over to Sally who arranged two chairs facing each other.

"Drink, Tom?"

"No, thanks."

"Ciggy?"

"No."

"Anything?"

"No, Sal, just get on with it, please."

Sally took a deep breath and started.

"I love you very much, Tom Goodman, but I have a past and I know that we all do, but mine is a bit more colourful, complicated even, maybe a little dark too. We have talked about your mum and the fact that your formative years were comfortable financially but emotionally traumatic, and of course, the fact that you do not know who your father is but that you may have some clues. Some clues that, in fact, we may be able to turn into knowledge. Well, my upbringing was difficult too and you know about my dad's suicide and the possibility that he wasn't my dad but that his brother, Richard, was actually my father, although that theory originated with the highly imaginative Helen."

"What I wanted to tell you was about what happened from my years in Saigon through to meeting you in Indiana."

Tom moved in his chair. "I think that I need that beer," he said. "You, Sal?"

"No, thanks, I want to keep a clear head."

Tom went into the van and emerged with a green bottle which he set on the edge of a hubcap and flicked the top off. He took a quick sip to stop the bubbles from pushing out and sat down again.

"Go on," he said.

"After my mum died, I realised that I was an orphan and, although I hadn't had a father for many years, I suddenly felt very vulnerable, so I did something out of character. I got a serving American officer drunk and stole his money and moved to Canada where I knew the entry requirements were minimal and hence where there was a large Vietnamese population. I then worked in Toronto in a family restaurant for a couple of years before moving to America."

Tom gulped his beer and said, "Well, those grunts in Vietnam had too much money. How much did you steal?"

"About sixty dollars. Ten went to a funeral for my mum and the rest on a standby flight to Toronto. Ten dollars buys a lot of funerals in Saigon, particularly if there is no family."

"That's the easy bit," said Sally. "I think the next bit is a two-beer minimum story." She rose and brought Tom another beer, removing the top in the same way that Tom had.

"I wanted to come to America, desperately, So I..." and here she poised. "Did something of which I am not very proud. I found out where the soldier that I had stolen the money from was posted in Vietnam and I wrote to him."

"Wrote to him, how, why?" Tom asked.

"Because I was a girl alone in a foreign country working in an illegal capacity and I was scared, Tom. I wanted to go to America."

"But how did you know where he was or even who he was?"

"I wrote down his name and rank when I stole his money and then, well the army is very efficient and I was cunning."

Tom took another large slug of his beer.

"I used a friend in Saigon to post on letters that I had written so that they would have a Vietnamese postmark and after a few weeks, and a lot of reticence, he agreed to meet me."

"But you were in Canada."

"Ahhhh," said Sally.

"Sal!" Tom said.

"I got my friend to meet him and she managed to talk him into contacting me in Toronto. Once he had gotten over his anger and shock, of course."

"You are going to tell me next that you married him," and the words hung in the air as an owl hooted in the woods nearby.

"Fuck, Sal, no! Really? How? Why?"

"I was going to say that it's a long story but it isn't," said Sally. "I used him, but in my defence, he asked me to marry him, which I obviously did, and it was his behaviour that ended the marriage."

Tom stood up and walking in aimless circles, finished the last of the beer. He then put one foot on the RV step before changing his mind and returning to his chair. He rightly decided that he needed a clear head to listen to Sally.

"Bloody hell, Sal. I mean bloody hell."

Sally went to touch his hand which was only half withdrawn and she read this as a good sign.

"It is no excuse, Tom, but I was lonely and scared, and I thought at any day that the Canadian authorities would find out that I was in the country illegally. So I hatched a plan to get to America and be able to stay there. I obviously didn't know you then and it was all that I could think of to do. Can I carry on?"

Tom exhaled. "Shoot," he said.

"I contacted Brad as I said and when he was back from his Vietnam tour, he agreed to meet me and then we got married; to be fair for three years we were pretty happy."

"Children?" Tom asked.

"No," replied Sally.

"Well, that's a blessing," and Sally noticed a further softening in Tom's demeanour. "And so what happened after three years?" Tom asked.

"Brad attacked his mother," said Sally.

"Jesus," replied Tom.

"He had a nightmare brought on by his service in Vietnam and attacked her as she peeked in on him sleeping. He thought that she was a Vietcong soldier. Fortunately, his father intervened and saved her but the fallout was enormous, obviously, and the next morning when I found out about it all, I just packed a bag and left."

"So, are you still married?"

"No, we divorced, amicably, within a year. He is an eminent psychiatrist in Nashville specialising in post-traumatic stress disorders now. His work is a direct result of what happened."

Tom was silent for a while and then said:

"Have you ever seen him since?"

"No, but I read about him a few years back and his work. I have an article about him if you want to read it?"

"No, thanks," said Tom, "or at least not now." He stretched out his legs and put his hands behind his head.

"Is that all?" He finally asked.

"It is," said Sally. "I was scared and alone and yes, cunning and manipulative, but I do love you so much, Tom, and that is why I did not want any secrets between us."

"I am going for a walk," said Tom and Sally just nodded. When he returned an hour later, Sally had not moved. Tom walked up to her and put his arms around her.

"No children. Definitely?" He said.

"No."

"No contact at all," he said.

"No."

"And you are divorced and an American citizen, yes?"

"Yes."

"Fuck it then," he said. "Onwards and upwards."

Ellena

"What the fuck? Who, who?" Ellena's father roared.

"Malcolm, please," implored her mother.

"Are you mad, woman? Do you expect me to hear news such as this and just react like I have a flat tyre on the car? Our daughter, our only child, who is just eighteen, who has her whole life in front of her, whom we have paid for the finest schooling, just pops in and announces that she is pregnant. And you want me to stay calm. Was it one of those Ivy League boys back from their fraternity houses? Eh? Was it, was it?"

Ellena's father paced to the window.

"Or one of those jobless ne'er do wells who are always hanging around combing their fucking hair and smoking? Well, who was it?"

Ellena was in tears and so was her mother.

Her father suddenly stopped pacing and stared at his daughter.

"Oh, please God, not one of those soldiers in skirts. Please say it wasn't one of those Scottish army boys," and Ellena fled the room.

"Jesus H Christ!" Malcolm Goodman shouted and reached for the whisky decanter in the tantalus while directing vitriol at his wife. "I blame you and your bloody lazy, good for nothing, shag them and leave them family. Aaaggghhh!"

He poured a large whisky, drank it in one, and then refilled his glass which he cradled in his hand while he fell back into an armchair, where sadness crashed over him like a wave.

Within a month, the situation had been both resolved and exaggerated. Ellena was quietly married off to a friend of her parents' thirty-five year old son. He was a successful attorney with a burgeoning practice and a reputation for intimidation both in the courtroom and amongst the staff in his practice. Prematurely bald and severely overweight, he was a conspicuous consumer of not only food and drink but also enormous Cuban cigars, which led to the most atrocious breath compounded by the fact that he rarely brushed his teeth and, until necessity took over in his forties, visited the dentist.

He was wealthy, odious, and now Ellena's husband. She hated him. To compound that hatred, he was disgusting in bed. He was violent and controlling mainly because he had a tiny penis which was rarely if ever properly erect. Sweating and gross, he would try to mount Ellena often having to change to a doggy position before finishing himself off by hand or worse still for Ellena in her mouth. After sex, he would verbally belittle her before rolling away and falling into a deep flatulent sleep. Waking early, he would slap her awake too before defecating noisily and very pungently in their én suite bathroom leaving the door open.

Ellena lost the baby six weeks after they had married but no appeal to her father would change her marital status. Divorce was unthinkable in stitched-up middle-class New York. Her husband made no allowance for her physical or emotional discomfort and her friends deserted her. The irregular letters from the deceased baby's father tailed away into nothing and she was glad that she had not told him of her pregnancy, although with a drink in her hand, she could still see his dark Celtic eyes and feel his hard body on hers. Ellena drank more and more and so did her husband.

She tried to get him so drunk most evenings that there would be no chance of him demanding sex and, eventually, it became a distant memory for both of them. He drank and she drank. His business never seemed to suffer, although he would delegate more than he used to, but Ellena was almost permanently drunk and in this state, she could meet his unpleasantness with unpleasantness of her own. They both operated on an alcohol-fuelled hatred of each other and of themselves.

In 1952, Ellena's parents and her husband all died. Her father had a heart attack and her mother died of attendant grief, which appeared as a fancy medical name on her death certificate. Her husband's passing was more spectacular. Enormous, drunk and ugly, he had a portal haemorrhage whereby he literally split open internally and the great chunks of his copious insides burst out of his mouth and coated his office walls. He wasn't missed by anybody so unpleasant was he and the coroner added a pencil notation to the medical report that just said 'vile' which was both true and erasable.

Ellena tried her best to control her drinking but she had crossed an invisible line and a handful of dry days saw her drinking even more when they had gone by. She was also wealthy too. Both her husband and her parents had her as their sole beneficiary and so her monthly income as well as her investments and property were substantial. Amongst the many awful decisions that she made after the three deaths was one exception and that was to hand over her financial affairs to a trusted lawyer, which meant that she was never impoverished. She also moved to the Upper East Side into an apartment where everything from the cutlery to the bedding was brand new with no trace of her husband or parents.

She was solvent, drunk, but content of sorts until one day the movie *Brigadoon* was being shown at her local cinema, and having watched it drunk and alone, she decided to go to Scotland.

She flew to London and spent a week there before catching a train to Edinburgh, where she spent another three days before travelling first class by train to stay at the Gleneagles Hotel. On the third day of her stay at the hotel, she dressed in a two-piece suit and a headscarf. The weather was mild but it was wet underfoot so she wore unbecoming but practical brogues. She carried a coat and a handbag in which was concealed a so far unused hip flask of whisky. She then arranged for a taxi to take her to Auchterarder and to wait for her in the village square no matter how long it took for her to return. The taxi driver was delighted and spent a good part of the day smoking cigarettes and eating his piece.

Ellena followed the route on the local map that she had bought to what she believed was the home of Jack Gow. She walked past the house once and then took a seat on a bench in the small park opposite. She desperately wanted some of the whisky but resisted and was glad that she had, as two hours after taking up her position, she saw him, the father of her, of their, dead child. He was not as fat as her deceased husband but he was portly and sloppy. He wore baggy grey trousers and a football team top which showed part of his belly. He was smoking and most of his hair had gone. He spat and she saw the gaps in his teeth.

He was ugly and old before his time, late thirties she guessed, just a bit older than her. He scratched and moved towards the bus stop where he took a small tabloid newspaper from his back pocket, looking down the road he went to start reading it when he glanced into the park and pinching his cigarette between finger and thumb, he leant forward as if he saw something of interest but he changed his mind, and within seconds, a bus had pulled up. Ellena watched as he made his way to the back of the bus and took a seat. He then took another glance in her direction but if he saw her, then she would never know, and then both he and the bus were gone.

Now she opened the hip flask and as she took a long gulp of the fiery liquid, she saw his house door open again and out came a woman, who may have once been pretty with three older children and one in a pram.

Ellena corked the hip flask and returned it to her bag, she then walked back to the taxi and shook awake the driver who was happily asleep. Returning to the hotel, she took a bath and then rang room service for a bottle of champagne. After two glasses only, she made her way to the room of the young chef called Michael whom she had been charming for the first couple of days of her stay and, over the next two nights, she set out to make another Scottish baby.

Mud, Mud Inglorious Mud

"Good morning, Miss Smith," they chorused. 'They' were the seventeen children, aged between nine and thirteen, that had enrolled in the Vincennes school for the inaugural first term, which unusually started in February but going forward would be one of three terms starting in January, May, and September.

"Good morning children," replied Eleanor and taking a piece of chalk from her desk, she turned and wrote on the blackboard 'Arithmetic' and then underneath, she broke the word into syllables 'A/rith/me/tic', and then further wrote in brackets adding, taking away, dividing and timesing. She knew that the last word was not very good English but it would serve until the children were educated enough to replace it with multiplication.

There was a collective groan from the assembled children as they contemplated nearly two hours of working with numbers. They would have much preferred a story read by Eleanor or to have done some drawing, or colouring themselves, but on some level, they understood the value of the maths lessons even though they didn't particularly like them. Eleanor spent a good deal of her spare time planning the curriculum and also ways of getting the younger children to work alongside the elder ones without impeding or intimidating either group.

Her hard work paid off and within a few weeks, the standard of all the classes was markedly higher. Eleanor was pleased and so were the parents. There were nine white children and eight black ones and so far, there had been no bad feeling, just a sense of collective community and support. Mary too was delighted because not only was her beloved church filled with enthusiastic young people but there was a knock-on effect with their parents, several of whom had been irregular church attenders, but were now a devoted part of the congregation.

Towards the end of April, and therefore the end of the school's abridged first term, Eleanor decided to set the children some tests. They were of a general nature but related to the work that they had done over the previous weeks. She split the children into two groups, the nine to eleven year olds and the late-born eleven year olds through to thirteen year olds. On the day of the tests, she aligned the chairs in three rows of four and one of five and the children were given boards on which to rest their papers.

Eleanor hoped that after the spring recess, the promised desks would arrive and that they could dispense with the boards, and she saw these tests, and what she hoped would be a positive outcome, as an incentive to speed the arrival of the desks.

As a reward for their hard work and, she hoped, good test results, Eleanor enlisted the help of several of the mothers to organise a party on the afternoon following the end of the school term when the results could be announced and the children could relax with their parents. There would also be some poetry and some songs from the children and the plan was to set everything out in the yard behind the church, which was close to the river, and to start around 5.30pm in order that as many parents as possible could attend after their working day.

The weather in Vincennes had been seasonably warm but very unseasonably wet and Eleanor was praying for a dry day. Mary and the others waited until the last moment to set out the chairs and lay the tables and then heap piles of glorious food upon them. There were ribbons and flower arrangements and as all the women looked upwards, they breathed a collective breath of relief as the sun shone down from a cobalt blue sky. It would not be dark until 8.00, and so it seemed like the gods had chosen to smile favourably at The Vincennes School Easter party.

Mr and Mrs Calvin Dark were out of town, so it fell upon Mary to thank Eleanor for all her hard work and then there was a hush before Eleanor stepped forward to announce the test results. There was an average of 67% across the age groups but there was one star pupil who had excelled. Her name was Hermione and she was twelve years old. Her prize was a certificate and a posey of flowers and she stepped forward to receive her award from Eleanor who took two steps towards the river and then turned to face the young lady. As she did so, the children cheered and the parents clapped, reaching a crescendo that was surprisingly noisy in a relatively small gathering.

However, it wasn't applause that was filling the air but it was the river bank breaking itself away from the body of the yard. Weeks of torrential rain had permeated beneath the sandy soil and destabilised it to such an extent that the action of fifty-odd people milling around upon it had caused a fissure that took six or seven feet of earth from under Eleanor and Hermione and pitched them

171

into the fast-flowing water. Both of them sank below the surface and emerged in a tangle wedged in the branch of a tree that was half in and half out of the river.

Eleanor's head was clear of the water but Hermione was lower down in the water but in front of Eleanor. As Hermione struggled, Eleanor felt an excruciating pain in her arm and saw that not only was it broken but also that the bone of radius was sticking through her skin and Hermione's hair was caught around the bone; however, she then further realised that it was only her arm, her broken arm, or to be clear the splintered bone of her arm which was wedged in the tree that was stopping the young girl from drowning.

With terrible agony, Eleanor moved her broken arm further back into the tree which pulled Hermione's nose and mouth above the water line and then both women in unison screamed for help.

"Somebody get a rope," shouted one of the men.

"Hang on, girls, hang on," came a universal cry.

"Oh my lord," said one of the women.

There was a splash as one of the black fathers dived into the water. It was Hermione's uncle, Joseph, as her father was still at work. The fast-flowing water took him past the tree but he managed to scramble to the bank further down the river and running back to the crowd of people, he immediately launched himself into the torrent anew. This time, he managed to get a grip on a branch of the tree further up its trunk and further away from the girls but from this position as the third rope was thrown successfully towards them, he managed to grab an end of it and wrap it securely around his upper body.

He then slowly edged his way along the trunk until he was within touching distance of his niece and her teacher and by looping his legs over the branch, he took Hermione by the belt of her dress and pulled her towards him which caused the broken bone in Eleanor's arm to shift painfully again. The coldness of the water and the damage to her arm were sending shockwaves through Eleanor's body and she was close to passing out. With strength born of desperation, the man took hold of Eleanor's waist too and then shouted to the men on the bank who were holding the other end of the rope:

"When I kick away from the tree, pull with all your might! Ready...now!" He held the rope in one powerful arm and Eleanor and Hermione in the other, and kicked himself free. All three of them spun over the upper branches and the current tore them away and towards the bank. The impact of the rope tightening and the weight of the women tore at Joseph's shoulders and he held on with all his strength until the force of the water and the arc of the rope swung the three of them towards the bank, where willing hands lifted Hermione and Eleanor and then Joseph onto the bank.

"Oh, thank you, thank you," said Hermione's mother, cradling and soothing her daughter. "Oh, my poor sweet girl," she kept saying. A cart was brought near to the river bank but not too near as there was a collective fear that the bank could give way again. Blankets were found in the church and another of the men removed and tore up his shirt so that the gentlest of the women could put Eleanor's broken arm in a sling. The cart was then driven slowly and carefully to the doctor's house in town.

Later, both Joseph and Hermione were returned to their respective homes, where Joseph's wife and Hermione's father delivered sympathy and rebukes but more of the former than the latter. Neither were the worst for wear although they both slept with a lit candle by the bed to prevent any nightmares.

Eleanor had her first taste of laudanum as the doctor set her arm and put it in a sling. Her nighttime problems were not of the mind but of a practical nature until she managed to fall asleep with her arm wedged between two pillows. The following morning, Dolores was inundated with lemonade in jugs, flowers in vases as well as cakes and pies. She strictly controlled the timing and number of visitors but took all the victuals and put them in the cool of the pantry. The eternally grateful Hermione and her parents were regular visitors and the teacher/student roles were reversed as the younger girl read aloud to her teacher.

On the fourth day after the incident, Joseph called at Dolores's cottage and found Eleanor rocking very carefully on the swing seat. He sat opposite her and they talked for a while and, on leaving, held hands and said a prayer of deliverance.

Kentucky

As the RV rolled along the roads of West Virginia heading for the eastern fringe of Kentucky, Sally looked over at Tom who had his feet on the dashboard and was reading a thick novel, or to be strictly accurate, the remaining pages of a once thick novel. It was her turn to drive and, like so many things in their lives, they were in accord about who drove and when. Neither of them had any ego when it came to taking the wheel and neither of them either liked or disliked the process of driving, so they merely took it in turns doing, roughly, hundred-mile stints and then swapping at a convenient spot. Sally spoke:

"How's the book you are reading going?"

"The truth?" Tom replied. "It's awful. Smug, convoluted, narcissistic, and worst of all, boring."

Tom had decided to read *Ulysses* by James Joyce as a test of his ability to concentrate and undertake a task that required diligence and resolve.

"And, Sal," he said. "I haven't even reached his forty-page sentence with no punctuation."

"Is that why you are discarding the pages that you have read? What if I wanted to read it?" And she paused for a second before saying, "Cancel that, I would rather stick hot pins in my eyes. Why don't you just throw it out of the window?"

"Well, two reasons, Sally. Firstly, that would be littering, which is both fineable and morally wrong. And secondly, I would be giving up, and yes, I know what you are going to say…life's too short, etc., etc., but I like a challenge and I am almost halfway through."

"It's your life, Tom," she replied but her look and her smile told him that in some quirky way, she admired his resolve.

"Eyes front," barked Sally and pointed to a sign by the side of the road which read:

"Yeeha!" Tom shouted, which on reflection was probably not relevant or appropriate but had seemed right when he said it.

"I do fancy hearing some bluegrass," said Sally. "Shall we park up soon and find a music venue for tomorrow?"

"Excellent plan," replied Tom and within a few miles, they had found a small rest area to stop. While Sally prepared some food, Tom took a beer and laid out the paper map on one of the picnic tables. He lit a cigarette and when Sally joined him, he said, "I think our best bet is to head for Louisville which is about three hundred miles away and right on the border with Indiana. We can ditch the Winnebago on a lot and take a taxi or train or whatever into the city and grab some food and then source a venue for some music."

"We could even have a night in a hotel and have a hot shower and a big bed."

"We definitely could," replied Tom.

"But in the meantime, there is some pasta congealing in the pot." Sally snatched the cigarette from Tom and after two drags, she scuffed it on the ground to extinguish it and then picked up the filter which she dropped in the trash in the van.

They had walked the ten paces back to the RV hand-in-hand and Tom took Sally's face in his hands, and said, "Sal, there is nobody on earth that I would rather be with than you, I love you."

Sally kissed him and said, "And I love you too but now supper."

Wrapped in a snowy white dressing gown and with the country music still ringing in her ears, Sally towelled her hair dry and clicked on the television. She flicked through several channels and then turned it off again.

"I don't really miss the television," she said. "It's either bad news delivered by impossibly beautiful anchors, both male and female I stress, or serials about very happy or very unhappy families. How do those women get to have such white teeth? It's not natural."

"They gargle with bleach," said Tom emerging from the shower with a towel around his waist. "I think after sex, a hot shower is the most wonderful thing that you can do."

"And as you have done both, mister lover lover man, you must be the happiest man in Louisville."

Tom smiled. "And the music was brilliant too." He raised a glass of water in the air and said, "To Louisville and all who sail in her."

"James Joyce?" Sally enquired.

"Fuck James Joyce," came the reply. "I am going to have a night off from that man."

With clean bodies and excited minds, they both fell into a deep sleep and awoke in the morning to make love again, to shower again, and then head out of the hotel to have coffee and reconnect with their Winnebago and the black-and-white photo of Eleanor Smith. Perry County was only about sixty miles away and they intended to take their time and arrive there in the afternoon.

Calvin and George

"How are you, honey?" Dolores asked, stepping into her lodger's bedroom after gently knocking on the door.

"This is the first day that I can truly say that my arm doesn't throb," Eleanor replied.

It was now three weeks since the accident at the river and as with all major events, both good and bad, the details of the event were starting to become hazy and the interest of the people who were not involved was starting to wane. None of the three people involved in the incident had the remotest trace of ego and all of them were keen to get back to normality. Joseph had quickly overcome the damage to the muscles of his shoulders and back aided by a balm made by one of his wife's sisters and by a fortnight of light duties insisted upon by his employer.

"We need you back at full strength, Joseph, so rest up and get well," was what he had been told and in addition, he often found a package of eggs or a poke of tobacco in his jacket pocket at the end of a day's work. He was fortunate that his boss was a decent man who cared for all of his workers whether they were indentured or not.

Hermione still had nightmares but they were starting to become less severe and also appeared less often. The certificate that had entered the water with her had been replaced and now stood in pride of place in her family home. The small posy of flowers that had been lost too had also been replaced many times over by both friends of hers and by friends of her parents. Hermione was young and on the mend.

The fact that the accident had happened on the last day of the term meant that there were fully three weeks while the victims could recover and while the church and the yard could be made safe. Ironically, since that day, the amount of rain that had fallen was significantly lower than it had been and with a bright sun and the resultant high water table, the yard and the surrounding countryside were in full bloom. The river had dropped to its normal seasonal level and the ground

177

had dried out. Several of the men spent their spare time building a post and rail fence around the yard, driving the posts deep into the earth and securing the rails with carpenter joints and copper nails.

Access to the river was by a gate which was padlocked during the school day and also in the evenings and at weekends. The children planted shrubs and flowers along the fence's margins partly as a school project but mainly because they wanted to.

Eleanor returned to school on the first day of the new term with the church bedecked with flowers and with the yard fenced and looking pretty.

"I never thought to ask you, child, but which hand do you write with?" Mary said.

"The right," said Eleanor.

"Thank goodness for that," she said, aware that it was the left arm that Eleanor had broken.

She hugged her friend carefully and said, "We are so happy that you are here and well, so happy."

Eleanor smiled and the children came into the church-turned classroom.

"Good morning, Miss Smith."

"Good morning, children," she replied. "We are going to start the term with the weakest of the subjects from the recent tests and that is multiplication."

There was a collective groan. School was back.

"So now that we are using the proper word for the discipline and not 'timesing', I want you all to spell it in your day book."

Fourteen were correct, two missed out on the second 'l', and one child needed to write it out ten times as punishment.

School was really back.

Eleanor found the first few days tiring and then she got into her rhythm. Dolores gently stepped back from being her nurse and within a couple of weeks, with the exception of the scar where the stitches had been placed and then later removed, as well as an occasional numbness in her left arm, it was as if nothing had occurred.

Calvin Dark visited the school and spoke to the children about safety and vigilance. His words and his presentation were exact and practical but there was little warmth and both Mary and Eleanor thought that the children were wary of him. Mary, of course, did not know what he had done and said to Eleanor but she had the intuition of a former indentured slave and that of a woman and mother too.

"I don't like that man," she said to her husband.

"Nobody does, Mary, but he is a force in this town and so we have to be careful around him and play his game."

"I know," she replied, "but that does not make it right."

Samuel soothed her and she took his lit pipe and drew on it for a while.

"That would make the white ladies of this town throw up their hands in horror if they knew." He laughed and gently took his pipe back. He kissed her and she smiled. It was likely but not certain that she was pregnant with their ninth child.

A month into the summer term, Eleanor was heading out of the church to check if the gate was locked when she heard a sob. She detoured away from the back door of the church towards the side in shadow where she found George sitting against the wall with his knees drawn up and his head hidden. George was Mary's third born, he was twelve years old.

"Hey, George," said Eleanor. "Are you alright?"

George started and stood up, wiping his face with the back of his sleeve.

"Yes, Miss."

"Really, George?"

George had a schoolboy crush on Eleanor and she often caught him looking at her but he would turn away quickly and look bashful if she returned his gaze; he would glance at her again quickly when his embarrassment had ebbed.

"Yes, Miss, really."

"Ok then, George, run along, but if you ever need to talk, then I am…" She trailed off as the dam of emotion inside him burst and he knelt and clung to Eleanor's skirts as a conscripted teenager on his first day in the mines would do many years in the future.

George sobbed and sobbed and Eleanor smoothed his hair and, eventually, sat him down on a stump and knelt beside him.

"Can I help?" She said and George gulped.

"Take your time," she added.

George wiped his face again and, summoning all his courage, he mumbled, "Mr Dark."

"What about Mr Dark?" She asked.

"He, he…he touches me."

"He what?"

"He touches me."

"He touches you where, George?"

"On my bottom and on my pencil."

"When does he do this, George?"

"When I have to go to the townhall for school stuff."

Eleanor realised that George was one of two monitors that she had appointed. They were positions of responsibility. Rewards really as the school was not big enough to need prefects. Ginny, a white girl, was the other monitor. Unwittingly, Eleanor's position of trust had put two children in danger.

"George. What about Ginny? Have you talked to her?"

"She says he touches her bottom and her front bottom and does other things, but she won't tell me and she won't tell her parents because her dad will kill her or kill him."

Eleanor blew out her cheeks.

"Jesus," she said. "Have you told your mum and dad?"

"I can't, Miss Smith, I just can't."

"Ok, George. I promise you that this will never happen again. Both you and Ginny will not have to go to the town hall, you will not be monitors and you will never have to be alone with Mr Dark again. Let me think about this and we will see what's to be done, but in the meantime, let's leave your parents out of this."

"Thank you, Miss Smith. Will you talk to Ginny?"

"I will, George, and I will also let you know what I have decided to do but in the meantime, try, try not to worry."

Eleanor went back into the church and prayed.

The next day, she got Mary to look after the children over lunch, which was not unusual, and she headed up to the town hall where she sought out Calvin Dark. One of the clerks said that he would be free in twenty minutes and she was to wait in the same room as the one that they had agreed to the setting up of the school.

Eleanor looked out of the window and heard the door open.

Calvin Dark entered with his thinning hair smeared down and his belly stretching the buttons of his waistcoat.

"Is your arm recovered enough to wank off the boys behind the barns like I am led to believe that peasant trash do?" He asked.

"It was my left arm," she said. "But I am ambidextrous, if you know what that means."

Calvin sneered and said, "What do you want? I am a busy man."

"I have come to strike a deal with you. If you leave those children alone," and she paused while he took in the knowledge. "If you leave those children alone, then I will help with your err...frustrations. Clearly, that pinched little frump that you are married to cannot get you hard but I can and will, but only if you leave the children alone."

Eleanor did not wait for a reply but she touched the bulge in Calvin's trousers and then curtsied again. Both these actions aroused and confused him in equal measure but he chose not to touch the children again, for now anyway.

Eleanor teased Calvin Dark until he caught up with her after church two weeks later.

"My wife is out of town for the weekend," he said. "Time to keep your promise."

Eleanor was careful but she agreed to meet him on a Saturday afternoon on the outskirts of town, where he would pick her up in his buggy and, in his words, 'go somewhere private'.

He was early and she was late and, during the short carriage ride into the woods, he constantly fumbled at her dress and bodice until he pulled the horses to a halt and hobbled the lead one. He then lunged at Eleanor but stopped as she pulled a hip flask from under her skirts.

"For courage," she said and took a swig.

He grabbed it and did the same.

The inside of the bottle had two sections. One with whisky and the other with laudanum. By using the tongue, you could move a valve to release either. One of her father's friends had invented it to cover up his prodigious use of moonshine. This was a copy and a good one. Eleanor drank whisky and Calvin Dark drank laudanum, collapsing within seconds onto the dirt.

Eleanor then used one of the horses and a rope to haul his inert frame back onto the buggy and then returned the horse to its harness. She then drove the team at a canter deeper into the forest before calling a halt. The horses did well because this was not a track or a path but a haphazard route into the trees. There was enough sun above the canopy to guide Eleanor back out of the forest but first, she dragged Calvin Dark off the buggy and removed his coat and boots. She crushed his eyeglasses under foot and then removed one of his socks.

From beneath her skirts, she produced a hunting knife and, running it across the heel of his left ankle, she severed his Achilles tendon with a pop. She left the

181

other one intact which would allow him some sort of movement and the possibility of hope and rescue. She then navigated the team out of the woods and in the lowering sun, returned to the edge of town. After supper with Dolores, she headed out into the dark when she knew the old lady would be asleep and retrieved the team and the buggy, leaving it at Calvin Dark's grand house in Vincennes with no neighbours and therefore, no witnesses.

As she entered the cottage to hear Dolores gently snoring, she yawned, it had been a long day. Just as she yawned, Calvin Dark awoke in the dark and heard the first eldritch cry of a wolf and then the responses of the pack. There was blood in the air and they were seeking it out. Calvin was confused initially and then furious before the sound of the wolf pack triggered terror. Pure prehistoric terror. He rose to run but collapsed, and in the dark, felt both the cut on his heel and the blood still oozing from it. The howl of the wolves was nearer now and the bears weren't far behind.

Years later, a hiker found a belt buckle shaped into the letters 'CD'. There was a tiny bit of leather attached to it but apart from that, nothing, except what looked like a couple of animal bones lying nearby. The hiker was not an Indiana man but lived in California, nor were his initials CD, so his bar room buddies often joked about the origin of his belt buckle. Complete Dork, California Dreamin', and CrossDresser were a few but never Calvin Dark.

Tell City

"Here's a bizarre article," said Sally. "It's from the South Bend tribune. South Bend is in Indiana by the way."

"Thanks, Sal, but I did know that."

"It reads: If you want an idea of what the Perry County Museum is like, then go to Pigeon Forge in Tennessee and stand in the middle of the town and rotate yourself three hundred and sixty degrees, during which time you will see hundreds of restaurants and casinos and bars, plus a half size Titanic and a full-size King Kong. There will be flashing lights and neon signs and a continual thump thump thump of music and announcements and general hullabaloo. Now imagine, if you can after that assault on your senses, the polar opposite of that, no noise, no lights, no sideshows, just a place of sanctuary and reverence, then that is the Perry County Museum in the South-West of our great state."

"Wow," said Tom. "I am not sure that you would have gotten out with your life if you had delivered that copy to the features editor at *The New York Times*," and they both laughed just at the moment that a slightly lopsided sign saying 'Welcome to Perry County, population 18,422' appeared in view.

"Here we are," said Tom.

"Here we are," echoed Sally. "The place where we, literally, had a meeting of minds."

If the population were indeed 18,422, then it seemed like the vast majority of those people were somewhere else or hiding away. The area was eerily quiet and so they headed for the county seat of Tell City, where several years back, he and his boss from the demolition firm had brought the contents of Eleanor Smith's homestead to the sheriff's office. They parked up in the town square and looked around. This was Hoosier country and the surrounding heavy forest gave it an enclosed, almost trapped, feeling.

"I don't remember it being so quiet," said Tom.

"Nor I," said Sally.

But just then, from a stoop of a house behind them, came a shout:

"You folks lost?"

Sally and Tom spun round and looked at the white lady sitting on her porch, knitting and watching the world go by.

"No, Ma'am," said Tom, adopting a ridiculous drawl. Sally nudged him and urged him to desist with her eyes.

"We are looking for the Perry County Museum."

"Well, you are close but no cigar," said the woman rising from her chair and coming down to the RV.

"Fancy set of wheels," she said.

"Thank you," said Tom.

"Where are you from?" She said warming to her task.

"New York," said Sally.

"Then what are you both doing around here?" She said and then chastised herself. "My manners! That is none of my business."

Sally moved forward and said to the woman, "We are also after some information too if you can help."

"If I can, honey," replied the woman.

"We are doing some research on a woman called Eleanor Smith and we know…"

The woman pulled her up short. "Eleanor Smith. Eleanor Smith. Everybody here knows about Eleanor Smith. Most of it is made up or she would have the biggest family in Indiana, but around here because of what she did and because of her relationship with Abraham Lincoln, God rest his soul, everybody knows about her. What type of research are you doing?"

Sally and Tom looked at each other and as they did, the woman spoke again:

"My manners again! The name is Ethel and I have lived here in Tell City all my life. Would you both care for some iced tea?"

Sally and Tom exchanged glances again and nodded. Here was a primary source presented to them without any effort at all. They followed Ethel up onto the stoop and sat in the indicated chairs while their hostess disappeared inside. She returned with a tray on which sat a jug and three glasses, plus a plate with what looked like brownies on it.

"Homemade," she said. "The iced tea and the brownies." She poured the drinks and offered the plate to them both, and Sally and Tom took a piece each.

"Wow," said Tom. "That's delicious," and their host offered the plate again to them both. Tom took another but Sally declined.

"Now what would you like to know about Eleanor Smith?" She said,

Tom gave Ethel the full background to their project and it was now her turn to be impressed.

"So you are the young man that found the items in the old Smith family farm that created all that interest a few years back?"

"That's me," said Tom, "but I was just part of a team that was assigned to demolish the buildings."

"I hear you, son, but even in a team, somebody has to score the touchdown, and you sure did that."

Tom smiled and he was transported back to the moment when with a crowbar in hand, he had discovered the items. Ethel continued:

"And I believe that one of Abraham Lincoln's papers that you found now sits in a fancy frame in the White House."

"It does," replied Tom.

"And have you seen it?" Ethel asked.

"I have," said Tom. "The vice president gave four of us a tour of the White House and showed us the framed document in the Oval Office. Unfortunately, Sally and I had only just met so she did not get a chance to visit with us but we were both involved in the ongoing investigation, in fact, that is how we got together."

"How lovely," said Ethel. "And now you are married?"

Sally laughed and Tom looked away. "Not yet," she said.

Ethel took her hand. "You will be, honey, I see it in his eyes."

Tom carried on:

"Sally was working in politics and I was a journalist and then a few months back, I was interviewing a woman called Kimberly Smith." Sally could feel Ethel was desperate to interrupt but she held herself back. "Well, one thing led to another and I found out that Kimberly was Eleanor's relation and at the same time, through an equally bizarre coincidence, I received a legacy which I had no idea about and so we decided to follow the trail back to Eleanor and maybe, just maybe, write a book about her."

"Now that is fascinating," said Ethel. "Kimberly Smith is a goddess in this state and I don't think anybody has made the connection between the two. Clearly, they have the same surname but most folks know that it's the maternal surname that gets lost down the years and the paternal one that prevails, and so two female Smiths over a century apart would have no familial ties."

"Coincidence," said Sally. "Kimberly was a Carter and it just so happens she married a Smith."

"Well, I never," said Ethel. "I wouldn't mind seeing those two together in a room full of self-important men; they would have them standing in the corner in dunces hats in no time," and she laughed until the tears ran down her face. "Men, eh, just boys in long pants," and she laughed again.

"I take it that you are not married then," asked Sally.

"Oh yes, I was, honey, forty-six years, passed on three years back; lovely man but there would be no frontier without the women and no empires without the memsaabs, if you get my meaning."

Sally nodded and Tom looked coy while he thought of a different woman, an angry drunk woman under the ground in New York.

"Now how's about this for an idea," said Ethel. "Why don't you both take a couple of days to visit the museum and enjoy the town, and I will get a small cross-section of locals to tell you what they know of Eleanor Smith?"

Tom and Sally glanced at each other in assent again and Tom demurred to Sally.

"Thank you so much, Ethel, that would be delightful."

"Come for supper on Tuesday at about 5.30pm," she said. "I make a mean pot roast."

"Lovely," said Sally. "And we will bring the biggest apple pie that we can find."

Ethel hugged them both and then went back to her knitting quite exhausted.

Dark Times

They were dark and not dark times in Vincennes over the next few weeks. Universally disliked but still a citizen of the town, and a senior member of the council, Calvin Dark's disappearance emerged slowly. As his wife was away and because he had few friends, his absence was noted but also enjoyed by his colleagues at work. The surprise was that he was not present in the council offices even though it was the weekend as there was rarely a day that he did not attend there and, any time a door opened, the people in the room expected him to burst in and start throwing his weight around. However, it didn't happen and neither did he appear on Monday morning.

This was when one of the senior clerks decided to visit the family home and he did so as Calvin Dark's wife arrived back from her weekend away. Together they entered the house and the silence was palpable. Mrs Dark went from room to room but concentrated on the kitchen where she expected to find unwashed items and a general mess but it was as she had left it. The carriage that Eleanor had returned was still in the drive, but most alarming of all was the fact that their bed had not been slept in. It was at this point that she decided to call the sheriff in and he arrived promptly with one of his deputies.

Several people from the council were questioned as was his wife but nothing they said gave the authorities any direction in trying to find him. The owners of the two nearest houses, which were both over a quarter of a mile away, had not seen or heard anything, so the sheriff cobbled together a reluctant posse which made three desultory searches of the surrounding area before disbanding. Mrs Dark had a perfect alibi and secretly hoped that he would not be found. Nobody at the school or the church was questioned as it was felt that they would never move in the same social circles as Calvin Dark, which was inefficient and preposterous detective work but a relief to Eleanor.

The wolves and the bears tore him apart and devoured most of his bulk and it would be well over a century before a hiker losing his way stumbled upon his belt buckle, by which time Calvin Dark was just a footnote in history.

Calvin Dark visited Eleanor once more when his torn and bloodied form leered over her as she slept but it was a nightmare, and it would be the only one she ever had but even so, she awoke drenched in sweat. She thought about telling Dolores but decided to keep the whole episode secret. Nobody had seen or heard them leave together nor had anybody seen or heard her return. She was the only witness and, therefore, she was the only person that could reveal what had occurred. Let it lie. Let it lie.

There was an atmosphere of levity in the town of Vincennes. Probity demanded that the residents acted in a conservative and solemn manner but Calvin Dark's presence was not missed and as the weeks passed, there was a certainty that he would not be returning. When people band together, there are always stories and those stories can get exaggerated by Chinese whispers. He had been kidnapped by Native Americans, fallen down a well, run off with a fancy lady, run off with a man, been shot, been hanged, lost his mind and wandered into the forest.

None of them was, of course, true and in due course, he joined the list of missing persons and then later, he just became a shadow that had been lifted from the town. The unpleasant Mrs Dark seemed to be happier without him but her demeanour didn't improve enough for her to be welcome without her odious husband and in due course, she sold their grand home and moved west to Colorado to live with her sister. With glorious irony, the town council bought the house at the knockdown price of sixty cents on the dollar and turned it into the Vincennes Elementary School, which two years later became the Vincennes Elementary and Intermediate School with forty-four pupils.

A summer of hard work from local families, both black and white, converted the house into a building with classrooms, a medical room, a staff room, and a study overlooking the magnificent yard which was used for recreation of all sorts. On the door of the study was a sign that read:

Miss Eleanor Smith
Headmistress

Twelve-Foot Lincoln

A twelve-foot statue of Abraham Lincoln with a lopsided smile and a sheaf of papers in his outstretched hand greeted visitors to the Perry County Museum. Tom and Sally pulled up next to it and they got out of the Winnebago and walked over to examine it up close.

"Not sure," said Tom.

"Well, we do know that this country is almost incapable of creating anything small. I quite like it. You carry on examining it and I'll park up the van. Back in a minute."

Sally swung the RV away to the right under a sign that said 'parking for cars and RV's only', which prompted the thought that there must be a parking area for coaches and if there was a parking area for coaches, then there must be enough demand from parties of visitors, some of whom would presumably be from out of state. Sally was secretly pleased. She locked the van, sat on a nearby bench and lit a cigarette, which was a rare thing for her to do. She could still see the twelve-foot statue of Lincoln and see Tom walking around it examining him from all angles.

She smiled to herself. *Quite a journey*, she thought, *from the North-East of England to Saigon, then Toronto, then New York, and now rural Indiana*. One broken marriage and two dead parents, although Helen's voice still rang in her head that her supposed father's brother might actually be her real father. This thought made her return to the vehicle and to check, to actually touch, the Steinbeck book that had been so important to her mother and to take out Anh's photograph now starting to fade with age. The fly page of the book still read:

From one ex-minor miner to another.
Good luck on your last old day and your first new day as you close the door and open the curtains.
Michael. Gateshead 16 June 1946.

And it had been written nearly fifty years ago. Was the author still alive? Did it matter? But the same niggle that Helen had flagged and that Tom had not dismissed, and that had kept this book close to her mother, was still there. Richard was certainly her uncle but possibly her father. He was most likely still alive because she felt that if he was not, then somehow she would have heard of his passing. The book had been an important keepsake for her mother and Sally realised as she tucked it safely away again, that it was important to her too or why had she kept it with her all these years?

One day she again thought, *one day I will find out about Richard and maybe who Michael is. But not today.* She stubbed out the cigarette and put the stub on the running plate of the RV, to be disposed of when cool, and then she waved and shouted:

"You are starting to look creepy! Let's go and look at the museum."

Tom waved back and did a pretend penitent run over to Sally kissing her when he arrived.

"Ok, babes," he said and they set off down the short track to the museum.

Of the five original buildings, only two remained. The larger of the two was now the museum and the smaller was a restaurant and restrooms complex. Tom put his head into the restaurant and asked:

"Do we have to book?"

A kind waitress in her later years replied:

"No, honey, just turn up, we work on a first come first served basis."

Sally said to Tom:

"Let's eat now, there is a coach park, which means coach parties, which means queues, and you, Tom Goodman, are not good with queues."

"True," replied Tom and they settled into a booth where they both had Hoosier burgers with fries and a Lincoln salad. The same waitress asked where they were from and Tom made the mistake of identifying himself as the discoverer of the Lincoln papers, which prompted several of the other waitresses and most of the people eating in the restaurant to crowd around the booth asking question after question. Tom even had to sign several autographs which was surreal. Eventually, the manager came over and suggested that they come back to the museum after closing time and he would give them a private tour.

Sally was relieved and they spent the afternoon reading and making notes in the RV until the crowds had dispersed and they met the manager outside the now-locked museum.

"Charles Albright," he said, shaking hands with them both. "But you can call me Chuck."

"Thanks, Chuck," said Sally. "We appreciate the chance to see the museum without the crowds; nice, though, they all were."

Tom swivelled back and said:

"Sorry, Chuck, but it was just over there that Sally and I literally, and I mean literally, bumped into each other." Tom pointed at the spot where he had tried to get into what he thought was his car and had clashed heads with Sally and explained this to Chuck.

"Wow," he said. "That's kismet or fate, whatever you prefer."

Sally squeezed Tom's hand and said:

"Love I think," and Tom smiled back.

Chuck led them into the building and, pointing, said:

"These are the real treasures, the rest of the items have been donated or bought because these exist."

Tom and Sally looked at the large glass case in which sat the remaining Lincoln papers that were not in the White House as well as the dolls, the gun, the notebook, and the silver dollar. Behind the items were descriptions and explanations of their provenance. The case was back lit and was impressive. The rest of the museum was not. There were all sorts of pre-civil war items as well as film clips and photographs but most of it was of little interest. Eleanor Smith's secret hoard was the main attraction. Tom and Sally spent a desultory hour, then thanked Chuck, and departed.

"What do you think?" Sally asked.

"Rather disappointing to be truthful," said Tom. "What did you think?"

"I thought it was what it was. A rural museum trying to leverage off a fading story. However, it is the springboard for what we want to do and Eleanor Smith and Abraham Lincoln were only teenagers when this story started, so I suggest we find a spot for the van, cook some food, drink too much wine, hike ourselves to a standstill tomorrow, buy a fuck off pie and see what the good people of Tell City know about Eleanor and Abraham over dinner at Ethel's."

"Agreed," said Tom blowing a kiss at the giant ex-president of the United States.

Eleanor Rising

Eleanor is a girl's name of Old French origin that was widely embraced by English aristocrats as early as the twelfth century. It has since become associated with enduring character and has been embraced for its refreshing wholesomeness.

If Eleanor were a stick of rock and you broke her in half, then the writing inside would say 'wholesome with enduring character' and a great deal more besides. Now in her late twenties, Eleanor was completely absorbed into the community of Vincennes. She had that extraordinary ability, as many women do, of being able to change from an attitude of studied concentration to light-hearted enjoyment in the blink of an eye. She had accumulated not only friends and colleagues but also admirers of both sexes and both black and white.

As Dolores once said of her, "The kindest person that I have ever met that doesn't suffer fools gladly." Mary agreed but also highlighted the desire of people of all ages to be in her orbit. George, Mary's son, who had recovered his confidence with the surprise departure of his tormentor Calvin Dark, followed her around like a puppy, until many months later, this behaviour changed. Even though Eleanor was rather relieved, she was also a little surprised, until she happened to notice him talking to one of the girls in the yard one day and she heard his voice jump from a boyish squeak to a manly growl.

She also noticed how tall he had grown and the width developing in his shoulders and realised that little George was becoming a man, and a very handsome one too. She laughed to herself and realised that the months were turning into years and she had been in Vincennes for quite a while now. It was 1837 and she was twenty-seven years old, and as George and the girl walked away together, she took the opportunity to lean on the yard fence and look out over the river that had nearly taken her life she took stock. She was happy here in Vincennes and in her work.

She saw her parents regularly but not often and knew that her father was physically old for his numerical years because of the work that he did but that he loved her mother, his wife, and that she loved him. One of her brothers had joined the army and that caused her to worry but her other brother had committed to the farm and was bringing in both new ideas and hopefully, in due course, more money that would enable her father to reduce his workload. So the family was never a burden but was always a niggle at the back of her mind. She sometimes wondered if she had stayed on the farm too and occasionally raised her doubts to Dolores.

"From what I know, child, parents are guardians of their children, and no more than that. They feed them, educate them, love them, and then send them out into the world and if by any chance, they come back now and again, so much the better. You would have shrivelled up in Perry County and no mistake."

"Thanks, Dolores, you always say the right things."

"And one more thing," said the old lady. "It won't be too very long before you have outgrown Vincennes. I see big things for you, Eleanor. Big things."

Eleanor didn't reply but hugged her friend and noticed for the first time, a small weight loss in her but she put this out of her mind. Sadly, by the end of the year, the kindly and much-loved Dolores would be dead.

As the river rolled by, Eleanor thought about the school and about her two deepest secrets. Firstly about J9ck and her rape. He too had joined the army but had deserted and, according to her brother, was either dead or living rough. She did not really care, what was done was done, but what she didn't want was for him to appear in her life again seeking revenge. What she didn't know was that his body and that of his horse were at the bottom of a ravine in Colorado after a drunken gallop in the dark.

Both J9ck and the horse had broken their necks in the fall and died instantly, and neither was ever found and therefore, neither was the small amount of money and a half-empty bottle of whisky that J9ck had ridden off with after a losing hand of cards. The other players were too sensible to chase him in the dark but kept his face in their minds just in case he ever returned, which he never could.

Secondly, she thought about Calvin Dark and his actions and her consequent response. He had never been missed, but the law had to follow its course, and Eleanor had breathed a sigh of relief when the case was closed. She was somewhat surprised that his disappearance had caused so little consternation and in fact, had almost been celebrated, but over the months, multiple examples of his behaviour emerged, not all of it sexual, which revealed a man capable of base, cruel, and often illegal acts. Good riddance was the overall consensus and

Eleanor pondered, not for the first time, making a trip into the forest to look for his remains. Again, she dismissed it and as she did so Mary startled her.

"Penny for your thoughts, honey."

Eleanor smiled and hugged her friend.

"I was just remembering some things," she said and subconsciously rubbed her left arm where the scar was now pale and usually covered by the sleeve of her dress.

"Now," said Mary, "some thoughts for you. There are some people who would like to see you this evening, nothing untoward, about 7.00pm in the town hall if that is ok?"

"What is it concerning, Mary?" Eleanor asked, noticing her heart rate quickening.

"Best you come along and see," said Mary. "Oh, and do come to supper first, say 6pm. Dolores too."

Eleanor looked puzzled but smiled.

"Thanks, Mary, we would love to. I think that I can speak for my landlady."

Both the invited women left the cottage ten minutes before the due time and strolled through the town in the warmth of the early evening. They both knew what to expect for Mary was a wonderful cook but she now had eleven children, so it would be a good-natured frenzy of conversation, food and competition. They were not disappointed. There was a semblance of control and restraint but when the stew, potatoes, and squash arrived, there was a mad dash to the table.

Fortunately, Mary and Samuel had prepared four plates in advance for the adults and they had seated their guests prior to calling the children in but any chance of second helpings looked increasingly remote when the ten children and one baby descended.

"Grace!" Mary shouted. "George, grace."

"For what we are about to receive may the lord make us truly grateful."

And then the ten tore in and all was quiet.

For pudding, there was a custard in a huge bowl and again there was a frenzy before one child after another noticed there was nothing left for the adults. Guiltily they sat at the table with full bellies and worried looks. Mary stared back, then rose, and left the room. The silence continued until she re-emerged with another bowl of custard and a big stick.

"Get back," she chortled and pretended to drive the children away like a master swordsman. As she did so, Samuel took the bowl and divided it into four smaller bowls, three of which he gave to the ladies and one he kept for himself. Dolores restored calm by bringing ten sticks of candy from the pockets of her dress.

As they too disappeared, Samuel shouted, "Chores!" With a collective groan, the army of children headed good-naturedly out to do what their father had asked.

"Time for coffee?" He asked the ladies.

"Indeed," they chorused and as Samuel brewed it, they all cleared and washed up.

"Is every night like that?" Eleanor asked.

"Pretty much," Mary replied.

"Goodness."

They drank their coffee and Samuel smoked a pipe and just before 7pm, they all rose and headed towards the town hall.

"Here they are," cried a voice and there was a cheer that went up from the assembled crowd. Eleanor looked left and right to see who was the object of their adoration. She felt a squeeze on her arm and then gradually, very gradually, it dawned upon her that she was the reason that the assembled people were voicing their approval and as the realisation crept into her consciousness, a hundred random thoughts followed it.

I have been here less than eight years, I am not yet thirty years of age, and I am a woman. These were the most prominent of the jostling thoughts but as she gathered herself and tried to control her trembling hands, there was a call for quiet from an immaculately dressed man Eleanor knew only as Mr Wilson.

"We are in the vanguard of change for the population of this great country of ours. Whether you are a woman or a man, black or white, young or old, this is a time of change and we in Vincennes, in the great state of Indiana, choose to embrace this change."

The crowd whooped, hollered, and waved their hats and bonnets. He continued:

"To drive this change and to fill the vacuum left by Mr Calvin Dark's absence," and here there was a general murmur of disapproval, "the council of Vincennes proposes to create a new structure and to welcome several new members to join it; two of these new members you already know." He pointed at two middle-aged men, one black and one white, who rose from their chairs to nod and wave. "And two you do not," and here he paused before holding his arms wide and then continuing, "Good people of Vincennes, with your approval,

195

we would like to invite onto the council of our great town Mary Bateman-Clark and Eleanor Smith."

There was a short pause before the loudest cheer of the meeting split the air and the crowd bellowed their approval.

"Motion carried I believe." In their amazement, both ladies looked into the other's eyes before hugging each other. The congratulations from most, but not all, of the assembled people, went on for what seemed like an eternity until eventually they stood side by side, and Eleanor said:

"Well, Mary, as you said to me when we set up the school, now the hard work begins."

Ethel's Stoop

It was a free for all of old age and experience. All the great and the good of Perry County had descended upon Ethel's stoop with both food, remembrances, and opinions. Sally was grateful that she had bought the biggest apple pie in the store but as she mounted the steps and saw more people emerging from inside Ethel's house, she wondered if it was big enough until she looked at the table groaning with every conceivable food item and another two apple pies. This was catering on an epic scale, on an American scale.

Ethel turned and saw Tom and Sally before greeting them like long-lost friends. She then called for quiet and addressed the gathering.

"Hush now," she said. "This is Tom and Sally, and no, they are not married… yet. They are writing a book about Eleanor Smith and Tom here was the young man that found the Lincoln papers in the old Smith place a few years back."

There was a collective murmur of assent and interest.

"When we have finished the delicious food, then perhaps we can take it in turns to tell them about what we know of Eleanor and, of course, her relationship with Abraham Lincoln."

At this, several of the people lay their arms across their chests and two men attempted to rise but gave up and looked at the American flag flying from a flag post on the stoop rail instead.

And they did tell Sally and Tom their stories, they really did. Their collective knowledge was astounding and there was a second round of memories when Ethel told them that the Indiana senator Kimberly Smith was related to Eleanor.

"But doesn't the surname travel down the male line?" One man asked as several others who had the same thought nodded.

"Coincidence," said Tom. "Kimberly was a Carter who just happened to marry a Smith. I have been fortunate enough to meet her and it was another coincidence on the day that we met that led us here today."

And the comments then started:

"The greatest president that this country ever had."

"I think that they may have been lovers, they were certainly friends."

"Hoosiers both, like I am."

"Me too."

"And me."

"Her contribution to banishing slavery and her stance on feminism were astonishing."

"A queen, a visionary, no, a goddess."

"They broke the mould when they made her."

"Pretty too."

"Beautiful, pretty does not do her justice."

The comments came thick and fast but all the contributors were polite and there was no talking over another person or contesting what they said.

"If only all public meetings were like this," said Sally and the women liked her for saying it.

Everyone who spoke added to Tom and Sally's growing pool of knowledge but there was one man who had been waiting patiently for his turn and then held everybody's attention. He rose when it was his turn to speak and ran a hand through his mane of grey hair.

"My father heard her speak," and he could picture the other guests doing the math. "I was a child from his second marriage, his first wife having died after forty years together. My mother, his second wife, gave birth to me in her early forties when my father was seventy. He was born in 1830, so he was about twenty years younger than Eleanor Smith and Abraham Lincoln, so yes, I am ninety years old give or take as I don't have a birth certificate because they forgot to register the birth."

"Anyhow, prior to the civil war, my father was working in Vincennes and went along to hear her speak and to coin a phrase, she was awesome. So my best advice to you, Tom and Sally, is to go to Vincennes."

The sun was starting to lose its warmth which meant that the gathering on Ethel's stoop was starting to break up. The senior population of Tell City had eaten and talked and were now ready for their beds. As they moved down the steps and out onto the street, lifts were offered and accepted, even if it was only a short ride home for the passengers. Within ten minutes, Ethel's guests were all gone apart from the handsome gentleman whose father had actually seen Eleanor.

He kissed his hostess, shook hands with both Tom and Sally, then he reached into his jacket and pulled out his wallet, inside which was a tired but still clear black-and-white photograph, from which stared back a gangly senator in a stovepipe hat and wearing a frock coat and an elegant grey-haired woman in a long dress and a slouch hat. Both Tom and Sally stared open-mouthed at the image.

"Is that?" Tom enquired.

"It is," replied the old man.

"Wow," said Sally. "How extraordinary."

"It's yours," he said.

"We couldn't possibly," said Tom.

"Please," said the old man. "It just sits in a box in a drawer gathering dust, I feel that you two will bring it back to life."

"Thank you so much," they chorused and Sally put it safely in a side pocket of her handbag.

"Promise me one thing," he said.

"Anything," said Tom.

"That I can have a signed first edition when you have written your book."

"Gladly," said Tom and Sally kissed the old man on the cheek.

Ethel said, "Now you young things go write your book while I pour my friend a night cap," and she then winked and shooed Tom and Sally into the night.

Vincennes

"There are two key dates after Eleanor's first few years here that I can see," said Sally.

"Ok, and what are those?" Tom asked.

"1837 and 1840," said Sally.

"And why is that?" Tom said.

"Well, from what we have established so far, there was her formative years in Perry County, including the time with Abraham Lincoln and her rape by J9ck, or rather Jack."

"The rape may just be rumour so we will have to be careful how we present that," said Tom. "Although I know that you will be sensitive."

"And then after that, we know when she left home and travelled to Vincennes, and when she set up the school and the near drownings, and also when she joined the council along with Mary. We have a hazy idea about Calvin Dark and his disappearance. Agreed?"

"Agreed."

"Well, there are lots of gaps to fill in but I know that in 1837, Dolores died and that she bequeathed Eleanor the cottage in her will, and that in 1840, Mary also died very tragically of dysentery after drinking poisoned water leaving Samuel and twelve children."

"Ok. I knew about Mary but not about Dolores, but my instinct tells me that the passing of her two friends might have been the springboard for her subsequent departure from Vincennes."

"And the shadowy Mr Gold who she allegedly married," added Sally.

"So in conclusion, there is a lot that we know but still quite a few gaps, so, babes, let's get out there and hustle the good people of Vincennes."

"Good plan, Tom," said Sally.

"Oh, Sal, one more thing before we head there. Any news from Helen about your letter to the British Coal board?"

"Nothing I am afraid, babe, I think that avenue is a dead end."

In the flat next door to Jonny's in New York, where Helen was now living with her boyfriend, amongst a pile of mail was a letter from the NCB identifying five Michaels who might fit the description in Sally's letter and wishing her luck in her search. The envelope had been delivered in error to the wrong apartment and would not be discovered until the occupant returned from a six-month work assignment in South America and went through his mail.

There is a PBS documentary called *Mary Bateman-Clark: A Woman of Courage and of Colour.* It is a glorious piece of film that has one of her descendants playing Mary in the church in Vincennes where both she and Eleanor worked and worshipped. In the film, there are also various friends and other descendants talking about her life and her influence. Tom and Sally watched the documentary and then set out to discover more about both Mary and Eleanor. Mary was a relatively open book mainly because of her colour, the church, and the fact that she had died in Vincennes where there was a monument erected in her memory.

Eleanor was remembered too, her life woven in with the church and the town, and the fact that she was an activist for both racial and female equality. Tom and Sally decided with the permission of a council member to hold an evening meeting where hopefully local people would attend and tell them of their memories. They advertised on the council notice board and got the permission of Mary's church to hold the meeting there after one evening's service.

"It's either going to be mobbed or just you and I and a stray dog," said Tom. "Coffee and doughnuts?"

"Ideal," replied Sally. "And then if nobody turns up, you can live on sugary confectionery for the rest of the week." Tom pretended to be an overstuffed doughnut eater and hugged Sally as he did so.

"Enough," she said.

On the day of the meeting, they loaded up the RV with doughnuts, milk, and sugar bought at the local store, and a huge coffee urn which they had rented from the local cafe. As they turned the vehicle onto the street where the church was located, Sally nearly drove off the road. There must have been fifty people on the church steps, many with food items, and another twenty or so walking towards the church.

"Fuck-a-doodle-duck," said Tom. Sally just whistled. The majority of the crowd were black but there were white faces too and the atmosphere was happy. They wanted to talk about their girls and so they did:

"Two rattlesnakes in a bucket," said one lady resting her arms on her ample bust.

"Quieten the noisiest farm dog," said another. "My mammy told me of the time that one of Eleanor's class had stuck his tongue out at her behind her back. Well, when she found out, that poor boy was standing on a barrel in the yard for the rest of the day in the hot sun. He never did that again."

"Mary left us too soon," said another woman.

A chorus came of, "Amen."

"Broke Eleanor's heart so they say what with Dolores passing on a couple of years before."

When the last of the attendees left the church, they knew so much, almost too much about Eleanor and Mary. Nobody had a bad thing to say about either of them but the overriding emotion was that neither of them was to be meddled with.

Sally waved to the last of the townspeople and thanked the handsome black woman, who happened to be a distant relative of Mary's, for staying late to lock up.

"The least that I could do. Thank you for bringing our girls back to life for an evening and good luck with the book," she said.

Tom and Sally had left the coffee urn to be picked up in the morning and drove to the yard of another kind local, who had welcomed them onto his land during their stay.

Tom parked up and climbed down from the van.

He lit two cigarettes and opened two cold beers while Sally unloaded two deck chairs from the trunk. They then sat under the stars on a warm Indiana night and Sally spoke first:

"There is enough there for a book on its own," she said.

"If we can remember it all," said Tom.

"I think we will, Tom, and if not, I have a piece of paper here with at least fifteen telephone numbers on it from people who would be happy to answer questions."

"Quite a girl," said Tom.

"They all were back then, Tom. We can only guess at what they all went through but by writing this book, perhaps we can shine a light on another time when the world was very different."

"Indeed," said Tom. "What I think is clear though, Sal, is that the deaths of Mary and Dolores were the springboard for the next part of Eleanor's life, and I think that's what we have to look at next."

They both fell silent and absorbed the beauty of the starlit sky as a hunting owl flew by on its quest for food.

ES9L

Eleanor could not and would not ever tell her parents that both Dolores and Mary had become more important in her life than they had. Both these ladies had brought her an understanding and a comfort that her young years in Perry County that they had not given her. It was love on the deepest level and when they had both died within three years of each other, Eleanor felt rudderless and bereft. She had expected Dolores to pass on because of her age but Mary's death was a shock to everybody and the result of a simple accident of nature, unfit poisoned water.

Samuel had twelve children to look after and, although the elder ones helped to care for the younger ones, it was an enormous task for a man deep in grief. The community helped and Eleanor was an ever-present support but the entire family was adrift. Their joy had left them far too early and they did not know what to do.

In 1842, Eleanor entered a marriage of convenience with a gentle soul called Daniel Gold, who became more of a companion to her than a partner. She had felt the pressure of her single status in a world where marriage was the norm and had succumbed to Daniel's courting of her with gratitude but not really love. They would stay married for the rest of his life and have two children, a boy and a girl, but all three were shadowy figures, and Daniel was happy to look after the children and their home in Vincennes, which was seldom visited after 1843 by Eleanor as her profile and her influence grew.

Daniel was a small-time lawyer in Northern Indiana but rarely took cases outside of Vincennes and never if they meant being away overnight. He was kind and supportive and, on the rare occasions that Eleanor returned to their home, courteous and engaging. They occasionally made love but Eleanor always left the marriage bed immediately afterwards to ensure there was not going to be a third child. It was a marriage of convenience and it worked. Neither child felt deprived and neither child went off the rails in their teenage years or in later life. Or if they did feel deprived, they never said so or acted out because of it.

What Eleanor did not know in her grief was the foundations that both women had given her became the cornerstone that enabled her to go on to achieve what she did. The constancy of their love and support had not only held her up but also pushed her forward. Their absence was a bottomless pit, not filled up by her new husband, or later by her children, but cavernous and dark.

By default, Eleanor was now the vice president of the Vincennes council as other members retired, or moved on, or, sadly like Mary, died. She was held in very high regard both at the school and in the town but she knew that she now wanted to achieve more. So during one of the school holidays, she took a two-week break and travelled to Washington on her own. Daniel as ever was supportive and reduced his work load to look after the children. Through the Lieutenant Governor of Indiana and Senator Jesse D. Bright, Eleanor was introduced to several influential people in the capital.

Although Bright would serve a lengthy term in the senate, he was eventually expelled for his confederate leanings even though he opposed the civil war. But this was years in the future and his knowledge and contacts were pivotal in giving Eleanor traction in Washington as was her ability to arm wrestle.

On the tenth day of her two-week visit, Eleanor was speaking at yet another poorly attended meeting in a hall many blocks away from the centre of influence.

"Cooking and cleaning is what you should be about as a woman," was the first male heckle.

"Or in the bedroom, girl," was another and at this, there was a gentle murmur amongst the mainly female attendees. Eleanor ploughed on with her standard speech highlighting the need for an end to slavery and rights for women.

"Waste of an evening," was a follow-up from the first heckler and he rose to leave. "And you lot," he said waving his hat at those sitting around him, "should leave too."

"And you, Sir, if you had any manners or the tiniest bit of intelligence, or any balls, would listen to what is being said rather than rehashing what your father and his father have wrongly indoctrinated in you down the years."

The man forgot that Eleanor was a woman and strode back down the aisle in a fury before checking himself. Eleanor jumped from the stage and met him half way, staring up into his face, she forgot all decorum and growled, "Come on then, you bigot."

"Who are you calling a…" he retorted but did not know the word and therefore could not repeat it.

"You…" At this point, the adrenalin started to leach out of both of their bloodstreams and they both took half a step back breathing heavily.

"Best of three," Eleanor heard herself say.

"What?" was the reply.

"Best of three. Arm-wrestling," and the man knew that he was beaten. If he backed down, he was a coward and if he took her on, he would be expected to win but if, heaven forbid, that he lost, then he would be a laughing stock; he was cornered. His slow mind eventually decided to defeat her gently as the only way out; however, he was overweight and slack despite his size and used to giving orders rather than working hard. He also didn't know that even the young wrestling champion Abraham Lincoln could not always beat Eleanor. It was all about technique she always told him, when her hand had pressed his down, and not about brawn.

The meeting was cut short and a table was placed on the dais with two chairs on either side. Eleanor knew as soon as she took his pudgy hand in hers, that it was no contest and within seconds, he was beaten and embarrassed. He slunk out of the hall along with his heckling friend and Eleanor was surrounded by adoring women. She could not have achieved more with the sharpest of oratory and the last four meetings before she returned to Vincennes were standing room only. Her star was firmly in the ascendance.

Eleanor was at the vanguard of the first women's rights convention in the United States, it was held at the Wesleyan Chapel in Seneca Falls, New York, on 19 and 20 July 1848. At that conference, activist and leader Elizabeth Cady Stanton drafted the Declaration of Sentiments, which called for women's equality and suffrage.

She was also a keynote speaker at the National Woman's Rights Convention of 1850 where speeches were given on the subjects of equal wages, expanded education, and career opportunities, women's property rights, marriage reform, and temperance. Chief among the concerns discussed at the convention was the passage of laws that would give women the right to vote. Although the convention became best known for its demand for women's right to vote, the Declaration of Sentiments covered a wide agenda, asserting that women should have equality in every area of life: politics, the family, education, jobs, religion, and morals.

And she made the concluding speech at The Woman's Rights Convention of 1852 which was the first convention held in Pennsylvania. The convention was held on 2 and 3 June 1852 at the Horticultural Hall in West Chester, Pennsylvania. The main objective of the meeting was to pursue legal, social, educational, and economic equality for all women.

Boundaries were being challenged as were rules and laws, and Eleanor was a pioneer in the movement. She was also heavily involved in the race debate. In the 1850s, the conflict over slavery brought the United States to the brink of destruction. In the course of that decade, the debate over slavery raged in the nation's political institutions and its public places. Congress enacted new policies related to slavery. The courts ruled on cases related to slavery. Of the four million black people residing in the United States in 1850, about 3.2 million were enslaved and about 430,000 were free.

While white men enjoyed increased citizenship rights and privileges as the century progressed, for African-Americans, the opposite was true.

Eleanor drove herself forward and championed the cause of both women and enslaved black people as she always had. By 1855, she was exhausted and guilty about her constant absence from home, so she gave herself permission to take some time off and after a week at home with Daniel and the children, she felt rested. There was, however, a growing need to see Abraham not only to seek reassurance and guidance but also to be with her childhood friend. By luck, he was going to be in Springfield the next week and so with Daniel's blessing, she set off to see her childhood friend.

Springfield 1855

President Abraham Lincoln issued the Emancipation Proclamation on 1 January 1863, announcing, 'that all persons held as slaves' within the rebellious areas 'are, and henceforward shall be free'.

Lincoln warned the south in his Inaugural Address: 'In your hands, my dissatisfied fellow countrymen, and not in mine, is the momentous issue of civil war. The government will not assail you...You have no oath registered in Heaven to destroy the government, while I shall have the most solemn one to preserve, protect and defend it.'

Lincoln thought secession illegal and was willing to use force to defend federal law and the Union. When Confederate batteries fired on Fort Sumter and forced its surrender, he called on the states for seventy-five thousand volunteers. Four more slave states joined the Confederacy but four remained within the Union. The civil war had begun.

The son of a Kentucky frontiersman, Lincoln had to struggle for a living and for learning. Five months before receiving his party's nomination for president, he sketched his life:

'I was born on 12 Feb. 1809, in Hardin County, Kentucky. My parents were both born in Virginia, of undistinguished families, second families, perhaps I should say. My mother, who died in my tenth year, was of a family of the name of Hanks. My father...removed from Kentucky to...Indiana, in my eighth year. It was a wild region, with many bears and other wild animals still in the woods. There I grew up...Of course, when I came of age, I did not know much. Still, somehow, I could read, write, and cipher...but that was all.'

Lincoln made extraordinary efforts to attain knowledge while working on a farm, splitting rails for fences, and keeping a store in New Salem, Illinois. He was a captain in the Black Hawk War, spent eight years in the Illinois legislature, and rode the circuit of courts for many years. His law partner said of him, 'His ambition was a little engine that knew no rest'.

He married Mary Todd, and they had four boys, only one of whom lived to maturity. In 1858, Lincoln ran against Stephen A. Douglas for senator. He lost the election, but in debating with Douglas, he gained a national reputation that won him the Republican nomination for president in 1860.

As president, he built the Republican Party into a strong national organisation. Further, he rallied most of the northern Democrats to the Union cause. On 1 January 1863, he issued the Emancipation Proclamation that declared forever free those slaves within the Confederacy.

But in 1855:

Eleanor had last seen Abraham in 1855 when he met up with his good friend and supporter, Joshua Speed, in Springfield Illinois. A colleague of hers had told her of the meeting and Eleanor was determined to travel there anonymously and to surprise her old friend. Her intelligence supplied the date but not the location, so Eleanor arrived in Springfield two days before they were due to meet and used the time to speak with officials in the town about a range of political issues always underpinned by the twin ideals of the abolition of slavery and of the promotion of the female cause.

As ever, there was a wave of positivity and a further wave of mistrust and antagonism but Eleanor was inured to the negativity and felt as she always did, the gentle tilt towards change. 'Sticks and stones may break my bones but words will never harm me', was her mantra but even her elephant hide could be pierced on occasion. On the evening before Abraham and Joshua were due to meet, Eleanor had been persuaded to address an anti-slavery meeting. The crowd was noisy and not entirely supportive, and at times, she struggled to make herself heard until near the end of her presentation, the hall fell silent in the way her classes back in Vincennes had done when she had entered the room.

Vanity made her think that it was her doing until she looked to the back of the room and saw a tall gangly man in a frock coat and stove pipe hat taking up the space where the central aisle arrived at the doors. Most of the crowd knew who the man was and those who didn't quickly picked up the respect that the majority were giving him. And then he spoke:

"Good people of Springfield, the skill of debate is to listen even if you don't agree with the content. Herbert Spencer once said, 'There is a principle which is a bar against all information, which is proof against all arguments and which cannot fail to keep a man in everlasting ignorance that principle is contempt prior to investigation'. To that I would add that, it is also good manners to listen to a lady without interruption. Pray continue, dear speaker."

Eleanor's talk was close to its conclusion, so she finished speaking and decided against taking questions from the floor. Instead, she offered up her thanks and walked down the aisle to enthusiastic applause arriving in front of the enigma that was Abraham Lincoln.

"Where to start?" He said.

"With a drink, I think," said Eleanor and went on tiptoes to kiss his cheek.

In the lounge of the hotel where Eleanor was staying, Abraham ordered drinks for Eleanor, Joshua, and himself. Joshua spoke first:

"I have heard so much about you from Abraham, Eleanor. I don't think that I would be embarrassing him by telling you what high regard he holds you in."

"Why thank you, Sir," she said, smiling and squeezing Abraham's hand. "And I of you."

Abraham made it as if to speak but Eleanor jumped in and answered the question that was hanging in the air.

"But how do we go forward? The Kansas-Nebraska Act is all that anybody talks about."

"I know it," said Abraham. "We will need to go back to go forward. Congress will not have me, and the Whig Party is struggling and so," and here he lowered his tone. "Myself and other influential people, mainly men I am afraid at the moment, Eleanor, but that will change, have decided to form a northern anti-slavery party to be named the Republican Party. By doing this, I can, if chosen, move the agenda forward and get elected to the senate. It will not be easy but then again, no cause that is virtuous ever is particularly when the financial as well as the emotional stakes are so high. We will need strong people like yourself and Joshua here to initiate that change, but with God's providence and our resolve, it can be done."

For the next hour or so, the three of them discussed the way forward until Joshua put down his glass and rose. He said:

"The hour is late and we have much to do in the next few days, so excuse me, Madam." Here, he clicked his heels and kissed Eleanor's hand. "And, Abraham, I will see you at the hustings. Goodnight."

Abraham shook his friend's hand and sat down again.

"Dear Eleanor," he said. "What a joy and a tonic. I have missed you."

"And I, you."

"Those days, so long ago and yet they are right now too when I look at you. Are you happy?"

"I am, Abraham. I have a family and friends, and a cause, and I have good health. Like you, there are barnacles beneath the waterline but that's where I keep them. And you, are you happy?"

"I am," he replied. "There is much to do but I have a loving wife and four children, friends, and a cause too. I don't know if it was the nature of our childhood years but adversity only seems to make me strive harder and I know that we will prevail. With God's blessing, we will prevail and live in a society where there is no slavery and there is equality for all."

"Amen to that," said Eleanor and they both sat back in their chairs with their legs just touching and enjoyed the silent intimacy of old friends while the fire crackled and spat.

1863

Four score and seven years ago, our fathers brought forth on this continent, a new nation, conceived in Liberty, and dedicated to the proposition that all men are created equal.

Now we are engaged in a great civil war, testing whether that nation, or any nation so conceived and so dedicated, can long endure.

We are met on a great battlefield of that war. We have come to dedicate a portion of that field, as a final resting place for those who here gave their lives that that nation might live. It is altogether fitting and proper that we should do this.

But, in a larger sense, we cannot dedicate, we cannot consecrate, we cannot hallow, this ground. The brave men, living and dead, who struggled here, have consecrated it, far above our poor power to add or detract. The world will little note, nor long remember what we say here, but it can never forget what they did here. It is for us the living, rather, to be dedicated here to the unfinished work which they who fought here have thus far so nobly advanced.

It is rather for us to be here dedicated to the great task remaining before us—that from these honoured dead we take increased devotion to that cause for which they gave the last full measure of devotion—that we here highly resolve that these dead shall not have died in vain—that this nation, under God, shall have a new birth of freedom—and that government of the people, by the people, for the people, shall not perish from the earth.

Early in 1863, Eleanor sensed that the president of the United States was weary. How could he not be? The first two years of his presidency had been taken up nearly entirely with the civil war and while all wars are horrendous, an internal conflict pitching brother against brother and family against family tore at the emotional heartstrings of the nation. The above Gettysburg address was an idea in his head and had no forum or format as yet. Eleanor was an agitator, a spokeswoman and a national heroine, but it would be another sixty years before the first female senator entered the chamber, a lady called Rebecca Latimer Felton representing Georgia, and then only for a day.

She operated from the wings while the politics of a nation, with male-only actors, took place on the stage. The newspapers carried pictures of Lincoln every day and in April 1863, Eleanor's intelligence told her that he was to visit the army of the Potomac and so she was determined to travel there. She was correct and with a mixture of stubbornness and female resolve, she managed to get General Joseph Hooker to allow her to stay at least until Abraham had arrived.

Stoic, calculated, diplomatic, and measured, the president was nevertheless taken off guard when he saw his childhood friend sipping Madeira with one of his generals. After the pomp and ceremony of his arrival had abated, he seconded Hooker's tent for an hour and spent two minutes admonishing Eleanor and the next fifty-eight relaxing in her company.

"I came because you need some kind words," and Lincoln smiled. "I do not have time to draw you a bath or cook you a meal but I can say some soft words and dilute the harshness of this war. You are my friend and my love and a force for good, Abraham, and my coming here represents thousands of people of all colours, religious persuasions, and ages who want you to know that. So courage and shuffle the cards."

Lincoln tightened the rope that held the flaps of the tent closed and returning to Eleanor, he pulled up his chair and lay his head in her lap. She stroked his hair and she said, "The beard suits you."

"Thank you," he said, which had nothing to do with his beard but all to do with their friendship and love of nearly fifty years.

In April 1865, when the coward John Wilkes Booth assassinated Abraham Lincoln, Eleanor heard the news five days later and was inconsolable. She was determined to seek Wilkes Booth out and do what she had done to Calvin Dark but a soldier called Boston Corbett had done that within a week of her getting the news and several days before Abraham Lincoln was interred. Eleanor could not bring herself to attend his funeral but years later, she did visit the impressive tomb in Springfield Illinois, and as the light faded, using a knife secreted in her petticoat-less dress, she carved 'ES9L'.

In 1893, at the age of eighty-three, Eleanor was as ever promoting the cause, her cause. In a hotel room in Denver, Colorado, her assistant had left her to have a ten-minute nap prior to that evening's presentation. Eleanor sat near the window in a hard-backed chair and watched the crowds moving about in the streets below. She had placed her bag on the table with her speech notes and glasses. She then closed her eyes and they would never open again. Half an hour later and worried about the time, her assistant knocked gently on the door which was slightly ajar. On entering, she saw Eleanor sitting quietly with her hands crossed on her lap, her thick grey hair brushed back, and a smile on her face. She had passed on.

In her bag was an oilskin sleeve with envelopes for her husband, children, and friends. Nobody had been forgotten, no kindness overlooked, and no service ignored. All carried the message of love and hope. The one addressed to 9braham Lincoln would never be opened.

Book Tour

"A book tour, a bloody book tour."

"I know, I know," replied Sally. "How brilliant is that?"

"In Great Britain, wow," said Tom. "And if it's successful there, then they may translate the book into other languages."

"I don't know what to say, I just don't know what to say."

They hugged each other and then Tom broke away and, opening a bottle of champagne from the fridge in their hotel room, he said, "A toast, Sal, to us and to Eleanor Smith."

"And to Abraham Lincoln," she said. "I think we both know that he gave us the leverage to get this project off the ground."

Tom picked up a copy of the book from the pile on the table. He examined the front cover which showed the picture of Eleanor Smith and Abraham Lincoln that they had been given by the old gentleman in Tell City. On the inside of the cover was an acknowledgement of his kindness in letting them use the image and the legality of that usage. Tom and Sally had kept their promise to him and they had ten signed copies delivered to Ethel's house in Tell City by FedEx because that was where he now spent most of his time.

The book was called *Eleanor Smith Pioneer* and at the bottom were the author's names: Tom and Sally Goodman. They had taken the opportunity to get married in a simple ceremony in Vincennes just before the book was completed with Ethel and her handsome beau as witnesses who had driven up from Tell City for the occasion. They honeymooned in the RV on the journey back to New York selling the vehicle on the day that they had the publishing confirmed. One week later, they heard about the book tour.

Tom put the copy back on the pile sitting on the table in their hotel room and topped up their glasses. He then moved the considerably slimmer and much more worn edition of *Of Mice and Men* onto the top of the stack and turned to Sally.

"Pride of place, Sal, I think that we both know that this book was the glue that stuck you and me and this project together. Let's go and sell some books and see if anything else comes to light over the pond."

"London town me old cock sparrer," said Tom to Sally.

"What?" She replied.

"Apples and pears, jellied eels, pearly kings and queens on every corner, warm beer, fish n chips."

"You, Tom Goodman," she said, prodding him in the chest, "have been watching too many movies."

"One in particular," he replied. "*The Long Good Friday*."

"The days when Yanks could come over here and buy up Nelson's Column, a Harley Street surgeon, and a couple of windmill girls, are definitely over!"

"Nothing unusual, he says! Eric's been blown to smithereens, Colin's been carved up, and I've got a bomb in my casino, and you say nothing unusual?"

Tom was about to rehash another line from the film when Sally held her hand up:

"Enough."

"One more."

"Enough."

"You were only supposed to blow the bloody doors off."

"Wrong film, Tom, that is Michael Caine in *The Italian Job*. Now be quiet or we will have a shooter in our North and South and end up brown bread."

Tom laughed. "Impressive me old China."

Sally headed to the bathroom saying, "I am going to take a shower; we have a big day today and I want to look my best."

"You always look your best, Sal."

Sally smiled and flicked the hem of her dress up. Tom went to follow her into the bathroom but he was too slow and the door was closed and locked. He knocked urgently but turned away when he heard the shower burst to life.

Over the next three days, they held signings at eight book shops and had a read-through and question and answer session at a literary festival on The South Bank. On two of the three days, they had dinners with interested, though not necessarily interesting people, but on the third evening, they were free and decided to take in a show. They chose *Miss Saigon* not just because of Sally's roots but also because of the profile of the production and they were not disappointed. Afterwards, they went for a walk through Covent Garden stopping for a drink when Tom said to Sally:

"Do you want to make a detour when we are in the North-East, Sal, and maybe look in on your family?"

"The truth is, Tom, that I want to let sleeping dogs lie. David is the father that I knew and he is dead as is my mum. I actually don't want to know if Richard is my real father. I am quite happy as I am. In fact, I will be glad when we have left."

Tom took Sally's hand and held it.

"I hear you," he said.

Each store in London that was stocking enough of the books was given a life-size cardboard cutout of Eleanor Smith which had been made using the picture that Tom and Sally had taped to the dashboard of their Winnebago. Tom had wanted to take one of these on the train journey up to Birmingham but Sally had vetoed the idea. The cutouts were impressive though and when doing their signings, Eleanor looked out into the room with a wisdom in her face which echoed the content of the book. From Birmingham, they headed to Manchester and then Newcastle-upon-Tyne, where Sally had a sudden nervous realisation that her uncle could turn up at the signings but, as far as they knew, neither he nor any of his family did so.

In fact, in a bizarre coincidence, Richard and his wife were staying at Gleneagles Hotel while Tom and Sally were in the North-East and, in a further twist, their trains passed each other just outside Edinburgh as Richard and his wife returned south and Tom and Sally journeyed to the Scottish capital, although, of course, neither party were aware of this.

Tom and Sally had three days in Edinburgh, most of which was tied up in promoting the book. They decided to add some of their own money to the expenses that the publishers had granted them during the tour and to use that money to stay at the George Hotel on George Street which ran parallel to Princes Street which was the main Edinburgh thoroughfare. In Jenners, the glorious department store on the corner of Princes Street and South St David Street, an elegant man waited patiently in line, glancing now and then at the image of Eleanor and Tom.

He was last but one in the line and gallantly allowed the woman behind him to go ahead of him and, when she had taken her signed book and exchanged a few words with the authors, he moved forward with his yet unsigned book.

"Hi," said Sally.

"Hello," said John Carnegie.

"Can we make this out to anybody?" Sally asked.

"Just to John please," he replied and glanced again at Tom who became slightly uneasy.

"Is everything ok?" Tom asked.

"Absolutely," John replied. "You just remind me of somebody, but on the basis that I was in the hotel trade for most of my life, that is not surprising."

Tom relaxed a little and said:

"Really and where was that?"

"Gleneagles," he replied. "The Riviera of the Highlands," which triggered some long distant memory in Tom's mind.

"I am told that it is very beautiful."

"It is, laddie, you should visit."

"Sadly," replied Tom, "we fly back to New York tomorrow."

"Och, well, never mind. However, if you need somewhere to dine this evening, go to 'Michael's' on George Street and mention my name, John Carnegie. The owner is a friend of mine and he trained at Gleneagles. It is a very fine cuisine indeed. Meanwhile, thank you, it was a pleasure to meet you both."

"And you," chorused Sally and Tom together watching him turn and head to the door but not before glancing back one more time at Tom and studying him again.

"Nice man," said Sally.

"Bit unnerving," said Tom. "He reminded me of the editor of the *New York Times*…a man not to be fucked with."

As Tom was packing, Sally said:

"Fancy it?"

"Fancy what?"

"Michael's."

"Why not?" Tom said. "Probably have to book so I will give them a ring."

"Ok," said Sally and rolled the suitcase neatly beside the door, the other one she left open on the floor to finish tomorrow.

"7pm or 9 pm?" Tom shouted. "That's all that they have got left."

"7pm," replied Sally. "We are flying tomorrow."

Tom watched cricket, which he didn't understand, and Sally closed her eyes while lying on the bed. At 6.45, they put on their coats and Sally picked up her large handbag in which was a couple of signed books just in case anybody wanted one.

They strolled down George Street on an unusually mild Edinburgh evening and Tom pushed open the glass doors of the restaurant to allow Sally in first. A pretty girl at the consul put a line through their booking and led them to a table near the window looking out over the street. Tom ordered a beer and Sally a gin and tonic and, on delivery of these drinks, the waiter left two menus and a wine list.

"Swanky," said Tom.

"Lovely," said Sally and they ordered starters and main courses. As they both put down their cutlery after the second course and thought about a dessert, a man walked up to them and asked how they were enjoying their evening.

"Delightful," they chorused.

"Excellent," said the man, continuing, "My name is Michael which is eponymous, should you require anything, then please do not hesitate to ask me or one of my staff." Like John Carnegie, he had a Scottish burr and he too was blessed with good looks. As he worked the tables, he twice glanced back at Tom, once unnoticed and once causing Tom to say to Sally:

"I feel like a film star or a crook," at which she laughed.

They decided against a dessert but both had coffee, with which there was a cognac on the house.

"Do you think that it would be a bit showy to give the owner a signed book?" Tom asked. "I fancy that he has some standing in the town."

"Good plan," replied Sally and made it as if to whistle for service. Tom put his hand on her arm and she laughed while quietly asking a waitress if they could please see the owner and emphasised that it was not to complain. A few minutes later, Michael arrived again at their table and politely asked how he could be of service.

"We wondered," said Sally, "if you would like one of our signed books?"

"How kind," said Michael. "John told me that he had been at your signing."

"John, the big scary man?" Tom asked and Michael laughed. "Not so scary, he just has a certain way about him."

Sally lifted her bag onto the table and Michael sat down.

"Any more drinks?" He asked.

"No, we are fine," said Sally, rummaging in the bag. She put the hotel key and lipstick on the table, followed by the ever-present *Of Mice and Men* before gently lifting a copy of *Eleanor Smith Pioneer* from the interior and setting it in front of Michael.

He picked it up, looked at Eleanor and uttered, "Impressive woman. Thank you so much." He placed it neatly on the table and then glanced at the tatty copy of Steinbeck's *Of Mice and Men*.

He said, "May I?"

Sally said, "Of course."

"One of the great novels. It kept me sane many years ago," and he flicked open the cover page, and then time stopped. It read:

From one ex-minor miner to another.

Good luck on your last old day and your first new day as you close the door and open the curtains.

Michael. Gateshead 16 June 1946.

"Are you alright?" Tom asked.

"That's me. That's my writing. Where on earth did you get this?"

Now it was Tom and Sally's turn to be amazed.

"You are Michael? How? Why?"

All three of them sat in stunned silence until Michael said, "I think we all need a drink. Do you agree?" Tom and Sally just nodded.

Michael handed over the end of service to his maître d'hôtel and ushered Tom and Sally into his office. Drinks in hand, he told them his side of the story about his two years away from Jedburgh as a conscripted miner in the North-East doing his national service from 1944 to 1946, and how he had met Richard on his last day in a pub when he had no money and Richard had bought him a few pints. All he had of any value was the book that he had read and reread during those two years, so he signed it and gave it to Richard.

"Richard is your uncle then, Sally?" He asked.

"Yes," she replied. "It's complicated," she said, "but the book was important to my mother."

"And who was your mother?"

"Her name was Anh and she met Richard's brother, David, in the Far East after the war and they got married on his return to England. I was born in 1956 but something went awry and Richard and David had a falling out. Sadly, David, my father, committed suicide and my mother took me back to Saigon when I was six where she died a few years later."

Michael chose not to pry further, although clearly there was a lot more to David's death than a falling out with his brother.

"And you, Sally? If you don't mind me asking."

"I went to America via Canada which is another long story and met Tom in Indiana when he discovered some early papers written by Abraham Lincoln and we have been together ever since."

"And the Eleanor Smith book?"

"Over to you, Tom."

"Well, I left home when I was eighteen, in fact exactly eighteen, 18 November 1972 as my mother chose my birthday to impolitely ask me to leave. From there, I travelled around America doing odd jobs until I started working for a guy who had a contract to demolish some buildings in Indiana, which is where I found the papers."

"Gosh," said Michael. "I vaguely remember the story. Didn't the papers end up in the White House?"

"A couple of them did and are framed in the Oval Office. Sally and I were lucky enough to be invited to go and see them in situ. After the discovery, Sally was asked to do some research on their origin and we met and fell in love in Indiana, later moving to New York where I became a journalist."

"And the book? Your book I mean?"

"Another coincidence," said Tom. "I was doing an interview with an ancestor of Eleanor Smith, an Indiana senator named Kimberly Smith which rekindled our interest in Eleanor. When I left her, I bumped into my mother's lawyer who had been trying to trace me because there was a reasonable legacy due to me by default and so we decided to spend some of the money on researching and writing this book. And that, Michael, is how we ended up in Edinburgh. The Steinbeck book and its connection to you is amazing."

"Have you ever seen Richard since that day in the pub?" Sally asked.

"No, I haven't. It crossed my mind a couple of times to contact him and I am sure that he would be easy to find, but if you remove the book from the story, we were just a couple of young guys sharing a few drinks. We didn't actually know each other."

"I hear you," said Sally, "but wow what a coincidence."

"And a great pleasure to meet you both. Do you mind me asking when you are leaving?"

"We have a flight tomorrow afternoon," said Tom.

"Well, would you mind if we met up in the morning for ten minutes to get a photograph of us with the book?" Michael asked.

"Not at all," said Tom.

"Say 10am in the lounge at the George Hotel," said Sally.

"See you then," said Michael. "I'll bring a camera and send you a copy when they have been developed."

"Awesome," said Tom.

The next morning, Michael had not just brought a camera but also a photographer. Sally stood between the men and held the book in front of her while the photographer snapped away. When he was satisfied, he took photos of the book on its own, including one of the messages on the inside page. Copies were promised to Michael for delivery the next day in colour and black and white.

"Safe journey," said Michael. "Oh, and write your address down for me so that I can send you copies. It has been great to meet you both and if you are ever in Edinburgh again, look me up."

"And the same applies to you in New York," said Tom passing Michael a folded piece of paper which he slipped into his wallet.

Michael shook hands with Tom and kissed Sally, and as he left the hotel, he took one more glance over his shoulder. *Strange*, he thought.

The next day, John Carnegie was in the office with Michael when a courier delivered the photographs. Michael opened them and said:

"Excellent," before passing them to John, who examined them before holding one up and closing one eye to stare at Michael in the flesh and Tom in the photograph.

"Do you know, Mike, there is more than a passing similarity between you and Tom? You could be doppelgangers, or brothers at a stretch." Mike looked at one of the other photos and made a face.

"Possibly," he said. "Same nose, same chin, same hair, although different colour, but in truth, just two good-looking guys and a pretty girl." He handed back the photo to John who looked back and forth between Michael and the picture.

As Tom and Sally waited in the airport, Tom touched Sally's knee and said:

"Here's a funny thing, Sal. I think that I wrote my name as Tom Goodperson on the piece of paper that I gave to Michael. A psychiatrist would be interested in that action."

"Weird," replied Sally, "but I think he will just use the address for the photos, so no big deal." She ruffled his hair just as their flight was called.

Tom and Sally flew back to New York and as they were in the air, Michael took the slip of paper from his wallet and slipped the photographs into a FedEx envelope along with a note. He then took out a fountain pen and smoothed the slip of paper with Tom's address on it.

Tom Goodperson
Apartment 85b
Calder Tower
East 55th Street
New York 10007
USA

"Bloody hell!" Michael said. "Bloody, bloody hell!"

As Tom and Sally put the key in the lock of the apartment after the long flight, they heard the phone ring. Tom dropped the cases, dashed into the living room and grabbed the phone.

"Tom Goodman speaking."

"Tom Goodperson?" Michael said, and then there was a long silence until Michael said:

"I think we need to talk, son."

Son: definitions:

1. Son is often used as a term of respect by an older person for a boy.
2. A male child or person in relation to his parents.

Printed in Great Britain
by Amazon

56476085R00123